THE MARAZION MURDERS

SALLY RIGBY

Storm
PUBLISHING

Ebook ISBN: 978-1-80508-594-2
Paperback ISBN: 978-1-80508-595-9

Cover design: Lisa Horton
Cover images: Shutterstock

Published by Storm Publishing.
For further information, visit:
www.stormpublishing.co

PROLOGUE

Theatre Magazine, March 1972

The Final Curtain: Britain's Lost Promise

The chandeliers of London's Mayfair Theatre still gleam as brilliantly as they did that fateful night in November 1969. But for actress Thea Drake, they serve only as a bitter reminder of the moment her star plummeted from the firmament of British theatre and cinema.

'She was absolutely luminous,' said veteran director Julian Harper, who worked with Drake on her breakthrough film *Night Shadows* in 1966. 'The camera didn't just love her – it was utterly besotted. You could film a crowd scene at Piccadilly Circus and, somehow, your eye would find Thea and be compelled not to look away.'

That magnetic presence had earnt Drake two BAFTA awards before she turned twenty-five, and she was already being heralded as the next great British star. Critics praised her ability to bring unexpected depth to both social realism and her lighter roles. Her portrayal of a young war widow in film *The Red Brick Wall* (1968) prompted *The Times* to declare her 'one, if not the, most promising British actress of her generation.'

But beneath the polished veneer of success, Drake was crumbling fast. Her former castmate Naomi Sindon remembers seeing the warning signs during rehearsals for Genevieve Hartwell's *The Last Guest* during the autumn of 1969. 'She'd arrive at the theatre wearing dark glasses, even in the London rain, and her hands trembled so badly she could scarcely hold her script during the read through. We all knew something was terribly wrong but nobody openly talked about it. In the theatre one learns to maintain a discreet silence.'

On November 12, 1969, during the second act of the production, it came to a head when Drake, playing Mrs Blackwood, Hartwell's mysterious hostess, faltered during the character's psychological breakdown scene. In what audiences would later call a chilling parallel to her own life, she seemed to lose her grip on reality before their eyes. Witnesses said Drake attempted to soldier on for a short while, her words slurring, before collapsing centre stage. The curtain descended as the audience watched in horror.

'I was in the wings that night,' recalled stage manager Eric Dartmouth. 'When we reached her dressing room, it was like stumbling into a chemist's shop. Pills everywhere – uppers, downers, prescription bottles of every sort. Empty gin bottles were hidden behind her costume trunk. It was the industry's worst-kept secret finally coming to light.'

The subsequent headlines were brutal: 'DRAKE'S DOWNFALL, 'STAR FALLS IN WEST END', 'BRITISH CINEMA'S NEWEST CASUALTY'. The promising career that had shone so brightly was extinguished in a single evening.

'The difficulty with being a young star,' said Dr Patricia Matthews, a Harley Street psychiatrist who specialises in treating entertainment industry patients, 'is that no one prepares you for the pressure. You're expected to be perfect, always available, and perpetually "on". Many performers turn to substances simply to keep pace with the demands placed on them. It's a well-known, darker side to the entertainment industry, and one that's accepted by those who work in it.'

Drake's path to that breaking point was paved with typical showbusiness expectations. Discovered at sixteen while performing in a school production of *Our Town* in her native Surrey, she was whisked away to drama school before she could complete her A levels. Industry executives packaged her as the 'sophisticated girl next door', a marketing strategy that proved remarkably successful and found her being in demand in both the UK and the United States.

'They wanted me to be everyone's ideal daughter and everyone's dream date at the same time,' Drake said in a rare interview given to this magazine in 1971. 'I tried living up to it until I could no longer remember who I was meant to be.'

The aftermath of her collapse revealed the darker side of the British entertainment industry. Within weeks, Imperial Pictures dropped her from their upcoming production of *The River's Edge*. Theatres followed suit, unwilling to risk their investments on an actress now branded as 'unreliable'.

'The industry has always operated on a double standard,' noted entertainment historian Margaret Sinclair. 'Male stars could have their demons and even build their reputation around them. But actresses are expected to maintain an impossible level of perfection. One misstep, and they're finished. As in the case of Thea.'

Today, at only twenty-eight years of age, Thea Drake lives a quieter life. She's appeared in small supporting roles on the stage and in film, but nothing on the same scale as in the past. Sources close to the actress say she's been sober for eighteen months, though the industry's memory is long when it comes to scandal.

'I saw her audition for a small part last month,' said casting director

Winston Blackly. 'There's no denying that the talent's still there – perhaps, in a way, even deeper, and nuanced, than it was before. But producers are a cautious breed and, quite simply, they don't believe in second chances.'

Those who remember Drake in her prime, and her extraordinary body of work, can't help but wonder what might have been. 'She had that indefinable quality that makes a true star,' Harper reflected. 'You can't manufacture it. You can't teach it. It just is. And when it burns out too soon, as it did for Thea, you feel we've all lost something rather precious and irreplaceable.'

In her 1971 interview, Drake offered a perspective tinged with both regret and resignation at what had happened: 'People speak of my fall from grace as if I'd been living in some sort of paradise. That my life was perfect. The truth is, I was falling the entire time and there was nothing I could do to stop it. That night on stage was simply when I finally hit rock bottom.'

As the British entertainment industry continues to produce new stars, each one packaged and promoted as the next big thing, Thea Drake's story serves as a cautionary tale. It reminds us that behind every carefully crafted image lies a human being, vulnerable to the same pressures and demons that plague us all. The lights of the West End and film studios may shine eternally bright, but they cast long shadows... shadows in which too many young talents have lost their way.

ONE

MONDAY FEBRUARY 10

Detective Sergeant Matt Price glanced at his watch with a grimace. He'd popped out of work at nine to meet the surveyor of the house he was intending to buy. The appointment was for nine-fifteen and the man was already five minutes late. Matt tapped his foot impatiently on the ground, while exhaling a frustrated breath. In his peripheral vision he caught sight of his mum leaving their house and heading towards him. The small, terraced house he'd made an offer on was only three doors down from his parents', where he currently lived with his three-and-a-half-year-old daughter, Dani, and had done since his wife, Leigh, had tragically died in a car crash not quite two years ago. He'd made the decision to move out after his dad's recent health scare to give his parents some space and a little peace and quiet, but he wanted to be close to them so they could continue taking care of Dani while he was at work. The house he wanted to buy seemed perfect for the whole family's needs.

The morning air was crisp, carrying the scent of woodsmoke from a nearby chimney. Matt had always loved this time of year, when the world seemed to be preparing itself for the emergence of spring. Already there were scatterings of yellow along the grass verge as the daffodils were beginning to peep out. The street was quiet, apart from the distant hum of traffic and the occasional cry of a circling seagull.

'Oh, I'm glad to have made it before you got inside,' his mum called out, slightly out of breath from hurrying up the uneven path, the sound of her trainers making muffled thuds on the concrete as she got closer. Her cheeks were flushed pink from the exertion and her short grey hair slightly dishevelled by the morning breeze.

'The surveyor's late, that's why I'm still outside,' Matt said, with a sigh.

'You don't mind if I come in with you while the surveyor's doing his bit, do you?' She was already peering around him at the property's windows, her curiosity evident in every movement. Matt smiled. Some things never changed.

He turned to face his mum properly, noting how she was dressed in her favourite powder-blue cardigan, the one she always wore when she was going out. She'd probably been planning this little intervention all morning, and just hadn't mentioned it to him earlier when he'd left for work in case he'd say no.

'Of course I don't mind,' he replied. 'But I'm only planning to have a quick chat with him and then leave him to it because I'm needed at work. Lauren's at court in Truro,' he added, referring to his boss, Detective Inspector Lauren Pengelly.

His mother's eyes lit up with that familiar sparkle of interest. 'That's okay, all I wanted was a quick peep inside. I know you said it's like our house, but it's still interesting to check out the decor and stuff. You know what I'm like... Nosy Rosy.' She chuckled at her own joke, pulling her cardigan tighter against the persistent breeze that whistled around them.

'I do indeed, and you're welcome to come inside with me,' Matt responded with a grin.

Dead leaves crunched beneath his mum's feet as she moved on the spot while checking her watch – the same one she'd worn for the past fifteen years, despite Matt's numerous offers to buy her a new one. She told him it was a waste of money while the one she wore was working fine.

'What time's the surveyor meant to be here?' she asked with a frown.

'By now,' Matt said, not even attempting to hide the irritation from his voice. 'I explained to him that I'd have to leave work to meet him here. I'll give him another ten minutes and if he hasn't turned up by then that's it. I'm going back to work.'

'Well, I can let him in if you like,' his mum offered, her hands clasped together in barely contained excitement.

Matt shifted his weight from one foot to the other, considering the suggestion. He didn't suppose it would hurt.

'Well, that should be okay,' he said slowly, watching as her face lit up even more. 'Normally the owner of the property would be here, but they've gone away, so they've given permission for me to deal with him instead. The estate agent has given me the key and—'

Matt's ringing phone interrupted him, the sharp tone cutting through his words like a knife. He glanced at the screen, instantly recognising the police station's number.

'DS Price,' he answered, watching as his mother pretended not to be listening intently to every word.

'Oh hey, Sarge, it's me, Tamsin,' the detective constable said.

'What is it?' He'd only gone out for a while, so surely it could have waited... Unless it was something important.

'We've had a phone call from Dr Carpenter at the morgue, and he wants you there straight away. There's been a suspicious death at Silver Fern Care Home in Marazion. He already has the body.'

Matt's stomach performed its familiar flip at the mention of the pathologist and the morgue. Even after all these years on the force, he still hadn't got used to that part of the job. The cool air suddenly felt even colder against his skin and he gave an involuntary shudder.

'Silver Fern? It's not a home I'm familiar with. But more to the point, why is this the first we've heard of it? If the body's already with Henry at the morgue, then the police should have been informed.'

He paced backwards and forwards, his shoes scuffing against the uneven pavement.

'I'm sorry, Sarge, you know as much as I do. All Dr Carpenter said was for you to get down there immediately. Well, he did ask for the DI, but when I explained that she was in court today, he asked for you instead. I told him you weren't here and said that I'd let you know as soon as you got back to the station, but he asked me to call you. So it must be serious.'

Tapping his foot on the ground, Matt nodded despite being on the phone. 'Okay, that's fine. I'll head there now. If anyone else asks for me tell them that I'll be back as soon as possible.'

Matt ended the call and sucked in a breath. He turned to his mother, who was watching him with that blend of concern and curiosity that mothers excelled at.

'Trouble?' she asked.

'It looks like it. I've got to head over to the morgue... unfortunately.' He grimaced, already feeling queasy at the thought. 'Hopefully, the body I'll be viewing won't be too bloody.'

Everyone at the station knew about his aversion to dead bodies and blood – it had become almost legendary. The running joke was that he was the only detective who managed to solve crimes while being determined to avoid coming face to face with a corpse. For ages he'd been contemplating having hypnotherapy to conquer his phobia of everything gruesome, but he'd never quite got around to it. Probably because the thought of discussing his fears with a stranger somehow seemed worse than facing them head-on.

His mother's eyes widened with interest, and he could practically see the wheels turning in her head. The wind rustled through her silver hair as she leant forwards slightly.

'Umm. I didn't intentionally listen, but when you were on the phone you mentioned Silver Fern. Do you mean the care home in Marazion?'

'Yes, that's the one.' He eyed her suspiciously, knowing that look all too well. 'Why, do you know it?'

'Well, I don't know it as such,' his mum said, excitement

creeping into her voice as she gestured animatedly, her hands dancing in the air like birds. 'But, you know, that's where all the famous people are. It's a home for retired entertainers. I'm almost a hundred percent sure that I saw someone... what was her name again?... but she used to be in one of the soaps... Anyway, the other day I saw her walking around town. It looked like she was on her own pushing a walker.' She paused. 'Although she couldn't have been on her own coming all the way from Marazion to Penzance. There must have been a carer somewhere...'

Ah. That explained it. His mum loved anything to do with celebrities. He hoped the death wasn't of someone she knew and loved.

'I don't know anything about that, and I also don't know who's died. So it's important that you please keep this conversation to yourself.' He tried to make his voice stern, but they both knew it was futile. His mother had never managed to keep exciting news to herself for more than a few hours, max. Providing she contained herself to only telling his dad, it should be okay. It wasn't like the news wouldn't be common knowledge soon enough.

'My lips are totally sealed,' his mum said, doing a zip motion with her fingers across her mouth.

'I'd better send Lauren a text and let her know what's going on.' He pulled out the phone again, his fingers moving quickly across the screen while he composed a message.

> Going to see Henry. Suspicious death at Silver Fern Care Home in Marazion. Will fill you in later after I've been.

The screen's blue light reflected in his eyes as he hit send.

Matt pocketed his phone, already mentally preparing himself for what lay ahead. The morning had grown colder – or perhaps it was just because of what awaited him at the morgue. His stomach churned uneasily at the thought of clinical white tiles, harsh fluorescent lighting, and the smell of disinfectant that never quite masked what lay beneath.

'Are you going now, then, love?' his mum asked.

'I've got to. Here's the key. Do you mind hanging around a while for the surveyor?' He tried to focus on the present moment, pushing thoughts of the dead body to the back of his mind.

'Of course I will,' she said, patting his arm affectionately, her touch warm and reassuring against the chill air. 'Your dad's okay on his own, and Dani's at nursery. I'm here for as long as you want.'

'Thanks. But don't wait more than ten minutes. If he hasn't turned up by then the survey will have to be rearranged. I'm annoyed that he hasn't phoned to explain why he's late.'

'Yes, that's not on. Off you go. You can tell me all about what's happened at the care home later.'

'You know I can't do that, Mum,' he said, trying to sound serious but unable to prevent the chuckle from leaving his mouth.

'Okaaay,' his mum said with a resigned sigh. 'Bye.'

As Matt walked back to his car, he could feel his mother's eyes following him. The weight of her gaze was as familiar as the sound of her voice or the smell of her perfume. He knew that despite his warning, she'd be bursting to tell someone about the mysterious death at the celebrity care home. Some things never changed, and his mother's love of a good story was one of them.

The morning sun continued its slow climb into the sky as he reached his car, its weak winter light catching the dew clinging to the vehicle's roof. He opened the car door and took one last look at his mum. She waved, and for a moment, he was transported back to his school days, when she'd wave him off every morning from their front door. A lifetime ago.

The car's engine rumbled to life, and Matt set off towards the morgue. He couldn't shake the feeling that this case wasn't going to be straightforward. If a celebrity really was involved, it would not just attract local media attention but it could go national. And that wasn't something they wanted.

TWO

MONDAY FEBRUARY 10

Detective Inspector Lauren Pengelly stood in the corridor outside the main courtroom of Truro Crown Court, pacing up and down the polished marble floor. Her heels clicked against the stone, echoing off the high ceilings as she tried to work out the questions she'd be asked. The familiar musty smell of the old courthouse filled her nostrils, mingling with the scent of furniture polish.

Sunlight streamed through the tall Victorian windows, casting long shadows across the floor and illuminating the dancing dust motes in the air. She usually enjoyed being in the courthouse, and seeing cases brought to a resolution, but today, it was the opposite.

Lauren was due to be a character witness for her aunt, Julia, who was accused of murdering her husband, Lauren's uncle Roy. The weight of this responsibility pressed down on her shoulders, a physical burden she couldn't shake. She assumed the prosecution would ask her what her uncle was like to live with – something she knew intimately, having lived with the whole family as a child after her parents were killed in a car crash. Julia was her mum's sister and she'd insisted that Lauren move in with them rather going into care.

Lauren paused her pacing, running her fingers along the smooth wooden panelling of the corridor wall. Memories of life with her uncle flooded back. The sound of his angry voice echoing through the house and the way Aunt Julia would flinch at any sudden movement. The constant tension hung in the air like a storm about to break. Lauren remembered hiding in her room, with headphones on, trying to drown out the arguments that seemed to shake the very foundations of the house.

'He was abysmal and mean-spirited,' she muttered under her breath. But she truly believed it wasn't her aunt's intention to kill him. Lauren had met her fair share of murderers, and Julia wasn't one of them. No way.

A young law clerk hurried past, his arms full of files. He offered her a sympathetic smile and Lauren nodded in return, her hand unconsciously moving to straighten her jacket. She'd chosen her court outfit carefully: a navy suit that projected the authority of her position in the police force but that wasn't so severe that she came across as too officious.

The older her uncle Roy had got, the worse he'd become. According to her aunt, his aggression had escalated to such an extent she'd suspected it was dementia. But he'd stubbornly refused to see anyone about it, however much Aunt Julia had tried to persuade him.

'Excuse me, Detective Inspector?' A woman from the court office approached. 'Can I get you anything? A glass of water perhaps?'

Lauren shook her head. 'No, thank you. I'm fine. Thanks for offering.'

But she wasn't fine. Her stomach was churning with anxiety, and it wasn't simply about testifying. It was the whole situation that bothered her. According to her aunt, she'd decided to try and calm Roy down by putting some of her anxiety medication into his food. But it had killed him. It turned out he'd been drinking before his meal, and the alcohol had interacted fatally with the drugs. When the police went to the house, Aunt Julia had told them what she'd done, but because of the awful life she was living, they didn't believe her, and so she was charged with murder. Deep down,

Lauren suspected that she'd have done the same if the case was in her jurisdiction.

Through the courtroom doors, Lauren could hear the muffled sound of voices. Someone was testifying, most likely one of the medical experts. Lauren checked her watch again, the face of it catching the sunlight streaming in from the tall windows.

Another court official passed by, nodding respectfully. 'Morning, Detective Inspector.'

'Morning,' Lauren responded automatically, forcing a smile.

She continued her pacing, her mind dwelling on her family's complicated history. The prosecution had wanted her aunt charged with murder, but Lauren would stake her life on her aunt's story being the truth. Julia was the only decent one in the whole family. Roy and Clint and Connor, Laura's cousins, were the bane of her aunt's life, but Julia had accepted it because that's the sort of person she was. Julia was kind and had sat up with Lauren night after night following her parents' deaths, braiding her hair and telling her stories until she could sleep without nightmares. Without Julia, Lauren's life would have ended up much different from how it now was.

The sound of a door opening made her turn and two barristers emerged from a side room, deep in conversation. Lauren recognised one of them from previous cases. He nodded in acknowledgement as they passed.

'Excuse me, Inspector Pengelly?' A court usher approached, his dark waistcoat slightly askew. 'Do you have a moment?'

'Of course,' Lauren said, straightening her jacket once more.

'I've just checked the schedule. It's looking like you won't be called until later in the day. If you'd like to go and come back this afternoon...'

'Are you sure?' Lauren asked. 'I don't want to miss giving evidence. This is... well, it's important.' She thought of her aunt sitting alone in the dock, despite being surrounded by people.

The usher nodded sympathetically, his kind eyes crinkling at the corners. 'Quite sure. The morning session's already running late. There's been a lot of technical evidence regarding the medication. We can call you if anything changes.'

'Do you have any idea what time specifically?' Lauren pressed, thinking about the mounting paperwork on her desk and the cases that needed her attention.

'Probably not before three-thirty, I'd say,' he replied, consulting his clipboard. 'The prosecution has several expert witnesses to get through first. They're being very thorough with the pharmacological evidence.'

Lauren nodded, her hand already reaching for her phone. 'Okay, thanks for letting me know. I'd appreciate a call if anything changes.'

'No problem, Detective Inspector.'

As the usher walked away, Lauren pulled out her phone, her fingers poised to text Matt. But she noticed that he'd already messaged her a few minutes ago, saying he'd been called to the morgue.

She quickly replied:

> I'll meet you there. I'm not needed in court yet. I'll be about forty minutes.

Looking up at the imposing courthouse ceiling, Lauren was torn between duty and family loyalty. Part of her was relieved for the delay, but another part wanted it over with.

Through a nearby window, she could see the courthouse steps where reporters had gathered, hungry for details about the case despite the court day having only recently started. Lauren thought about how they'd already portrayed her aunt in the papers. *Killer Wife Drugs Criminal Husband.* They hadn't mentioned how Julia had spent decades managing his rages and protecting others from his temper. They also hadn't yet realised that Julia was Lauren's aunt. Once they did find out, they'd go to town on it. She could imagine the headlines.

Lauren gathered her things, taking one last look at the courtroom doors. 'Hang in there, Aunt Julia,' she whispered, before heading for the exit, her footsteps echoing through the corridor like a countdown to the testimony that could determine her aunt's fate. As she pushed open the heavy doors, she silently prayed that the jury would see what she saw. Not a murderer, but a woman who had in all innocence done something to make living with her husband more bearable, except that it had backfired.

Stepping into the bright February sunshine, Lauren flinched, her eyes taking a moment to adjust after the courthouse's dim interior. A lone seagull wheeled overhead, its cry cutting through the murmur of voices from the gathered press. She quickened her pace, hoping to avoid being recognised, but it was too late.

'Detective Inspector,' a woman with a sleek bob and predatory smile said, breaking away from the group, her phone extended, presumably set to record. 'Is it true you're related to the accused?'

Lauren felt her blood run cold. So they knew already. She kept walking, her face a professional mask that had taken years to perfect.

'No comment,' she replied, a response she'd given countless times but never from this side of an investigation.

The reporter persisted, matching her stride. 'Sources say you lived with Julia and Roy Cave as a child. How does it feel to testify against your own family?'

'I'm not testifying against anyone,' Lauren said before she could stop herself. 'And I'd appreciate you respecting the ongoing proceedings.'

More reporters were noticing now, breaking away from their huddles. Lauren spotted her car across the square and increased her pace.

'Will this affect your position with Devon and Cornwall Police? Surely there's a conflict of interest,' called another voice from behind.

Lauren reached her car, fumbling slightly with the keys. DCI Mistry, her boss, had asked the same question during a tense meeting last week, but she'd explained there was no conflict and he'd accepted her word.

Once inside her car, Lauren took a deep breath, her hands gripping the steering wheel tightly. She glanced at her reflection in the rearview mirror, noticing how pale and uptight she looked. She couldn't bear the thought of her aunt spending the rest of her days in prison. She'd had an awful life and now with Roy out of the way, her remaining years should be less stressful. Providing, of course, that Connor and Clint left their mother alone.

Lauren started the engine, and she allowed her mind to leave the current situation and instead focus on what Henry had for them at the morgue.

THREE

MONDAY FEBRUARY 10

Matt sat in his car in the hospital car park, his fingers drumming nervously on the steering wheel as he stared at the building which housed the morgue. Despite it being morning, the hospital car park was almost full, and that was before visiting hours started after lunch. He'd planned on waiting for Lauren, but as time was getting on, he decided to face the waiting dead body alone. He was about to get out of his car when he heard a car's engine and he turned to see Lauren pulling into the empty space beside him.

'Morning, Matt,' Lauren said, buttoning up her jacket as she stepped out of the car. 'It looks like good timing on my part. You won't have to go inside alone.'

Matt gave a relieved smile. Lauren didn't mind his squeamishness when around anything gory and had become sympathetic... almost. A big leap considering when he'd first joined the team, she'd questioned his competence because of both this and his slight limp, which was the result of having been shot in an undercover operation when he worked for Lenchester's Criminal Investigations Department. He'd proved himself within a few weeks of joining, and she'd been the first to admit her mistake, which he admired her for. Not all bosses would have been prepared to acknowledge so quickly that they'd been wrong in their assessment. It was the start of a good working relationship and, if he said so himself, he'd provided a positive bridge between her and the rest of the team. They now worked as a cohesive unit, rather than the *us* and *her* that he'd witnessed on his arrival.

'Yes, I must admit I'm glad to have you with me,' Matt replied, managing a self-deprecating smile. 'Not that I'll be hiding behind you, obviously. How on earth did you make it here so quickly?' He patted his pocket, checking for his notebook and pen. Writing things down gave him something to focus on at times like these.

'I used my siren and floored it,' she admitted, grinning. 'Although I'm surprised you're not in there yet.'

They pushed open the heavy double doors and walked down the sterile hospital corridor, their footsteps echoing off the polished floors. The familiar antiseptic smell made Matt's nose wrinkle slightly.

'I hoped you'd make it here quickly so hung around outside for a bit. How's the court case going?' he asked, in part to distract himself from their destination, but also because he knew how much it had been on her mind.

Lauren's expression turned thoughtful as she considered his question. 'Too early to say, I think. Being a witness means I've not been inside the court, but from what I've been told the prosecution is going into an awful lot of detail with their expert testimony on the drugs administered to my uncle, including the amount and the specifics of how he would have been affected. It's like they're trying to prove Aunt Julia was a chemist and had an in-depth knowledge of pharmaceuticals. It's ridiculous, considering she left school at sixteen with hardly any qualifications, none of which were in science.' She pushed a strand of hair behind her ear, a gesture Matt had come to recognise as a sign of her anxiety. 'It's not easy being stuck outside, unable to see how it's all progressing, but there's nothing I can do about it.'

'I'm sure it will be fine,' Matt said, hoping to console his boss, but realising that his words sounded trite. 'Sorry, I didn't—'

'It's okay,' Lauren interrupted. 'I understand what you mean and appreciate your concern.'

They lapsed into silence until they arrived at the entrance to the morgue, its metal doors gleaming under the fluorescent lights. Lauren pushed the door open. The temperature dropped noticeably as they entered.

Dr Henry Carpenter was regarded as the best pathologist in the county, and he was sitting at one of the desks, poring over an open manila folder on his desk. His white lab coat was a stark contrast to the organised chaos of files spread across his workspace.

'Morning, Henry,' Matt called out, causing the pathologist to look up from his work, his half-moon reading glasses perched precariously on the end of his nose.

'Ah, good. I'm glad you're here,' Henry said, dispensing with any pleasantries, sliding the chair back and standing. He rubbed his back, as if to ease the stiffness. 'I've got something to show you.'

He led them through to the main morgue area, where a single body lay draped under a white sheet on the stainless-steel table. The overhead lights made everything appear even more stark and clinical. He pulled on a fresh pair of latex gloves, snapping each one of them against his wrists. 'This is Dawn Cross, aged ninety-two,' Henry began, drawing back the sheet just enough to reveal the elderly victim's lined face. 'She was brought in by the paramedics because her death was unexpected. She lived at Silver Fern Care Home in Marazion. According to her medical records, she was relatively healthy for her age; the only medication prescribed was a low dose blood pressure tablet.'

Matt shifted his weight from one foot to the other, maintaining a safe distance from the table. 'If she was healthy, then why was she in the care home? Surely she could have taken care of herself.'

'I don't have that background information, because it's not relevant to my investigation,' Henry replied. 'What I can say is that while the death initially appeared to be from natural causes, the toxicology results tell a different story.' He moved to a nearby counter and picked up a manila folder, from which he extracted several papers covered in chemical analysis data.

'The victim ingested antifreeze from eating chocolates,' Henry continued, pointing to specific highlighted areas on the report. 'The fascinating part is how we discovered it. During the post-mortem, I noticed some unusual crystallisation patterns in her kidney tissue which is a telltale sign of ethylene glycol poisoning... which is the main component in antifreeze.'

Lauren leaned in to examine the report. 'Chocolates?'

'Yes.' Henry nodded, moving to another table where several evidence bags were laid out. 'The last things she consumed were several chocolates. Three of these appeared to be strawberry creams.'

Matt screwed up his face, taking an involuntary step back-wards. 'How can you tell what she ate so specifically? By the time it's gone down into the stomach—'

Henry held up a hand, to silence Matt, his eyes lighting up with professional enthusiasm. 'Excellent question, young man. In most cases, you'd be right that stomach contents can be difficult to identify. However, this case is unique for several reasons. First, the antifreeze didn't kill her immediately, which allowed us to trace the method of delivery. We found partially dissolved chocolate residue in her oesophagus and, more importantly, there were distinctive traces of the strawberry cream filling still present in her mouth cavity.'

He moved to a microscope and gestured for them to look. 'If you examine the tissue samples, you can see the characteristic crystalline structures formed by the antifreeze. But what's particularly interesting is how they're distributed. The highest concentration was found mixed with the chocolate residue, suggesting the poison was introduced through the strawberry cream centres specifically.'

'But wouldn't she have tasted it?' Matt asked, keeping his distance from the microscope but taking careful notes.

'That's another clever aspect of this poisoning,' Henry

explained. 'Ethylene glycol has a sweet taste that would have blended perfectly with the chocolate and its cream-filled centre. The victim would have had no reason to suspect anything was wrong; all they would have tasted was the chocolate combined with the filling.'

Lauren frowned, her detective instincts clearly engaged. 'So what do you have for actual time of death?'

Henry consulted his notes. 'Based on body temperature, rigor mortis, and the state of decomposition, I believe it was Friday afternoon between four and seven. You should be able to check with the care home's logs regarding when she was last seen alive, and when and from whom she received the chocolates.'

'Can you tell how long the poison had been in the chocolates before she ate them?' Lauren asked.

'Not from what was retrieved from the victim's stomach.'

'And if we find any others that haven't yet been eaten?' Lauren continued. 'There might be some in the victim's room.'

'It's a possibility. Bring them to me, if you discover any.'

'Would death have been immediate and was it painful?' Matt asked, hoping that the woman hadn't suffered much – or at all.

'The progression of the poisoning would have been relatively slow at first. Ethylene glycol poisoning typically occurs in three stages. The initial symptoms would have appeared similar to her being drunk. She'd have been confused, had slurred speech, and maybe felt dizzy. This would have progressed to cardiopulmonary symptoms, and finally, severe kidney failure.'

'Could she have been saved if it had been caught in time?' Matt asked, his pen poised over his notebook.

'Absolutely,' Henry replied, his expression grave. 'If recognised early enough, there are effective treatments involving either ethanol or fomepizole, which compete with the ethylene glycol for the same metabolic pathway. The key is early detection, but the initial symptoms can be misleading, especially in an elderly patient where confusion or disorientation might not immediately raise alarm bells. Or if she was alone in her room, then no one would have noticed.'

'So when she was discovered, it would have looked like she'd simply died with no outer signs of there being something wrong?' Matt asked, with a frown.

'Yes,' Henry replied, matter-of-factly.

Lauren began pacing slowly around the room, her heels clicking rhythmically on the floor. 'So, we're looking for someone with access to both antifreeze and the knowledge of how to incorporate it into chocolates without detection. Acquiring antifreeze would be easy enough but the latter not so.'

'Indeed,' Henry agreed.

'Were you able to tell whether the poison was injected into the middle of the chocolate or coated it?' Matt asked.

'I'd need to see one that hadn't been eaten, but it's my educated guess that it would have been injected. That way the victim most definitely wouldn't have tasted anything out of the ordinary.' Henry paused a moment, as if considering something else. 'Also, whoever did this would have needed to know enough about the victim's routine to ensure she would eat the chocolates relatively soon after receiving them.'

'Why? Would it have affected the effectiveness of the poison?' Lauren asked.

'No. My reasoning isn't scientific. I assumed that if there'd been too long a delay between receiving and eating the chocolates, someone other than the victim might have consumed one. And to my knowledge, she's the only person to have been poisoned at this point.'

'That makes total sense. Thanks, Henry. We'd better get going. If the victim didn't poison herself, which I'd have thought most unlikely, we now have a murder on our hands and need to begin investigating. We'll let you know if we discover any more of the chocolates in the victim's possession.'

Matt sucked in a breath and closed his notebook, trying to process all the information Henry had imparted. The case had become much more complex than a simple care home death. Whoever planned this murder had been methodical, patient, and possessed of some very specific knowledge. The question now was: who had wanted Dawn Cross dead badly enough to plan such an elaborate poisoning?

FOUR

MONDAY FEBRUARY 10

'Attention, everyone,' Lauren called out as she strode into the office with Matt following close behind.

Glancing around, she took in her team seated at their respective desks. Detective Constables Tamsin Kellow, Clem Roscoe, Billy Ward and Jenna Moyle were all present, each seemingly absorbed in their own tasks. The office had a familiar, comfortable buzz about it: the sound of keyboards clicking, papers shuffling, and the ever-present hum of the aging heating system.

Tamsin was squinting at her computer screen, twirling a strand of her dark hair around her fingers, as if deep in thought. Clem had spread a number of what looked like crime scene photos across his desk, while Jenna was on the phone, speaking in hushed tones. Billy, as usual, was leaning back in his chair, tossing a stress ball from hand to hand.

Luckily, they weren't particularly busy and the cases they did have were mundane, day-to-day affairs, like petty theft, graffiti and suchlike. But that was about to change and Lauren didn't envisage any problem diverting them to the murder investigation. She could already anticipate Billy's inevitable quip about it.

'Sergeant Price and I—' Lauren caught herself. 'Matt and I have just come back from seeing Henry at the morgue. As I'm sure you might have already guessed, we have a suspicious death on our hands.'

'Oh, not another one,' Billy groaned dramatically, letting his chair fall forwards with a thud. Lauren grinned to herself. She'd been right about his reaction. 'This place is like a murder magnet. And it's all down to you, Sarge,' he said, nodding in Matt's direction. 'It was quiet before you arrived and—'

'So you keep telling me, Billy. *Every time,*' Matt said. 'Surely it's time to change the tune.'

'Why would I want to do that?' Billy asked, feigning innocence. 'I like to give you something to complain about. Anyway, at least it makes the job interesting, doesn't it?' He glanced around at the rest of the team, who had now finished what they'd been doing and were giving Lauren the attention she'd asked for.

'Right,' Lauren said, perching on the edge of the empty desk positioned next to the whiteboard. 'Someone from the Silver Fern Care Home in Marazion has—'

'Isn't that the place where all the old stars go?' Billy interrupted, his eyes lighting up with interest.

Clem stretched in his chair, running a hand through his greying hair. 'They're not all stars,' he corrected, his voice carrying the patience of someone used to explaining things to Billy. 'The home is for retired entertainers, and the majority have ended up there because they were unable to look after themselves or had no family to take care of them.'

'How do you know that? Some might have gone in there so they could hang out with other famous people, rather than boring people. Because there are *definitely* some famous people there,' Billy insisted, leaning forwards eagerly. 'That's what my mum told me and she knows everything.'

'I didn't have you pegged for a mummy's boy,' Tamsin said, chuckling.

Billy flushed a deep shade of red. 'I'm not but—'

'Enough,' Lauren said, holding up her hand to silence them. 'I accept that some residents might choose to live among their peers despite being self-sufficient, Billy. And to clarify your other point, yes there are some entertainers living there who were very well known in their day,' Clem acknowledged, sharing an amused look with Jenna. 'But not all of the current residents were famous, by a long shot. Most were jobbing actors, or singers or musicians, or whatever.'

'Well, of course old Clemipedia would know that,' Billy responded with a smirk, using the nickname he'd given the older officer a long time ago because of his encyclopaedic knowledge.

Lauren cleared her throat, drawing their attention back. 'Now we've established all that can we please focus,' she said, her tone firm but not unkind. 'One of the residents, Dawn Cross, died on Friday, sometime between four in the afternoon and seven in the evening. Initially, it appeared to be of natural causes, but after the paramedics attended, the pathologist was instructed to undertake a postmortem because she hadn't been ill and her death was unexpected.' She paused for effect, noting how her team leant in slightly. 'It turns out she'd been poisoned by chocolates, specifically strawberry creams, containing antifreeze.'

'Antifreeze?' Tamsin said thoughtfully, tapping her pen against her desk. 'Well, that means the killer has got to be a woman.'

'Why do you say that?' Billy swivelled in his chair to face her.

'It's well documented that women prefer using poison to murder, but men don't,' Tamsin explained, looking to Lauren for confirmation.

Lauren shook her head, crossing her arms. 'That might be the case in the literature, but it wouldn't be prudent to base our investigation solely on that,' she said, watching Matt nod in agreement from where he stood close to her. 'Initially we'll be investigating all of the residents and the staff at the care home.'

'So until this murder's solved, all leave's cancelled,' Matt added, his deep voice carrying across the office.

'But Sarge... ma'am.' Billy's face fell dramatically. 'I'm meant to be visiting Ellie in Lenchester this weekend.' He slumped in his chair, his bottom lip protruding like a pouty child.

Lauren felt a twinge of sympathy. When Tamsin had broken her leg and Ellie had been seconded to them temporarily from Lenchester where she worked as a DC, Billy had struck up a relationship with the young officer. Lauren knew it was hard for them to maintain their connection from a distance, but there wasn't anything that could be done about it. Lauren also missed Ellie, particularly her extraordinary research skills, the like of which she'd never come across before. DCI Whitney Walker at Lenchester was very lucky to have Ellie as a part of her team.

'Sorry, Billy. There'll be other times you can visit, once this case is over,' Matt said softly.

'Okay, I suppose so,' Billy replied sullenly, though Lauren could see he was already accepting the situation. 'Unless you magic up another murder for us to investigate.'

'I'll try my hardest not to,' Matt responded, with a smile.

Lauren moved to the centre of the room. 'Matt and I will visit the home and get details of staff who work there, look at the visitor logs, and generally peruse the crime scene. I suggest the rest of you tidy up what you're doing so that we can all concentrate on this case. Once you've done that then start looking at the home for anything that's been in the media recently. When we come back, we'll allocate more specific tasks as needed, but it's good to get background on it. Also, Tamsin, can you look into Dawn Cross's background. She might have had a stage name, so bear that in mind.'

Tamsin was already pulling up search engines, while Clem began clearing his desk of the previous case's materials. Jenna reached for her notebook, ready to begin fresh notes on the new case.

'Any questions?' Lauren concluded, exchanging another meaningful glance with Matt. They both knew that if this case involved well-known personalities, the press would be breathing down their necks soon enough. They needed to move quickly and efficiently.

Jenna raised her hand slightly, her silver bangles jingling. 'Before you head out, ma'am, I might have something relevant.' She rifled through a stack of papers on her desk. 'I was working on the series of petty thefts at care homes in general last month. There could be a connection.'

'Go on,' Lauren said, her interest piqued.

'Nothing was ever proven, but there were complaints about small items going missing: jewellery, cash, even medications.' Jenna found the file she was looking for and held it up. 'Silver Fern wasn't one of the homes involved, but the pattern might be worth looking into. I know theft isn't murder, but it's certainly something.'

'Good thinking,' Lauren said. 'We can cross-reference the staff lists, once we have them, and see if anyone from Silver Fern worked at any of the places where there had been thefts.'

'Hey, look at this. Silver Fern made the local papers three months ago,' Billy called out, his fingers flying across the keyboard. His previous sulking was clearly forgotten in the excitement of a new lead. 'Something about a resident's family complaining about the standard of care there.'

Tamsin rolled her chair over to peer at his screen. 'Was it Dawn Cross's family?'

'No, different resident,' Billy replied, scrolling through the article. 'But it mentions high staff turnover in the past year. It could be relevant.'

Lauren felt the familiar surge of energy that came with a case picking up momentum. She loved watching her team like this, each person contributing their piece to the puzzle.

'That's great. Follow up on it. Matt and I will head to Silver Fern now. I want a full media report when we get back. Don't forget social media too. We need to know as much as possible about the home, the staff, and Dawn Cross herself.'

As she spoke, Lauren noticed Matt's thoughtful expression. She'd worked with him long enough to recognise when something wasn't sitting right with him.

'What is it?' she asked quietly as the others dispersed to their tasks.

'I was thinking about the method. Poisoned chocolates. It's very personal, isn't it? And certainly not random. Whoever did this to her knew her routine, and her preferences.'

'And had access to her room,' Lauren added. 'The care home will have strict protocols about visitors and gifts, I'd have thought, which means that either someone bypassed the rules or...' She allowed her words to tail off.

'Or it was an inside job,' Matt finished grimly. 'And if that's the case, does that mean all the other residents are in danger?'

Lauren's mind was already racing ahead to the interviews they'd need to conduct. 'We'll speak to the manager of the home first and find out which staff were around at the time of, and leading up to, Dawn Cross's death. I doubt they'll still be on duty though, if they were working nights.'

'Yes,' Matt agreed, as they headed towards the door. 'At this time of day the night staff will probably have gone home.'

Before they left, Lauren turned back to her team one last time. 'Remember, everyone, this needs to be handled delicately. Some of these residents would have spent their lives in the public eye. If word gets out about a murder in their midst, the media circus will make our jobs impossible. So, let's keep this to ourselves, at least for now.' She glanced at Billy, who was holding his mobile phone. 'I'm sure you're not phoning your mum are you, Billy?'

He flushed a deep shade of red.

'You were, weren't you?' Tamsin said, jabbing a finger in his direction.

'No, I wasn't,' Billy muttered, hitting one of the keys on the phone and putting it down on his desk.

'Of course you weren't,' Tamsin said. 'I'll make sure he doesn't, ma'am,' she added, looking at Lauren.

'Billy understands, and won't do it,' Matt joined in. 'Right?'

'Yes, Sarge. Ma'am,' Billy responded.

'Good. I don't know how long we'll be, but I'll forward to you anything that needs looking into straight away,' Lauren said.

'Including the CCTV,' Clem said. 'Assuming they have any.'

'Yes, including that,' Lauren said with a nod. She hadn't considered that, which was remiss of her.

As they left the station and made their way to the car park, Lauren couldn't shake the feeling that this case had the potential to be much more complex than she'd initially thought. Something about poisoned chocolates in a care home full of former entertainers seemed almost theatrical. It was like the plot from a play or TV show that one of them could have starred in. She just had to hope that they weren't embarking on something where real life ended up imitating art.

'My car?' Matt asked.

'No we'll take mine,' Lauren said, keys in hand, her mind already organising the questions they'd need to ask. 'Let's go and see what the stars have to tell us.'

FIVE

MONDAY FEBRUARY 10

Lauren pulled up to the front of Silver Fern Care Home, an impressive large old manor house on the outskirts of Marazion. The Georgian architecture stood proud at the end of the sweeping driveway, which curved elegantly through manicured lawns dotted with statues, several bird baths and carefully tended flower beds. In the far distance she glimpsed St Michael's Mount, which rose from the bay, stark against the grey sky.

The setting was idyllic.

'Wow, this is a really nice care home,' Matt said, nodding his approval as he glanced around at the grand facade. 'Not that I've seen many, but I'm sure there aren't many in such beautiful surroundings.'

Lauren's eyes swept across the pristine grounds, her mind already cataloguing potential entry and exit points, in case anyone tried to get away, but she doubted that would happen considering they had no suspects yet. 'Nothing more than I expected. If someone famous wants to spend their retirement here, it needs to be luxurious and special.'

'But it's still got to be affordable for those entertainers who weren't famous. Do you think they have social services funding for those people?' Matt asked, his brow furrowing.

'I've no idea,' Lauren replied, reaching for her warrant card. 'I imagine there would also be other requirements for people to live here. Maybe an Equity card, or something like that. We'll find out more when we get inside.'

They walked through the heavy oak doors into a small reception area, separated from the main building by an imposing glass partition. Lauren approached the reception desk, where a smartly dressed woman sat behind a computer screen. She held up her warrant card.

'Good morning. I'm DI Pengelly and this is DS Price. Is the manager here, please?'

'Yes, she is. I'll ask her to come out,' the receptionist responded efficiently. She reached for an internal phone system and pressed a button. 'Gill Trelawny to reception, please. Gill Trelawny to reception.'

Her voice echoed through the building's PA system and Lauren exchanged a glance with Matt. The announcement sounded more suited to a supermarket than an upscale care facility. They stepped to one side of the reception area to wait for the manager and Lauren continued to assess the layout and security measures in place. She noted a camera, indicating they did in fact have CCTV. Hopefully that would be of some use.

After a couple of minutes, a tall slim woman in her fifties, wearing black trousers and a black and cream striped blouse, came through the glass door, her heels clicking against the polished floor. 'Hello, I'm Gill Trelawny. How may I help you?'

'We're from Penzance police. We're here regarding the recent death of Dawn Cross.' Lauren watched carefully for the woman's reaction.

The manager's professional smile faltered slightly. 'Oh. Is there a problem?'

'Is there somewhere private we can talk?' Lauren asked, not wanting the news to spread through the home before they'd interviewed the manager.

'Yes, of course. Come with me. Hold all calls until I instruct otherwise,' Gill Trelawny said, turning to the receptionist.

'No problem,' the woman answered with a nod.

Gill then walked over to a security box beside the glass doors and quickly keyed in a code which automatically opened them. Lauren and Matt followed her into a wide, open-plan area. The space was furnished with elegant Georgian-style furniture and circular tables, the high ceilings adding to the grandeur of the setting. The period features had been carefully preserved while incorporating modern necessities.

They headed down a long corridor and into a side office, where Gill gestured to two high-backed chairs positioned in front of a substantial antique desk.

As they settled into the chairs, Lauren was aware that Gill Trelawny's demeanour had shifted to being more guarded. The manager took her place behind the desk, her hands clasped tightly together. 'What's the problem?'

Lauren leant forwards slightly, keeping her voice steady and measured. 'Dawn Cross's postmortem revealed that her death was not from natural causes, as originally believed. It's now being treated as suspicious.'

The colour drained from Gill Trelawny's face, her composure cracking further. 'What happened?' she asked, her voice barely audible.

'According to the pathologist, Dawn was poisoned after ingesting antifreeze. We believe it was administered through chocolate.'

'Dawn certainly loved her chocolate,' Gill murmured, almost to herself. 'She was very well known for it.'

Lauren's interest sharpened. 'Did anyone bring her any recently?'

Gill shook her head slowly, her forehead creasing in concentration. 'To be honest, I'm not sure, but she would often buy her own. There was always an open box in her room.'

'Do you know whether she had a particular favourite?' Lauren asked.

'Oh yes,' Gill responded immediately, some animation returning to her face. 'She loved the tinned assortments. Everyone knew that. There wasn't one in the selection that she didn't like, even the toffees, which she'd complain would stick to her plate. But that didn't stop her from eating them. Although her absolute favourite were strawberry creams. She couldn't get enough of them.'

'That's very useful, thank you,' Lauren said. 'We need to have a look through her room, but I'd also like to speak to the staff who were on duty on Friday between the hours of eight and ten in the evening.'

'I can check the rota for that,' Gill said, turning to her computer.

'I noticed you have CCTV at the entrance to the building. Do you have it elsewhere?' Lauren pressed.

'Yes, we have cameras in all of the corridors and outside the front office, but not at the rear of the building.'

'Why's that?' Matt asked.

'The camera needs replacing and to be honest, I hadn't got around to doing so.'

'I suggest you do so, as soon as possible. Please could you send the footage from all cameras to my office,' Lauren instructed, handing the woman her card, her tone making it clear this wasn't a request. 'Have you had any visitors in the building recently, in particular towards the end of last week?'

The manager nodded, seeming relieved to have something concrete to offer. 'As well as family and friends visiting the residents, we did have some electrical work done. The electrician we use, Hazel Dunston, has been with us for a long time. She works for Northside Electrical. She was here Thursday and Friday. We usually ask for her because she's good and the residents know and like her.'

'Please send me the company details, and also the name and number of Dawn's family so we can inform them about the death now being suspicious.'

'Her son visits regularly. I'll text his details.'

Lauren nodded, her mind already organising the next steps of the investigation. 'Thanks. Back to the staff on duty on Friday.'

Gill pulled her keyboard closer and clicked the mouse, scanning through the information. 'There were five staff on, not counting myself.'

Matt's eyebrows rose. 'How many residents do you have?'

'Thirty.'

'That's not many staff,' Matt replied.

Gill shifted uncomfortably in her chair. 'We follow the national guidelines for care homes. They're not so strict as they are for nursing homes because the care required is very different. We would normally have had six carers on duty on the Friday evening shift, but two of them were off sick.'

'Is that usual?' Lauren's eyes narrowed slightly.

'It's not uncommon; there are so many germs around at this time of year.' Gail's explanation seemed rehearsed, causing Lauren's instincts to prickle. Being understaffed would make it easy for someone to bypass protocols and get into Dawn Cross's room without being noticed.

'And are any of the four staff working at the moment, apart from you?'

Gill gave a sigh. 'I'm afraid not. Sorry. Do you want me to phone and ask them to come in?'

'Not yet. Did you notice anything out of the ordinary on Friday from mid-afternoon until seven?'

Gill shook her head. 'No. Not until Dawn was found dead.'

'At what time was that?'

'Just gone nine. The staff were doing their rounds to check if anyone would like a drink before going to bed. Although many of the residents are asleep by then. Only a few will stay up late.'

'What about Dawn?'

'She was one of the residents who sat up late watching the television.'

'Where was she found exactly?' Lauren asked.

'In her recliner. The member of staff went in and saw her. He then called me and after ascertaining that she was no longer alive I called for an ambulance.'

'Did anyone go into Dawn's room between her being discovered and the paramedics arriving?' Lauren asked, concerned that whoever poisoned the woman might have gone in there to remove any evidence.

'I don't believe so but can't be one hundred percent sure. After we called for the ambulance her bedroom door was closed and she was left in there.'

'I assume the CCTV footage of the corridors will confirm that she was left alone?' Matt asked.

'Yes, although there are some parts of the corridors that aren't captured because of the angles.'

'How is the home set up?' Lauren asked.

'It's divided into four separate wings: Olivier, Gielgud, Plowright and Richardson. Dawn was on Plowright,' Gill responded. 'Two wings are upstairs and two are downstairs.'

Lauren stood, her movement decisive. 'We'll take a look at Dawn's room. For now, please contact the staff who were on duty during the time Dawn died and ask them to be here first thing in the morning for an interview. After we've looked around the room, we'll speak to the residents.'

As much as she'd like to interview the staff sooner and go into more depth with Gill Trelawny regarding how the home operated, Lauren had to be back in court and couldn't spare the time. At this early stage in the investigation she wasn't prepared to leave the interviews to anyone else.

'Most of the residents are involved in a rehearsal of the play they're putting on. It's a production of *Arsenic and Old Lace*. Come with me and I'll take you to Dawn's room.'

Gill Trelawny led them out of the office and Lauren's mind was already racing, analysing the information they'd gathered. The limited staff, the possible missing CCTV coverage, the theatrical production's darkly appropriate title... all added up to something that made her increasingly uneasy.

SIX

MONDAY FEBRUARY 10

Lauren and Matt followed Gill Trelawny through the large entrance hall towards the magnificent sweeping staircase of polished mahogany, its elaborate balustrade, with intricately carved spindles, twisting beneath the smooth, highly polished, handrail.

'Do you have a lift?' Lauren asked, giving a quick scan of the area but unable to see one.

'Oh yes, there's one for the residents, but I thought we'd take the stairs so you could enjoy the splendour of the building. It's beautiful, isn't it?'

'Yes, it certainly is,' Lauren acknowledged.

'The home originally belonged to the family of one of Queen Victoria's ladies-in-waiting. It was bequeathed to the Entertainers Collective fifty years ago, by one of the descendants who was a well-known patron of the arts, to be turned into a care home for retired entertainers. There are strict rules of acceptance.'

'What are the rules?' Lauren asked, interested in finding out how it all operated.

'Residents must have been a member of Equity during the time they were actively working in the industry.' Gill paused. 'Equity is the UK's trade union for performers and those in the creative arts,' she added.

'Yes, we do know about Equity,' Lauren said, with a nod.

'Sorry. Some people don't,' Gill explained.

'What about funding? It can't be cheap to live here,' Matt asked, gesturing with his hand to the luxurious surroundings.

'Residents who are not able to fund themselves are assisted by the Entertainers Collective, who have a fund available for this.'

'What about social services?' Matt asked, with a frown. 'Won't they assist?'

'It's tricky because we're selective and only take ex-entertainers. It's something the Board of Directors are working on,' Gill said with a sigh.

'It's a lovely place to work, for sure,' Matt said, with a smile. 'Have you worked here long?'

'I've been here three years, after being an assistant manager at a home in Devon. It's lovely, but the residents are very different from what I'm used to.' Gill paused.

Was she worried that she'd said too much?

'In what way?' Lauren asked, picking up on it.

Knowledge of any conflict would be useful for the investigation.

'Without being disrespectful, let's just say the residents are much more demanding than I've been used to, and are not backwards in coming forward when it comes to making their feelings heard. But I love my job,' Gill hastily added, as if suddenly she felt awkward for complaining about the residents.

Lauren got it and certainly wouldn't judge the care home manager. She could imagine some of the residents being prima donnas – something she'd be mindful of during the investigation.

'You mentioned residents having visitors. Do they get many?' Lauren asked, wanting to refocus on their task at hand.

'Not really, to be honest. That's why they want to live here, so they can be amongst their peers. It gives them a sense of purpose and stops them from whiling their time away doing nothing.'

'What about Dawn?' Matt asked.

'Her son visits most Sundays, and that's it.'

'You mentioned they're performing a play?' Lauren asked.

'Every season the residents put on either a concert or a play, or maybe some readings. This time round it's a play. Dawn had a part in it.'

'And they're still going ahead?' Matt asked, arching an eyebrow.

'Oh yes, they decided to continue with it, in honour of her. They're currently rehearsing in the big ballroom, which is where the performance will take place. There's a stage at one end. Right, her room's just along here.' Gill nodded along the corridor.

'How long was Dawn at the home?'

'Coming up for three years, when she became fed up with living on her own. She refused to move in with her son, who wanted her there with him, but she wanted to live here.'

'Why didn't she want to live with him?' Lauren asked.

'She said that as much as she loved him, he was too inflexible. She knew she wouldn't enjoy living with him and didn't want to spoil their relationship.'

'What was she like as a resident? Was she one of the demanding ones?' Lauren asked.

'Actually, no. Dawn was one of the nicest residents in the home. I very often wished they were all like her. She was popular with the other residents, too, and could be a calming influence, especially as some of the others can be a little temperamental. All the staff liked Dawn, too. I never heard a bad word about her. Also, because she was so healthy she was easy to care for and didn't take up much of the carers' time.'

'We'll take it from here,' Lauren said when they came to a stop outside a room with Dawn's name on the door. 'This is now a crime scene, so please make sure that nobody comes in after we've gone and before forensics arrives.'

'Her son is due to come by either today or tomorrow to take all her belongings. We do give relatives a week to do that after someone passes.'

'Well, he won't be able to do that until we release the room,' Matt said firmly. 'We'll let him know when we speak to him.'

Gill left them and Lauren, followed by Matt, stepped into the room, the space holding that stillness unique to a recently vacated room. She pulled on some disposal gloves, the latex snapping softly in the quiet room. There was a faint smell of lavender coming from a small bowl of potpourri on the windowsill.

A collection of framed photographs caught her eye. There were younger versions of Dawn in various theatrical poses, her vitality captured forever behind glass. Lauren moved closer, noting how her smile remained unchanged across the decades.

Lauren then turned to the wardrobe in the corner. It was solid oak, its brass handles polished to a warm gleam.

'This is very nice,' Lauren said, running a gloved hand along the polished door of the wooden wardrobe. 'If a little small.'

'I suppose the residents all downsize when moving in here, and so don't need much space,' Matt suggested.

'True,' Lauren said with a nod.

Her attention was drawn to a half-finished knitting project on the chair: a burgundy scarf, the needles still stuck through the yarn as if waiting for their owner's return. The sight unexpectedly made her throat tighten.

The television mounted on the wall displayed a blank black screen, but beneath it sat a neat stack of DVDs, mostly old musicals and theatrical performances.

'She clearly never really left the stage behind,' Matt said.

Lauren's eyes scanned the titles; most of them she hadn't heard of.

A gentle breeze, coming in from the top window that was open slightly, rustled the cream-coloured curtains, carrying with it the distant sound of piano music from somewhere else in the building. The juxtaposition of life continuing while they stood in this room of death wasn't lost on her.

Lauren's gaze settled on the small tin of chocolates on the bedside table, sitting innocuously next to a well-thumbed copy of

An Actor Prepares by Stanislavski. The book was marked with numerous coloured tabs, suggesting that Dawn had been studying even in her final days.

'The chocolates,' Lauren murmured, turning to Matt and pointing at the square-shaped tin, with its lid firmly in place. She moved carefully around the bed, covered with a floral bedspread. 'We'll leave everything until after forensics have been here. Apart from the chocolates because I want to get these to Henry. I'll take a photo of the way they were positioned.' She pulled out her phone, took several photos and then placed the chocolates in an evidence bag.

She walked over to where Matt was standing, staring out of the window at the manicured gardens below. A group of elderly residents sat on benches in the sunshine and one woman was gesturing dramatically, apparently acting out a scene while her companions watched with rapt attention.

'They clearly have no idea of the tragedy that took place here,' Matt said with a shake of his head. 'Are you going to ask the manager to inform them that Dawn's death is suspicious?'

'Once we've interviewed the residents in the ballroom it won't take long for the news to spread. So it probably won't matter. Unless they want to offer some counselling.'

'Do we want a family liaison officer to come out?'

'I've been thinking about that but decided that in such a large place it might be tricky and not very productive. We'll leave it for now and revisit if needs be.'

They moved from the window and Lauren returned to the small wardrobe in the corner. On opening it she revealed a collection of carefully preserved costumes. There were some everyday clothes squashed to one end, and the rest comprised sequined gowns, feathered headpieces, and a variety of fancy shoes all arranged by colour. 'Look at this. It's like she's kept her whole life's work.'

'She was clearly performing until the end,' Matt murmured. 'And I think the script for their current production is on the bedside table. She's made loads of notes in the margins, so what else could it be?' He moved it slightly with a gloved hand. 'Ah yes, I was right. The title's on the front page. *Arsenic and Old Lace.*'

'Leave it where it is. I think we've seen all we need to for now,' Lauren said, feeling a little uneasy. 'Let's interview the residents in the play.'

The room's perfection needled at her detective's instincts. No scuff marks on the floor, no water rings on the bedside table, not even a wrinkled tissue in the waste bin. It felt more like a stage set than a lived-in space. Had the room been cleaned after Dawn's death, or did she always keep it this way?

'Okay,' Matt agreed. 'I'll message Clem first and ask him to check out Hazel Dunston the electrician.'

As they prepared to leave, Lauren noticed a small calendar hanging by the door. Dawn had marked the date of the play's opening night with a star, and beneath it, in elegant script:

The show must go on

The irony wasn't lost on her.

She paused in the doorway, taking one final look at the room. 'Someone made sure everything was perfect here... too perfect. The question is, were they cleaning up evidence, or just wanted it nice for when her son came to visit?'

'I've no idea, but either way, it's quite the performance,' Matt replied, with a shake of his head.

They closed the door quietly behind them, leaving Dawn's life frozen in time while they sought answers about her death. The sound of the piano music grew stronger as they walked away, an inadvertent soundtrack to their grim task.

SEVEN

MONDAY FEBRUARY 10

'Right, let's go and find the residents who are performing in this play,' Lauren said as they walked down the corridor. 'Whatever it was called, I can't remember...'

'*Arsenic and Old Lace*,' Matt said.

'Oh, you know the play, do you?' Lauren asked, turning to him, not hiding the surprise in her voice.

'Not the play. The film starring Cary Grant. It was from around the 1940s, I think.'

'Get you.' Lauren smirked. 'I didn't know that you were into old movies. You're clearly old before your time.'

'I'm not. And I'm not,' Matt replied with a grin. 'Cary Grant's my mum's all-time favourite actor and whenever his films were on the telly she insisted we sat down and watched them. It was pointless complaining. To be honest, I don't remember at all what it's about. Apart from poison, obviously, from the title.'

'Hmmm. It's certainly ironic when we consider how Dawn Cross died.'

'Ironic or perhaps relevant,' Matt added.

'Good point,' Lauren agreed with a sharp nod. 'Okay, let's head for the ballroom. I assume it will be on the ground floor.'

When they got to the bottom of the sweeping staircase, Matt

turned to the right. 'I can hear some voices over there.' He pointed in the direction of the sound.

They hurried over, finding the door was ajar. Lauren turned to Matt, placing a finger on her lips, indicating she wanted to listen before entering.

'The settled humour of this piece requires some precise comic timing if that's at all possible, and not your usual slapdash approach,' spoke a very loud, demanding voice.

Lauren and Matt exchanged a glance. Could the man be any more pompous?

'Sorry, Ken old fruit, I can't help it. My Roosevelt's more Blackpool Tower than Broadway,' came a jovial response, followed by the sound of exaggerated stomping.

'That's *Kenneth* to you, Charlie, and if it's not too much trouble I'd request that you please respect the playwright's intention,' Kenneth huffed, his voice hitting a pitch that suggested his blood pressure was rising. 'You were supposedly a professional, after all.'

Lauren sucked in a breath. Talk about cutting.

'Still am, darling,' Charlie responded, not sounding at all offended. 'I did the circuit until I was seventy-five, and that was without my walker. I've had an idea. What if Teddy Roosevelt thought he was Richard III instead? A walker. A walker. My kingdom for a walker.'

Lauren glanced at Matt, who raised his eyebrows as they heard a few people in the room dissolve into laughter.

'Need I remind you all, I played Malvolio at Stratford,' Kenneth said, sounding defensive.

'Of course you did, love,' Charlie said. 'And I played Blackpool Pier in February. That's proper theatre, that is. At least no one fell asleep during my act.' There was a pause which Lauren assumed was for dramatic effect. 'Well, except that one bloke, but it turned out he was dead. That was a right carry-on, let me tell you.'

'Some of us dedicated our lives to the craft of performance—'

'And some of us had to make drunk people laugh at two in the morning in Rotherham,' Charlie said, interrupting Kenneth. 'Now there's a tough crowd. You ought to try doing Shakespeare for a hen party from Sheffield and see the response you get.'

'Can we forget about what you did in the past and get back to the play,' Kenneth said, his voice strained. 'Like I said, this requires subtle observation, a delicate touch—'

'Like what I had to use when hecklers were drunk enough to throw chairs but not sober enough to thump me,' Charlie mused.

'Charlie, your constant references to working men's clubs are hardly relevant to this masterpiece of theatre. Are you so stupid that you don't understand?'

'What I'm saying is relevant. You just don't get it,' Charlie responded, his voice remaining calm, despite the increasing amount of abuse Kenneth seemed to be subjecting him to.

A loud shriek of laughter came from a female voice, and Lauren looked at Matt, who was clearly struggling to maintain his professional composure.

'Come on, let's go in.' Lauren pushed the door open, fighting back her own smile. 'Hello, sorry to interrupt.'

They stood in the entrance, and she scanned the exquisite room.

'Who are you?' The loud, demanding voice clearly belonged to Kenneth, who was now drawing himself up to his full, over six-feet, height. His commanding frame was topped by a silver comb-over that was slightly askew, probably from his earlier agitation. He took a step towards them.

'I'm Detective Inspector Pengelly, and this is Detective Sergeant Price. And you are?'

'Kenneth Blencoe,' he announced with theatrical gravitas, as if expecting applause. 'I'm directing this production.'

'Ex-RSC, darling,' Charlie stage-whispered behind a hand to Matt, but loud enough for everyone to hear. 'He never lets us forget it.'

'And standing next to you is Charlie,' Kenneth said through gritted teeth.

'At your service.' Charlie gave an elaborate bow that nearly sent him toppling into a chair. 'Though I should warn you, the last time I dealt with the police, it was when someone threw a frozen chicken at me during my comedy set in Barnsley.'

Lauren noticed Matt tensing his jaw to keep from laughing. It was the same for her. How she managed to hold back her mirth was anyone's guess.

'Yes, that'll do for now,' Lauren said, trying to maintain professional authority in a room full of dramatic personalities. 'If you could all come a little closer, I wish to speak to you and don't want to shout.' She gestured for the group to gather round. About fifteen residents gradually shuffled forward, each trying to position themselves centre-stage and in Lauren's direct eyeline.

'I'm Fred,' a small man in a beige cardigan with dark brown buttons announced, clearly not wanting to be left out of the introductions.

Lauren nodded at him and then took a deep breath. 'Thank you. Unfortunately, we have some rather serious news regarding Dawn Cross, who died last week—'

'Oh, that was dreadful,' interrupted a tall slender woman in a floral dress, clutching at the pearls which hung around her neck. 'Such a shame. It was so sudden. She was a lovely person. We're really going to miss her.'

'I'm sure you will,' Lauren acknowledged, kindly. 'What I must inform you is that following the postmortem, the pathologist has concluded that Dawn's death wasn't due to natural causes. It's now being treated as suspicious.'

'What?' Kenneth's voice echoed off the high ceiling. 'Explain "suspicious".'

'She didn't die of natural causes,' Lauren repeated and then paused for her words to sink in. 'She was murdered.'

The room erupted in gasps worthy of a West End production.

'Murdered?' Charlie gave a low whistle. 'Blimey. And here's me thinking the most dramatic thing that happened round here was when Kenneth's toupee fell off and landed in his soup last Tuesday lunchtime.'

'It's not a toupee,' Kenneth hissed, self-consciously patting his hair.

'Please,' Lauren continued firmly. 'This is serious.'

'Sorry,' Charlie muttered. Kenneth nodded in agreement.

'Thank you. We'd like to know a little bit about Dawn as a person.'

'Well, she was quiet and friendly,' a woman piped up. 'Apart from when she used to be on the stage. Then she was a bit up herself,' she added with a theatrical eye roll.

'Don't speak ill of the dead,' Kenneth said.

'I'm not. It's true and Dawn would be the first to admit it,' the woman responded, not appearing at all intimated by the man.

'And you are?' Lauren asked.

'Veronica Waite,' the short, well-rounded, silver-haired woman replied. 'I've known Dawn for years. We used to be in rep together. She was much nicer as an older woman. More chilled and fun.'

'Was Dawn in this play?' Matt asked, gesturing to the scripts scattered around.

'Yes,' Kenneth said, dabbing his eyes with a silk handkerchief, although Lauren couldn't detect any tears. 'She had one of the larger parts. Aunt Martha.'

'How was the allocation of parts decided?' Lauren asked, wondering if this could have anything to do with her murder.

'Bribery,' Charlie piped up, seeming unable to take the situation seriously.

'That's enough,' Kenneth said. 'I've already told you it was a fair process following auditions. As the play's director, the allocation of parts was down to me. It's not like we have a large pool to choose from. Because believe me, if I did have more of a choice you'd be sitting on the sidelines.'

'Try it and see what happens,' Charlie responded with an exaggerated smile.

'Gentlemen, please,' Lauren said, holding up both hands to silence them.

'Who's going to play Aunt Martha now?' Matt asked.

'Bertha was understudying the role, so she is,' Kenneth replied, pointing to the tall woman who'd spoken earlier.

'Didn't you think to cancel the production in deference to Dawn?' Lauren asked.

'No.' Kenneth raised a hand to his chest. 'Absolutely not. We're doing the play in *honour* of Dawn. The show must go on, my dear. That's what she would have wanted, without question.'

'That, and for someone to figure out who topped her,' Charlie muttered, earning himself another glare from Kenneth.

Lauren glanced at Matt, who was scribbling notes while trying not to smile. 'Did any of you notice anyone hanging around the home who shouldn't have been last week? Someone you didn't recognise?'

They all shook their heads, several adding dramatic flourishes to their gesture.

'Did anything out of the ordinary occur?' Lauren added.

Charlie let out a bark of laughter. 'Everything's out of the ordinary here, daaarling. What do you expect when you get a group of performers together all vying for attention?'

'Thespians,' Kenneth corrected, emphasising each syllable. 'At least most of us are.' He glared in Charlie's direction.

'Well, whatever.' Charlie shrugged. 'Though I must say, if this was one of my old working men's clubs, we'd have solved the murder by now. Nothing gets past a crowd of drunk northerners on a Saturday night. Not that you'd ever know.' He smirked in Kenneth's direction.

'If anybody thinks of anything that might be useful,' Lauren said loudly, before Kenneth could respond to Charlie's quip, 'please let Gill Trelawny know, and she'll get in touch with us.'

'Can we go back to rehearsing now?' Kenneth asked, holding up the script.

'Yes, by all means,' Lauren said, nodding for Matt to follow her to the entrance of the ballroom.

'Right. From the top. And Charlie, for the love of all that's holy, stop suggesting we replace the elderberry wine with WKD Blue.' Kenneth's voice boomed out as they left.

Matt frowned.

'That's vodka,' Lauren explained.

'Oh, I didn't realise. And now I feel really old if people of that age know more than me when it comes to trendy alcohol. How come you know about it?' he asked with a frown.

'It's not that trendy, it's been around for years. I'm surprised you haven't come across it,' Lauren replied.

'Yeah, well, that's because my life is one long round of work and childcare. Not that I mind,' Matt clarified. 'Where to now?'

'Dawn Cross's son, Quentin, to inform him of the latest, and to also ascertain if he knows anything that might help the investigation.'

'Do you think a resident in the home could have killed Dawn Cross? For all the craziness, nothing struck me as being a red flag.'

'I honestly don't know. But they would have had to get hold of antifreeze and know the intricacies of how to deliver it.' Lauren paused. 'Though I must say, in a building full of amateur dramatists performing *Arsenic and Old Lace*, it does seem a bit on the nose.'

From behind them came the sound of Kenneth's voice: 'No, Charlie, you can't add a tap dance number.'

EIGHT

MONDAY FEBRUARY 10

'Do we know anything about Quentin Cross?' Lauren asked, drumming her fingers on the steering wheel, as they were heading from the care home to see the victim's son.

'Well,' Matt replied, shifting in his seat to face her, 'according to the text I've received from Billy, he's a retired solicitor.' I assume he must have put his mother in the home because it's less than twenty minutes away from where he lives.'

'Or she might have insisted on living there because of the type of place it is.'

'True. Interesting he didn't follow in his mother's footsteps and go into the entertainment business. Unless it was something he did before going into the legal profession,' Matt mused, more to himself.

Finally they arrived at Crowlas, a small hamlet on the outskirts of Penzance where narrow country lanes wound between ancient drystone walls and hedgerows that were thick with bramble and wild fuchsia. The landscape changed from coastal views to more rural as they pulled up outside an imposing detached Victorian property, which had climbing ivy across the front.

Lauren parked on the street, and they walked up the long drive to the dark red painted door. The garden was perfectly manicured with not a leaf out of place. It was almost as if each blade of grass had been cut with a pair of nail scissors.

Lauren rang the bell and after a few minutes, a tall, well-built woman with curly, grey hair hanging loose to her shoulders, answered. A black velvet headband topped with a cluster of pearls held her hair back off her face. Her posture was rigid, defensive almost, as if she was worried about something.

'We're looking for Mr Quentin Cross,' Laura said.

'That's my husband. Who shall I say is calling?'

'DI Pengelly and DS Price from Penzance police,' Laura said, holding out her warrant card.

Matt studied the woman as she grimaced slightly at the sight of their identification. Her fingers tightened on the doorframe.

'Ah, please come in. If you'd like to take a seat in the drawing room, I'll fetch Quentin from his study.'

She led them into the house, her footsteps eerily silent on the carpeted floor. They walked into a square room which had two large sofas facing one another across a low, light oak coffee table. Long curtains matching the cream floral sofas hung from floor to ceiling.

While they waited, Matt wandered over to look at the different books lining the walls. The whole place made him feel uncomfortable. It seemed too perfect, too arranged.

'There's a mixed collection of books here,' he said quietly to Lauren. 'Some law books, and also some paperback romance novels.' He smiled wryly. 'Oh well, each to their own. I'd much prefer a thriller.'

Lauren nodded, her eyes scanning the room with professional interest.

Matt was about to head over to the photos on the fireplace when the door opened and a tall man with silver hair entered. The way he held himself was of someone used to commanding attention. Exactly what Matt would expect from a solicitor, if his past experience was anything to go by.

'Good morning, Officers. How can I help you? Please, sit down.' His voice was clipped and controlled.

'Mr Cross—'

'Please call me Quentin,' the man said, interrupting Lauren.

Considering the man's appearance, Matt was surprised at this informality.

'Okay, Quentin,' Lauren said, with a friendly smile.

Cross settled onto one of the sofas, his hands clasped tightly in his lap, knuckles white. Clearly, he wasn't as relaxed as he wanted to make out.

'Unfortunately, we have some news regarding your mother's death. Firstly, we're very sorry for your loss,' Lauren said, after they'd sat on the opposite sofa.

'What is it?' Cross's voice wavered slightly.

'Initially, it was believed she died of natural causes—'

'Well, she was ninety-two, but very sprightly,' Cross interrupted, a hint of pride in his voice.

'Yes, so we understand. Following the pathologist's initial report, we're now treating your mother's death as suspicious.'

Cross paled. 'Murder?'

The word hung in the air like wafts of smoke.

'Yes. I'm sorry,' Lauren said.

'Oh my goodness.' The colour leached even further from his face, and he gripped the arm of the sofa. His wife, who had been hovering in the doorway, rushed to his side and rested her hand on his arm.

'We'd like to ask you a few questions if you're up to it,' Lauren asked.

'Yes, of course I am,' Cross said, pulling himself together, his professional mask slipping back into place. 'I used to be a solicitor and am well used to in-depth questioning and dealing with the police, at all ranks.' He spoke as if to reassure himself more than Lauren and Matt.

'What can you tell us about your mother, in particular her career?' Matt asked, pulling out his notebook and pen.

A tiny smile crossed the man's face. 'She was a very successful actress in her day, especially in film and later TV. Although she didn't tend to be offered leading roles, she very often had the second-to-leading roles.'

'Was there a reason for this?' Lauren asked, tilting her head to one side.

Cross gave a shrug. 'To be honest, she wasn't classically beautiful in the way they wanted in those days, and that's why she always had either the part of the friend or, as she got older, the mother. She didn't mind because it meant she was gainfully employed for many years.'

Cross's posture noticeably changed when discussing his mother's career – he sat straighter and was more animated. He seemed proud of what she had achieved.

'What about in later life?' Lauren asked.

'Sadly, her career faded as she got older. It's not like nowadays when there are plenty of parts for older women. Once women got to a certain age in my mother's day, there was very little for them to do in films or on television.'

'Was she still able to work on stage?' Lauren prompted.

'Yes, she worked for the Royal Shakespeare Company and also for local repertory companies around the country.'

'Was this while you were growing up?' Matt asked, glancing up from his notes.

'Yes. When I was young, I'd often travel with her, and once I was older, I was sent to boarding school.' A shadow crossed his face at this memory.

'Is it just by chance that you live here and she ended up being in Silver Fern Care Home?' Lauren asked.

'Yes and no.' Cross shifted uncomfortably. 'We wanted to move to Cornwall and I bought into a law practice here. The home was close by which was a factor. Mother was getting to the stage when she couldn't really look after herself. Although she was healthy, her memory was getting poorer and it worried me that something would happen and she wouldn't be able to raise the alarm. We offered for her to live with us but she didn't want to be a burden.'

Cross's wife twisted the hem of her cardigan around her fingers and stared down at her lap.

Was there an issue?

'So it worked out well for all of you, then,' Matt stated, keeping his eye on her.

'Yes.' Cross glanced at his wife, a stern look in his eyes.

'Were you not happy with the arrangement, Mrs Cross?' Matt asked.

'Of course I was. It's great living here,' the woman replied, although Matt wasn't buying it. He'd park that for now, though.

'Since you mentioned suspicious circumstances' – Cross leant forward – 'how was Mother murdered?'

'Initial findings are that she was poisoned with antifreeze,' Lauren replied.

'Who on earth would do that?' Quentin responded, shock shining from his eyes.

'Do either of you know anyone holding a grudge against your mother?'

Cross sat there for a while, staring ahead. 'Not really,' he finally replied. 'I mean, she could be a bit of a madam when she was younger – that's no secret. It meant she occasionally rubbed people up the wrong way. But like I said, she was in her nineties and a gentle old lady.' His voice rose slightly. 'Who on earth would want to kill a woman of that age?'

'Do you think it was deliberately her they were targeting, or just an old person in a care home for whatever reasons? You read all sorts of stories about serial killers,' Mrs Cross asked, a puzzled expression on her face.

'We don't know yet, Mrs Cross, but it's certainly an avenue we'll be considering. We'll keep you both informed once we know more,' Lauren assured her. 'Where were you both on Friday between four in the afternoon and seven?'

'Why?' Quentin asked, frowning at them.

'We believe it to be during that time that your mother was murdered,' Lauren replied.

'Are you accusing me?' Quentin's eyes blazed.

'We want to eliminate people from our enquiries, as I'm sure you understand,' Lauren answered, in a non-accusatory way.

'Yes. Yes. I understand. We had lunch with friends in the local pub and arrived home at five. We didn't go out after that.'

'That's correct,' Mrs Cross agreed. 'Quentin fell asleep in the chair, and I sat in my craft room quilting.'

'Thank you. Is there anything you can think of that could assist our investigation?'

The couple exchanged glances.

Were they hiding something? Matt couldn't tell.

'Not really, Officer. I'm sorry,' Mr Cross said, his wife nodding in agreement.

'That's fine. If you do remember anything, please contact me. I'll arrange for a family liaison officer to be with you during this time,' Lauren said.

'No, absolutely not.' Cross's outburst seemed to startle even his wife. 'I refuse. I know all about family liaison officers. I've witnessed a few in my time when I was working, and no offense to yours – I'm sure they're wonderful people – but I don't want someone in my house with us.'

There was more to this than met the eye. What had happened in the past to make him so opposed to it? And was whatever it was relevant to the case?

'As you wish,' Laura said calmly. 'But if you change your mind, here's my card. Also, if you do think of anything that might be relevant, please let me know.'

'Okay,' Mr Cross said, taking the card from her.

Lauren stood, and Matt followed.

'We'll see ourselves out,' Lauren said.

'No, you won't. I'll escort you,' Cross said sharply, jumping up from the sofa.

Matt paused and looked at him, his detective's instincts tingling.

Was he worried they might start looking around the house on their way out?

They wouldn't. Not without a search warrant. But nevertheless, for the man to think that it begged the question: what was he hiding?

Cross practically herded them to the door, his wife trailing behind like a shadow. Once they got on the street and had climbed into the car, Matt turned to Lauren.

'Well, he was acting strange,' Matt said, loosening his tie.

'Yes. And I'm sure he didn't want us to see ourselves out because he thought we might have a nose around the place,' Lauren agreed.

'Exactly what I thought. Is he hiding something do you think? Or just being a typical solicitor?'

'It could be either. Did you notice how the wife seemed to be in his shadow? I'm sure she wasn't happy being close to her mother-in-law.' Lauren pulled over the seatbelt, clicked it in place and adjusted it over the front of her jacket.

'Yes, I did. And what's with not wanting a FLO?' Matt asked, putting on his seat belt, too. 'Do you think something happened in the past to make him so opposed to them?'

'It's certainly something we need to investigate – get one of the team onto it.'

'Will do. Where to now?' Matt asked, checking his watch, conscious of Lauren's need to return to Truro.

'I need to get back to court. I can't miss being called. I'll drop you off at the office and you can get the team working. We need to find out as much as possible about the care home residents, and also Quentin Cross and his wife, including any interactions they've had with FLOs in the past.'

'Yes, ma'am.'

As they drove away, Matt couldn't shake the feeling that there was more to Quentin Cross than met the eye. The perfectly maintained house, the controlling behaviour, the refusal of a family liaison officer – it all added up to something, but what the hell was it?

And, more importantly, would he kill his own mother?

Matt had seen enough cases to know that family ties didn't always mean what they should. He pulled out his notebook and started reading through them, to make sure they were firmly in his head. They needed to investigate Dawn Cross's theatrical career too. Maybe there were old grudges there – though killing someone in their nineties over ancient history seemed far-fetched.

The grey clouds gathering overhead matched Matt's mood as they headed back to the station. This case was going to be anything but straightforward.

Matt pushed open the door to the office, noting that he was the first to arrive. He glanced across to Lauren's office to check whether she was already there but couldn't see her shadow through the frosted glass panel in the door, so assumed that she hadn't. He hung up his jacket on the coat stand in the corner and headed over to his desk, intending to check his emails and tidy up anything outstanding, to ensure he could concentrate fully on the Dawn Cross murder case.

'Good morning, Matt.'

He started at the sound of Lauren's voice and glanced up to see her standing in her doorway smiling. She must have gone in through the other door into her office.

'Morning, ma'am,' he said, jumping up from his desk and hurrying over. 'How did it go yesterday afternoon in court?'

'Come on through and I'll tell you.' She gestured for him to sit on one of the low chairs surrounding the glass-topped coffee table, and she did the same. 'Well, to be honest, I was way more nervous than I thought I'd be,' Lauren said, fidgeting with her watch as if the nervousness remained, despite her part in the proceedings being over. 'I've never felt like that when giving evidence in court before which, as you know, I've done countless times.' She shook her head.

'That's because in the past when you've appeared in court it's been part of your job and not because you're acting as a witness for a relative. You wouldn't be human if it didn't affect you. This was personal.'

'Yes, you're right,' Lauren replied, nodding. 'Anyway, nerves aside, I think it went okay. I managed to answer all the questions the prosecution asked without dropping my aunt in it.'

Matt frowned. 'Surely you're not saying you lied on oath? I can't imagine that.'

'No, not at all,' Lauren quickly assured him. 'But you know what the prosecution can be like. They jump on the tiniest thing and try to push you on it. They especially wanted to know what life was like living with my uncle when I was a child.' She paused, running her fingers through her hair. 'I gave my evidence as well and concisely as I could. It was weird because I could feel Aunt Julia staring at me the whole time. It was almost like she was channelling what she wanted me to say, but she didn't obviously. I said what I knew to be the truth.'

Lauren leant back in her chair as if considering her words. 'I genuinely don't believe she killed my uncle intentionally. Yes, she did have an awful life with him and her sons, but that doesn't mean she set out to kill him. It was a mistake. She wanted to give him something to calm him down. I don't blame her; he was bad enough before he started to get dementia. He must have been unbearable after. She'd no idea that he'd been out drinking, or that the combination of the drug and the drink would be fatal.'

Lauren exhaled loudly. The stress of the case was clearly affecting her more than she'd admitted. Matt dreaded to think how it would affect her if Julia ended up in prison.

'When do you think the case will end?' he asked.

Lauren gave a tiny shrug, 'It shouldn't be much longer. We might get a result later this week.'

'And if they find her guilty of murder?' Matt broached, so he could explain that he was there for her, whatever happened.

'I'm not even thinking about it... but we can appeal,' Lauren said, straightening her shoulders. 'Right, less about me. We need to get the team cracking on the case, as they've now arrived.' Lauren tilted her head towards the open door and the others beyond, and rose from her chair.

That meant he didn't have the chance to explain how he'd be there for her but he'd tell her another time. He followed her back into the office where the rest of the team had arrived, their faces expectant.

Matt's stomach tightened with anticipation as they walked over to the whiteboard.

'Attention please, everybody,' Lauren said. 'As you know, we have a suspicious death. Dawn Cross. But what we don't know yet is the motive and whether she was specifically targeted or just an unlucky victim.'

Clem raised his hand, his face thoughtful. 'I've been thinking about the timing. Did the murderer intend for Dawn to die between four and seven? It's a busy time in the home, with dinner, and after that most residents will have returned to their rooms. There wouldn't be any activities. It would make it easier for someone to move around without being noticed.'

'Good point.' Matt nodded, his mind racing through the possibilities. Could the killer have known the care home's routine? It seemed likely.

'Also, if the timing was planned it could mean the murderer actually handed the chocolates to Dawn,' Clem added.

'It's not something we can ascertain at the moment,' Lauren said. 'We've had a chat with some of the residents, who spoke highly of Dawn, but none had seen anything. We haven't yet questioned the staff who were on duty Friday evening because they weren't working, but we'll go back and talk to them. There was also an electrician working on Friday in the home – Hazel Dunston – and we intend to visit her before going back to the home.'

'Did any of the residents mention if Dawn had any enemies?' Jenna interjected.

Matt's attention shifted to the victim's photo on the board. A smiling ninety-two-year-old woman. Who'd want her dead?

'Not so far,' Lauren responded. 'But let's examine what we do know. For a start, was Dawn Cross using social media? At ninety-two, I'm guessing probably not?'

'You're right, she wasn't,' Clem said, glancing at the screen on his desk. 'But the care home has a social media page, and they frequently include photos of different events and activities held there. There are plenty of photos of Dawn Cross on there, along with the other residents. Sometimes they post videos as well.'

'What about the home itself?' Matt asked. 'Did anyone discover anything negative against the home in the media, apart from that complaint, which we still need to follow up?'

'No, Sarge,' Jenna said. 'They advertise when they have concerts or plays and report on them after with photos. I looked at all the comments made on their posts and everything I've read is positive. There's been nothing bad said about them. It certainly seems a good place for the residents to live.'

Matt rubbed his chin, contemplating. 'Well, something isn't adding up. Why would someone target a well-liked resident in a reputable care home?'

'That's what we need to find out,' Lauren said. 'Who checked the CCTV footage that the home sent us?'

'I did, ma'am,' Billy said, nodding at his screen. 'I've watched people coming in and out of the place during the day and I reckon some of them were visitors and some weren't but we'd need to check. There was nobody acting suspiciously and no one was carrying a tin of chocolates.'

'Well, let's keep digging. Look in more detail into Dawn Cross and check her son to see if there's anything suspicious about him.'

'Surely you don't believe that he killed her? Especially at her age,' Billy said with a shake of his head.

'You should know by now that we don't take anything for granted,' Lauren replied firmly. 'Everyone needs investigating, however remote the possibility is of them being the killer.'

'Yeah. Of course. Sorry, ma'am,' Billy replied, lowering his head.

Lauren turned back to the whiteboard, her expression focused. 'I want to concentrate on Dawn's routine. We know that the only regular visitor she had was her son most Sundays. See what else we can turn up.'

'There is something that may, or may not be relevant,' Clem added. 'The care home had a recent change in senior management. New protocols were put in place about visitor sign-ins and resident outings.'

Matt's interest piqued. 'When was this change? Gill Trelawny didn't mention it.'

'Three weeks ago, after a social services inspection during which security procedures were questioned,' Clem replied. 'Maybe she didn't think it was relevant.'

Matt turned and faced the whiteboard, studying the timeline. 'You could be right, but now we know, we'll ask her about it. We need to focus on the chocolates which Dawn loved and would eat often.'

'Yes, they were the perfect vehicle to use, in my opinion,' Lauren added. 'What did you turn up about the electrician?'

'She's been with the company for five years, and doesn't have a criminal record,' Clem said. 'But there was something interesting. She was originally scheduled to work on Monday and Tuesday, but the appointment was changed at the last minute.'

Matt's pulse quickened. 'Who changed it?'

'That's just it,' Clem said, leaning forward. 'The person I spoke to at the company had no idea.'

Lauren's head snapped up. 'Maybe Hazel Dunston did, herself. We'll ask her.'

'Do you think the killer wanted the electrician there doing the work because it would mean the place would be busier than usual and make it easier for them to do their stuff?' Billy asked.

'It's a possibility, but I'm not jumping to any conclusions,' Lauren replied.

'Or the electrician could be the killer. Though why would she be there on a Friday? Thursday could have done just as well,' Billy mused, more to himself.

Matt studied the victim's photo again. Dawn Cross smiled back at him, her eyes bright and alert even at her age. Who would want to harm someone like her? It made no sense... Unless...

'Ma'am,' he said slowly. 'I've had a thought. What if Dawn saw something she wasn't supposed to see and she was killed simply to silence her? With her room overlooking the parking lot she could have easily witnessed something she shouldn't. And it would certainly explain why someone of her age was murdered.'

'Yes, Matt, that's certainly something to consider. Motive aside, we need to check if any other residents had regular evening routines that would have put them near Dawn's room at the time she ate the chocolates. Or they might have witnessed who delivered them. But for now, we need to interview Hazel Dunston and then return to the care home.'

The team dispersed, each with their tasks, but Matt lingered for a moment at the evidence board. Was this personal? If so, why? If not and it was random, did that mean that the other residents in the home were in danger?

TEN

Matt and Lauren drove out to Northside Electrical in Penzance to enquire about Hazel Dunston. The building was unremarkable, a small square grey structure with a corporate logo that had seen better days. Rain began spotting the windscreen as Lauren pulled into an empty parking space, and she flicked the wiper on and off.

Matt stared out of the window, his mind focusing on Dawn Cross and her final moments. Was it luck that no one had gone into her room while the poison was taking effect? Or did the murderer plan it, knowing that the staff would be otherwise occupied with the evening meal, or shift changes?

The front entrance of the company was flanked by several wilting potted plants, their leaves drooping as if they too had given up on the place. As they walked through the door to the front desk, Matt was hit by the sterile smell of cleaning products that seemed to permeate every professional space, underlaid with the sharp tang of electrical burning that reminded him of blown fuses and faulty wiring.

A woman who looked to be in her forties stood behind the counter, her fingers tapping against the keyboard in an irregular rhythm. The nameplate on her desk read 'Sian Moore' in gold-painted letters that were beginning to peel.

'We'd like to speak to Hazel Dunston, please,' Lauren said, holding out her warrant card.

The receptionist's eyes lingered on the identification, her tapping fingers still going. 'Ohhh.' She drew the word out, her gaze flicking between them. 'Actually, she's out on a job. Can I ask what it's about?'

'Sorry, we can't discuss that. I'm sure you understand,' Matt said, watching the woman's shoulders tense at his non-answer. 'Is the manager here?'

'Yes, I'll just fetch him.' She stood, smoothing non-existent creases from her skirt.

Did she know more than she was letting on?

They stood by the desk and Matt's attention diverted to the various safety certificates lining the walls. Most were outdated with renewal dates from the previous year. Lauren kept checking her phone, presumably hoping to hear about her aunt's case.

After several minutes, the receptionist emerged from the office behind the front desk, followed by a broad-shouldered man whose jacket stretched tight across his large stomach, straining the buttons.

'I'm Bert Walker, the manager here. How can I help you?' His voice had the forced cheerfulness of someone who'd spent too much time in customer service.

'DI Pengelly and DS Price,' Lauren said, holding out the warrant card again. 'We need to speak to Hazel Dunston urgently regarding the job she was on last week at Silver Fern Care Home.' Lauren's tone was professional but with an edge that Matt had learnt meant he'd better be helpful or there would be repercussions.

The manager's eyebrows lifted slightly, and he tugged at his collar. 'She always goes there. What's the problem?'

'We need to speak to her,' Lauren repeated firmly, not answering his question. 'Is she close by?'

'Yes, she is.' He glanced at his watch. 'She's doing a job down the road. I don't like taking my guys off a job, because it puts everything back. And customers get twitchy about it. But if it's important...' His voice fell away as if hoping they'd explain what it was about.

Nice try. But there was no way Lauren would tell him.

'Yes, it is, or we wouldn't be here.' Lauren stared directly at the man. 'I understand Hazel was originally scheduled to work at the home last Monday and Tuesday but this was changed at the last minute. Do you know why?'

The manager frowned and looked at the receptionist. 'Sian?'

'Yes, I did it because of trying to fit in an emergency that cropped up.'

'How come when my officer phoned here no one knew about it?' Lauren asked, annoyed that they hadn't been told the truth.

'I don't recall taking the call. It could have been our work experience girl. Sorry. I'll speak to her about it when she's next in.'

'Thank you,' Lauren replied. 'Now, Hazel,' she added, staring directly at the manager.

'I'll phone and ask her to come back straight away. But if you can keep it brief that would be very helpful,' he replied, folding his arms across his chest.

'We won't keep her any longer than necessary,' Lauren responded.

'Good. If you'd like to wait over there until she gets back.' He nodded towards a small waiting area.

'Thank you,' Lauren replied.

They sat down on hard blue plastic chairs which had seen better days and were worn and shiny from years of use. A coffee machine gurgled in the corner, producing a smell that was more industrial than appetising. Matt picked up a magazine from the table and began flicking through the pages, while at the same time keeping an eye on the clock, each second seeming to stretch longer than the last.

Finally, after fifteen minutes a woman in her late twenties or early thirties, wearing navy overalls, her dark hair pulled back into a ponytail, walked in the front entrance and headed straight to the reception, without giving them a second glace. Had the manager informed her they were waiting and she'd deliberately ignored them, to pretend she didn't know?

'Bert asked me to come back,' she said to the receptionist, her voice pitched slightly too high.

'Yes, the police are here. They want to speak to you.' Sian nodded in their direction.

'What, me?' Hazel turned, one hand rising to her chest in what appeared like a carefully rehearsed gesture.

She'd clearly been informed they were there.

Lauren and Matt got up and strode towards the electrician. The movement seemed to make Hazel nervous and she took half a step back, her shoulders touching the wall behind her.

'I'm Detective Inspector Pengelly, and this is Detective Sergeant Price,' Lauren said, looking directly at the woman. 'Is there somewhere quiet we can talk?'

Hazel's fingers twisted together briefly before she dropped them to her sides. 'We can go to the staff room if there's no one in there.' She glanced at Sian.

'It's empty,' the receptionist replied.

'Oh, okay, thanks.'

They followed Hazel down a narrow corridor lined with motivational posters that had faded to near illegibility. The staff room smelt of stale coffee and microwaved meals, with an underlying hint of something Matt couldn't quite place.

Hazel chose the chair nearest the door.

Was she planning to do a runner?

'What is it?' Hazel asked, adjusting the collar of her Northside Electrical overalls, even though it didn't appear to need any.

'Thank you for coming back to see us,' Lauren said gently. 'I don't know if you've heard that Dawn Cross, one of the residents at Silver Fern Care Home, died on Friday.'

Matt scrutinised the woman's face for any giveaway signs of deception.

Hazel's eyes widened. 'No, I didn't know anything about it. Nobody told me.'

Her reaction appeared genuine enough.

'Would you have expected them to?' Matt asked, leaning back in his chair.

'I suppose not. But I've been going there a while to do their electrical work and I know Dawn. I know all of them. What happened?'

'You don't believe it to be from natural causes, then?' Lauren asked, tilting her head slightly to the side.

'Ummm... I don't know. I thought because you're here that something must have happened. That's all.' The woman twisted her hands nervously in her lap.

'You're right. We're treating Dawn's death as suspicious. We wish to speak to you because you were working at the care home on Friday.'

'Oh... You mean... she was murdered?' Hazel's words fell away and her face paled. 'Yes. Yes. I was there on Thursday and Friday. I can't believe...' She shook her head.

'What were you doing there?' Lauren asked.

'I was PAT testing. That's portable appliance testing,' Hazel clarified. 'There are loads of them in a place like that. Every telly, computer, laptop, hair dryer, etc. etc.'

'Did you go into Dawn's room during the week?'

'Yes, I went into all of the residents' rooms, offices and communal areas.'

'Do you remember the day you tested Dawn's appliances?' Matt asked.

Hazel glanced away and wouldn't meet his eyes. 'Umm... Friday afternoon.'

'I see. What exact time did you go in there, and how long did the testing take?' Lauren asked.

'I can't remember the exact time, but I did test her television, bedside lamp, Kindle, laptop and hairdryer.' Hazel's fingers drummed against the table. 'Oh... and there was a small fridge she had in the corner of the room.' Her brow furrowed. 'I don't remember if there was anything else, sorry.'

'And was Dawn in there at the time?' Matt asked.

'Yes, she was... no wait... she did go out for a rehearsal. They're doing a play. That means I must have been in her room before two in that case.' Hazel nodded.

'Did you notice a tin of chocolates on the small table when you were in there?' Lauren asked.

'Yes. Because Dawn offered me one.' Hazel's right hand twitched slightly and she covered it with her left.

'Did you take it?' Matt asked.

'I nearly did but then said no because I'm trying to cut down on my sugar. It's not good for you.' She gave a tiny shrug.

'Did Dawn have one when she offered you it?' Lauren asked.

Good question.

'Yes, she did. She laughed and told me that it was her dessert because she didn't like what they had for lunch.'

'Did you notice which one she had?'

'No, sorry.'

Lauren suddenly changed the subject. 'Do you drive?'

Hazel frowned. 'Yes, of course I drive or I couldn't go out to jobs.'

'Do you use your own car for work?' Lauren continued.

Unsure where his boss was going with this line of questioning, Matt sat back and waited for it to become apparent.

'I don't own a car. I use a company van.' Hazel's voice steadied slightly.

'So you're not responsible for topping up with antifreeze, for example?'

Ah ha. That was it.

'No.' Hazel gave a brittle laugh. 'In fact, I wouldn't even know where to put it. The vans are looked after by the company.'

An electrician who didn't know where to put antifreeze. Matt found that hard to believe.

'Do you remember seeing anybody who was acting suspicious close to Dawn's room during the week?' Lauren asked.

'Not really. I mean, there are often people coming in and out. Residents do have visitors, although not as many as you'd think.' The words began tumbling out faster. 'I remember Dawn telling me one time that her son comes to see her once a week, but even then, sometimes he misses it if something else comes up. No one else visits her.' She shook her head. 'I thought it was very sad, especially for people like them.'

'What do you mean?' Matt asked.

'Well, they're so used to being in the spotlight, and now they're at this home and very few of them have visitors. It must be very hard. But most of them are cheerful and they do put on shows for the public which gives them some purpose. Although, to be honest, they're not very good. Please don't say I said that,' Hazel added. 'I wouldn't want to upset them.'

'I'm surprised the shows aren't good given the famous people living there?' Matt asked.

'Yeah, that's what I thought. You'll understand if you meet them. Most of them are stuck in their ways and they find it hard to work together. But it's better they do the shows than sit around in their rooms all the time, I suppose.'

'Did Dawn ever mention the shows?'

'Oh yes, whenever I saw her, she'd be talking about whatever it was they were doing. She had a big part in this recent play but...' She swallowed hard. 'That's not going to happen now, is it?'

'The show's still going ahead. Dawn's understudy will play the part,' Matt said.

'Oh... I might go then. To show my respects.'

'What time did you leave the home on Friday?' Lauren asked.

'At five.'

'Then where did you go?'

'Back to the office to drop off the van and then I walked home.'

'Can anyone vouch for you?' Lauren asked.

'My boyfriend was at home when I got there at around six-thirty.'

'You must have walked slowly,' Matt said.

Hazel flushed. 'Not really. I stopped at the supermarket to pick up something for dinner.'

'If you do remember anything,' Lauren said, staring directly at the woman, 'please let me know. Anything that you think might assist us in our enquiries.'

Hazel's fingers knotted together on the table. 'How was Dawn killed?' Her words tailed off, leaving the question hanging in the stale air.

'Sorry, we can't divulge that until the pathologist has completed his investigation,' Lauren replied, using it as an excuse, despite the fact she'd already informed Gill at the care home. There was no need for this information to be common knowledge.

Hazel's expression flickered for a fraction of a second before settling into what looked like concerned curiosity. Was there something she wasn't telling them? Or was Matt seeing something that wasn't there?

As they left the staff room, he caught Lauren's eye and knew she'd seen it too. They wouldn't be eliminating Hazel from their enquiries yet.

ELEVEN

TUESDAY FEBRUARY 11

Lauren strode up to the reception desk at Silver Fern Care Home, Matt at her side.

'DI Pengelly,' she said, showing her warrant card. 'Please could you fetch Gill Trelawny.'

'No problem,' the receptionist responded, her fingers hovering over the keyboard. 'I'll call her.'

Gill was with them within a couple of minutes.

'We're here to interview the staff who were here when Dawn was murdered,' Lauren said.

Gill nodded, clutching a folder to her chest. 'Four of the staff are here, but one of the agency staff isn't. She was meant to be on duty today, but she called in sick this morning.'

'Did she know about us visiting the home today when she called in?'

'Yes, she did.' Gill sucked in a breath through clenched teeth. 'Do you think it's connected?'

'We don't know but please text me her contact details.'

Again Gill looked uneasy. 'I'm sorry, but all I have is the agency's details. We don't require agency staff to complete our application form.'

'That's fine,' Lauren reassured her. 'We'll be able to contact her through the agency. What's her name?'

'Natalie Baker and she's with Redwood Agency in Penzance. Would you like to speak to the other staff in my office? You'll be interviewing three permanent staff. Brian Carson, Lynn Tremaine and Rose White. Then there's one from the agency, Mary Collins.'

'Yes, please – that will be a suitable place for us to see them,' Lauren readily accepted. 'Before we do that: I understand you've had a high turnover of staff recently. Why's that?'

'I suppose you saw it in the local paper. But it's not true. Yes, a couple of staff left at the same time three months ago, but that's all. I'd hardly call that a high turnover.'

'Yes, that is where we discovered it. The article also mentioned a complaint about the standard of care.'

Gill sighed. 'Yes, there was a problem but it wasn't as bad as the paper made out. A bell in one of our residents' rooms wasn't working properly. Sometimes it rang on our system and at others it didn't. This meant that the resident was left unattended when they wanted to use the commode on several occasions and they had an accident. When their daughter found out she kicked up and took her father out of the home. She then told the press.'

'How did you discover that the bell was at fault?' Matt asked.

'A process of elimination. It was fixed immediately,' Gill explained. 'If that's all, I'll take you to my office where you can interview the staff.'

Gill escorted them to her office, opened the door and ushered them in.

'Thanks,' Lauren said. 'Please send the first one in.'

After the manager had left, Lauren and Matt settled into the cramped office, its walls lined with regulatory certificates and staff schedules. Shortly after, a medium height, balding man walked in huffing and puffing as if he'd been engaged in some heavy lifting.

'I'm Brian Carson,' he said with a nervous smile. 'You want to speak to me?'

Lauren gestured to the chair opposite her and Matt and waited until he was seated. 'Brian, you were on duty on Friday when Dawn Cross died, I understand?'

'Yes, I was.' The man's face fell. 'We're well used to residents dying, it goes with the territory. But when it happens it still takes it out of you because we get so close to them. Well, not all of them obviously... It depends on how well they are, if you know what I mean.' His voice drifted away.

'Yes, of course, I understand,' Lauren said.

'We thought Dawn died of natural causes – like what usually happens. But now the boss told us that it's murder.' He shakes his head. 'That's awful. I don't get why anyone would do that. Dawn was a lovely lady.'

He seemed genuinely concerned and wasn't doing anything to make Lauren suspect him – but that didn't mean she'd totally dismiss him as a suspect.

'Yes, it is,' Lauren responded sympathetically. 'Which is why we need your help. Did you notice anything out of the ordinary happening on Friday or any of the days leading up to it?'

The man was quiet for a few seconds, as if searching his memory. 'No, I don't think so. It was business as usual.'

'And Dawn? How was she?' Matt asked.

'There was nothing different about her from what I remember.' Brian shrugged, his hands resting casually in his lap.

'Did she have her lunch and tea in the dining room on Friday?' Matt's pen hovered over his notebook.

'Yes, I'm pretty sure she did,' Brian confirmed with a small nod, his brow furrowing slightly.

'Did that mean her room was left unattended at those times?' Lauren kept her voice gentle, not wanting to sound accusatory.

'Yes.' Brian shifted uncomfortably in his chair, his fingers drumming on his thighs. 'But that's usual for all the residents.' He stared directly at Lauren. 'Do you think someone went in there and hid until she got back?'

'We don't know. Was she in her room all the time between her meals?' Lauren asked.

'No, there was a rehearsal in the afternoon before tea,' Brian responded, confirming what they'd been told by Hazel Dunston.

'And what about after tea?' Lauren pressed.

'She went back to her room straight away because she likes to watch one of the TV quiz shows. Dawn was very predictable in her behaviour.'

'Thank you. Do you recall the tin of chocolates on the side in her room?' Lauren asked.

'Yes. It would be odd if there wasn't any there.'

'Do you know where this particular tin came from?' Lauren asked, tapping her fingers on the desk.

'Actually I do. She bought them herself. I'm sure you've been told about her almost obsessive love for chocolates.'

'Yes, we have. Do you know when this tin arrived?'

'Last Wednesday. I know because I was the one to take the package to her.'

'There were a lot missing,' Matt said. 'Is that usual?'

'Dawn's chocolates never lasted long because she'd offer them to everyone. All the staff at some time or another would have taken one from her.' He paused, a wry smile crossing his face. 'Apart from the strawberry creams. We all knew not to take them because they were her favourite. In fact if someone did accidentally take one, she'd instruct them to put it back.' He laughed and then stopped, as if realising that he shouldn't do that when discussing someone who had been murdered.

Lauren exchanged a significant look with Matt. That would mean the killing was an inside job... or at least someone who knew Dawn's preferences because Henry had only found strawberry cream chocolates in her stomach.

'So anyone could have gone into her room, unnoticed, when she was at rehearsal or tea?'

Brian's face paled slightly. 'Well, yes, I suppose so. We're always busy helping the residents with their meals, so if anyone...' He trailed off. 'Oh God. Do you think we could have prevented it?'

'We can't surmise that,' Lauren responded kindly.

'But I didn't see anyone who shouldn't have been there. If I had then I'd have approached them.' He lowered his head.

'You can't blame yourself; you were doing your job at the time.'

'Thank you.' Brian looked up and met Lauren's eyes. 'Is there anything else? I've promised Charlie to run through his lines with him.'

'No that's all. Thanks for your help. If anything else springs to mind please let Gill know and she'll contact us. Could you please ask Rose White, Mary Collins and Lynn Tremaine to come in?'

Brian nodded and hurriedly left the room as if he couldn't wait to be as far away from them as possible.

'How come you want speak to them together?' Matt asked, once they were alone.

'I expect their responses won't be much different than Brian. I'm more concerned with this agency staff member who knew we were coming in and then decided to call in sick. That's a definite red flag, if ever there was one.'

'True. Good plan,' Matt agreed.

As Lauren had suspected, the subsequent interviews with the three women yielded similar information to Brian, although Lauren noted their body language seemed more guarded, particularly when discussing the chocolates. Was it because they shouldn't have taken any offered from the victim, or because they knew that she'd been poisoned by them? Even though it wasn't officially known, these things had a way of leaking and she wouldn't be at all surprised if it was common knowledge.

After dismissing them, Lauren and Matt returned to the reception only to find Gill Trelawny seated behind the reception desk.

'Can we have a quick word please?' Lauren asked, pleased that the manager was readily available.

'Of course. We'll go back to my office, if you like.'

Lauren agreed and once they were in there and seated, she turned to Gill. 'Before we leave, we'd like some more information about the agency staff member who didn't turn up today, despite being asked to and knowing the reason.'

Gill's brow furrowed. 'Natalie has only worked a couple of shifts so far. The day of the murder, which was her second time on duty, and earlier that week.'

'How long was her shift?' Matt asked.

'We operate on a twelve-hour shift rota, starting at either eight in the morning or eight in the evening.'

'Goodness, they're long hours,' Matt said, his mouth dropping open a little.

'It's a common enough system among care homes and the carers do have regular breaks. We find it works well and the staff are happy with it.'

'How did you find Natalie's work?' Lauren asked, tilting her head with interest.

'It's early days and obviously anyone new has to get used to our working practices, but from what I witnessed she did well and the other staff didn't make any complaints about her – that's usually how I discover any issues.'

'Did you notice anything suspicious about her?'

'I didn't have much to do with her because I was busy with the usual admin and overseeing.'

'Did her calling in sick ring any alarm bells?' Lauren asked.

'Not really,' Gill replied. 'It was a bit annoying, being last minute and all that but there are always so many bugs going around. I just had to deal with it, like usual when these things happen.'

'Did you phone the agency and ask them to send a replacement?' Matt asked.

'I didn't bother because it would have been unlikely that they could find someone at such short notice. Demand outstrips supply with agency staff, I'm afraid.'

'Yet it's a poorly paid profession,' Matt mused.

'Don't get me started on that,' Gill said, shaking her head. 'It's seen as a vocation, and with all jobs like that, the pay isn't good.'

'I see and—'

A knock at the door interrupted her.

'Come in,' Gill called out.

The door opened and Brian appeared.

'Sorry, to bother you, but there's something I remembered that you might want to know.' He stared directly at Lauren.

'In that case, I'll leave you to it,' Gill said, getting up from her chair and heading to the door.

'Thanks,' Lauren said.

Once the manager had left, Brian sat in her seat.

Lauren kept her expression neutral, though her pulse had quickened. 'Go on.'

'On Friday evening, when I did my rounds, I noticed Dawn's tin of chocolates was in a different place. Usually, she kept it on her bedside table, so she could reach it when she was in bed but when I saw it, it was on the chair. I didn't think anything of it at the time but you were asking about the chocolates and suddenly it came to me.'

'What time was this?'

'Around eight-fifteen, I think.' Brian nodded. 'Yes, definitely then.'

'When we saw the chocolates, they were on the bedside table,' Lauren said.

'That's because I put them back after discovering she'd died. Should I have left them?' He grimaced, appearing worried.

'No, it's fine,' Lauren said, because it was pointless telling him that yes, he should have, when they could do nothing about it. 'Did you mention this to anyone?'

'No. Like I said, it didn't seem important then, and it went out of my mind.' He paused. 'There's something else, as well. The agency worker Natalie asked me about Dawn's routine that day. She wanted to know when she took her evening medication and what it consisted of.'

Matt and Lauren exchanged glances. Now they were getting somewhere. 'Did that strike you as unusual?'

'At the time, no. New staff often ask about residents' routines. But...' He shifted in his chair. 'She seemed particularly interested in when Dawn would be alone. At least that's how I interpreted it.'

Lauren felt the pieces starting to slide into place. 'Did Natalie interact with Dawn at all during her shift?'

'Yes, she helped her back from the dining room after tea. She said Dawn was feeling a bit wobbly.' Brian's face suddenly showed concern. 'Oh God, do you think...?'

'We don't know. At this stage we're investigating all possibilities. While you're here, what can you tell us about the dynamics between the residents? Are there any tensions that we should be aware of?'

Brian's eyebrows rose. 'Well, they're all entertainers so you know how it can be. Some are bigger personalities than others.'

'Was Dawn one of those bigger personalities?' Lauren asked, already knowing who of the people she'd met would be classed as *bigger*.

A slight smile crossed his face. 'Not really. She was one of the easiest to deal with. Now, Margot Stevens. She's our former West End star. She needs... careful handling – and that's putting it mildly.'

'How so?' Lauren asked, anxious to learn as much as possible about these people.

'She always has to be centre stage. Even at breakfast.' Brian shook his head. 'She and Dawn had a bit of a run-in last week during the play rehearsals. Margot kept telling her how to act in certain scenes.'

Ah ha. Lauren leant forward. 'How did Dawn take that?'

'She was upset. I heard her telling her son on the phone that she was tired of being pushed around by "that theatrical old bat".'

Brian chuckled and Lauren and Matt joined in.

Even in her nineties, Dawn clearly had her wits about her and had a sense of humour.

'Are there other residents we should know about who are tricky to handle?'

Brian glanced at the door before lowering his voice. 'Well,

there's Gerald Morton, who used to be a magician. He can be...
difficult. Especially when it comes to the ladies.'

'Difficult how?' Lauren asked, frowning.

'He tries to get extra attention from female residents and staff.
Dawn complained about him a few times. She said he was always
trying to show her his "special tricks".' Brian made air quotes with
his fingers. 'Nothing serious, mind you, but uncomfortable.'

'And how did he take the rejection?'

'Not well. He's used to being adored, you see. Last Wednesday,
he made a scene in the dining room because Dawn wouldn't watch
his new routine. He said she was "destroying artistic greatness" or
some such nonsense.'

Lauren made several notes. 'Anyone else?'

'There's Kenneth and Charlie; they're always clashing but
sometimes I think they do it for the sake of it.' Brian shifted in his
chair and shrugged.

'Yes, we've already met them,' Matt said, pulling a face and
rolling his eyes.

'They're harmless enough, although can be annoying, that's for
sure,' Brian added, checking his watch.

'Is there anyone else we need to know about?' Lauren asked,
tapping her pen against her notepad.

'No that's about it. I really must go.'

'Of course. Thanks for the information,' Lauren said, rising to
shake his hand.

After Brian left, Lauren turned to Matt. 'We need to track
down Natalie, but first we should continue our chat with Gill
Trelawny because I want to pick up on some of those things that
Brian's told us.'

TWELVE

TUESDAY FEBRUARY 11

As they returned to the reception, Matt was mulling over what they'd recently learnt. Something wasn't sitting right.

'I take it you're thinking the same as me,' Lauren said, glancing at him.

'That our agency worker was way too interested in Dawn, but also the tensions between residents seem to go deeper than we'd first thought?' Matt nodded. 'We need to know what the manager knows about these theatrical tensions.'

'My sentiments exactly.'

When they reached the reception, Gill was sitting there.

'Can we have a word, please?' Lauren asked.

'I thought you'd finished here,' Gill said, with a frown.

'We had but now have further questions for you. We want to know more about the dynamics between your residents,' Lauren said. 'Particularly around the entertainment aspects of life here.'

Gill's expression shifted almost imperceptibly. 'Ah. You've heard about our little dramas, then?'

'We've heard some,' Matt replied. 'But we'd like your perspective as manager. How do you handle the more... challenging personalities?'

'Let's go back to my office and we can discuss further. Walls have ears, if you get my meaning.' Gill nodded at two of the residents who were coming in from outside.

Once back in the office, Matt and Lauren settled into the chairs opposite her desk.

'So, what can you tell us?' Lauren asked, as Gill simply sat there, staring in their direction.

Gill let out a long breath. 'To be honest, it's like managing a theatre company sometimes, only with more medications and mobility issues.' She reached for a file on her desk. 'Take Margot Stevens, for instance. Wonderful performer in her day, but she still expects star treatment from all those around her. Dawn was one of the few who wouldn't pander to her whims. Not that she was aggressive about it. Dawn wasn't like that. Not at all.'

'Did Dawn's behaviour towards Margot cause problems?' Lauren asked.

'Margot would complain about Dawn's lack of professional courtesy. Said she was bringing down the tone of the place.' Gill raised her eyebrows. 'But I think she was jealous. Dawn was a well-known and respected performer in her day. Not leading lady material, but always in good productions. Plus she still had a following.'

Matt leant forward. 'How come? Surely at her age she didn't still perform?'

'Only in our concerts. But Dawn had a regular column in one of those nostalgia magazines. Nothing huge, but it meant she was still working... still relevant, even at her age. Margot... well, let's just say the phone stopped ringing for her years ago and she's buried her head in the sand about it.'

'Why didn't you mention this to us sooner?' Lauren asked, her lips in a tight line.

'I'm sorry, I didn't think about it. I mean it's not like Margot was going to murder Dawn because she thought her disrespectful.' She paused, a confused expression crossing her face. 'I mean... surely you don't think...'

'We don't know, that's why any information you have is very important, even if it's just to eliminate people from our enquiries,' Lauren replied. 'Can you think of any altercation that was particularly nasty between the two of them?'

Gill nodded slowly. 'Actually, there was one incident, that happened the day before Dawn died.'

Matt exchanged a glance with Lauren.

'Go on,' he pushed the manager to continue.

'Well, I overheard Margot telling Dawn that it was unfair she still got the attention considering her total lack of talent.'

'Wow,' Matt said, his mouth dropping open. 'How did Dawn react to that?'

'She laughed and told Margot where to go – in no uncertain terms. Dawn always did use colourful language. It was part of her charm.' Gill gave a laugh.

'Did you intervene to stop it going any further?' Lauren asked.

'I didn't need to because Dawn turned away and headed off. At the time I was tied up dealing with Kenneth and Charlie, who at the time were having another of their rows, and this one was so loud I wouldn't be surprised if it could have been heard outside.' Gill rubbed her temples. 'Those two are constantly at each other's throats. At times, it's a bloody nightmare, let me tell you.'

'We did witness them having a go at each other during the rehearsal we watched. Tell us more about them,' Lauren asked, leaning forward.

'Kenneth Blencoe and Charlie Wright. They're like oil and water.' Gill reached for the water bottle on her desk and took a sip. 'Kenneth's a former Royal Shakespeare Company actor and occasional director. And he never lets us forget it. Charlie spent much of his career as a stand-up comedian, mainly working the clubs in the North. They're the complete opposite ends of the entertainment spectrum.'

'And they don't get along?' Matt prompted.

'That's putting it mildly.' Gill gave a wry smile. 'Kenneth thinks Charlie's style of comedy is "beneath the dignity of our theatrical establishment". Charlie says Kenneth's got a telegraph pole stuck up his... well, you get the idea. They're both playing the Brewster brothers in *Arsenic and Old Lace*, and Kenneth keeps trying to make it more "dramatically profound" while Charlie is determined to play it for laughs. You can imagine how that's all working out.'

'We've been told that much of their antagonism is done for the sake of it. Do you believe that underneath it all they sort of like each other?' Lauren asked.

'Well, they've known each other for years, so that's probably a good description of the pair of them. To be honest, I expect they'd be lost without each other to spar with,' Gill acknowledged.

'How did Dawn handle Kenneth and Charlie while rehearsing the play?'

'She did well. As one would expect. She used her years of repertory experience to help Charlie with his comedy beats, while respecting Kenneth's need for...' Gill adopted a pompous tone, '"proper theatrical gravitas". She'd had comedic and straight roles during her career, you see. It meant she was comfortable in both areas.'

'Yes, I do,' Matt said. 'Back to the huge row you witnessed between Kenneth and Charlie, what was it over?'

'Kenneth had a meltdown during rehearsal. It just so happened that I was watching at the time. He complained that Charlie had got a bigger laugh than him in their big scene together. He started ranting about "music hall buffoonery destroying the sanctity of the stage". Dawn tried to intervene and suggested they try it different ways, but Charlie accused her of taking Kenneth's side.' Gill shook her head. 'It got quite nasty. Charlie made some crack about Kenneth's failed West End career, and Kenneth... well, he threw a prop bottle at him.'

'A bottle?' Lauren's eyebrows raised.

'Just a plastic one from the props table. But it shows how heated things had become.'

'Tell us about the actress taking over Dawn's role,' Lauren asked.

'Bertha Meadows. She was the understudy.' Gill's expression turned thoughtful. 'Actually, she was quite eager to step in. I happened to be talking with Kenneth on Saturday morning and she came up and asked to play the part. At that time I didn't even know that they wanted to continue with the play.'

'It does seem a bit quick,' Matt observed.

'That's what I thought. But Bertha's always been ambitious. Despite most of her career spent understudying.'

'And will she be able to do the part?' Lauren asked.

'Well, Bertha's been hanging around Dawn's rehearsals an awful lot. She said she was "just being prepared" but it made Dawn uncomfortable.'

'How so?'

'Dawn told me Bertha kept questioning her about the blocking and there was an incident with Dawn's script. Pages went missing and turned up in Bertha's room. Bertha claimed she was just making notes, but it all seemed very odd.'

'What did you do about it?' Matt asked.

'I asked Melody to deal with it. She's very good at dealing with the residents when they go off on one and had even offered to help Bertha run lines one evening, just in case she was needed.'

'Did she report back that it was all sorted?'

Gill frowned. 'I meant to follow up, but then there was a crisis with another resident's medication, and...' She spread her hands helplessly. 'You know how it is here. Always putting out fires and dealing with fragile egos. But I'm sure Melody was able to calm the situation.'

'Brian mentioned that Natalie Baker, the agency carer, asked a lot of questions about Dawn during the two shifts she worked.'

'Oh. I don't know about that. But it sometimes does happen. Carers are star struck occasionally, if they're looking after someone they've seen on the telly or at the cinema.'

'So it doesn't ring alarm bells then?' Lauren asked.

'Not really. Actually, I've had a thought. I'm not sure if this is relevant, but recently Dawn was talking a lot about writing her memoirs from back in the day. She said it would prove most illuminating.'

'Had she been approached by a publisher to do it?' Lauren asked.

'I'm not sure, sorry. But maybe she had. Why else would she suddenly start talking about it?'

'Did Dawn say that it would be *explosive*?' Matt asked, remembering how celebrity memoirs often used that language.

'Not exactly, but she's always said she knew stuff about other actors that the public would find most interesting. Then again, what entertainer doesn't say that to make sure their book sells. Although Dawn had said that long before she mentioned her memoir.'

'Did Dawn tell you what things she knew, and about whom?' Lauren asked.

'No, and I didn't push her. Some things are best left unsaid. I particularly didn't want any gossip circulating if it was about anyone living here, or who might live here in the future.'

'That makes sense,' Matt agreed, although for gossip to circulate, surely it wouldn't be going via the manager.

Lauren stood and Matt did the same.

'Well, thanks for your help. We'll no doubt be returning but for now we're going to track down Natalie Baker,' Lauren said. 'You have my card if you need to get in touch.'

Once they were outside, Matt turned to Lauren, his mind spinning.

'Could Dawn's memoirs be the reason behind her death, do you think? You know how damaging they can be. I bet that was something to do with it – if she knows something that could cause problems should it come to light.'

'You're right. It's certainly given us a new angle to pursue –

and a potential motive that goes beyond the theatrical squabbles of retired performers,' Lauren replied with a sigh. 'Please contact Jenna and ask her and the team to investigate any incident that occurred in plays that Dawn Cross was in over the years. Something might come to light that will point us in the right direction of her accusations.'

THIRTEEN

TUESDAY FEBRUARY 11

The Redwood Agency was nestled in the heart of Penzance's town centre, its entrance squeezed between two small shops. Matt followed Lauren up the narrow staircase, noting how the worn carpet had been patched in places. The small office at the top was cramped but orderly; the sunlight filtering through the dusty office window caught motes of dust in its beam. A middle-aged woman sat behind a large dark wood desk that dominated the space.

'Good morning,' Lauren said, showing her warrant card. 'I'm DI Pengelly and this is DS Price. We'd like to speak to the person in charge, please.'

'That would be me,' the woman replied in such a strong Cornish accent that Matt struggled to understand, despite him having lived down there for a while now. The woman straightened in her chair, a worried expression on her face. 'My name's Elaine French. What can I do for you?'

The woman maintained steady eye contact, though her fingers nervously adjusted the stack of papers on her desk. Matt shifted his weight, the floorboards creaking beneath the worn carpet.

'We've just come from Silver Fern Care Home,' Lauren continued. 'We're investigating the suspicious death of one of the residents. We understand that one of your agency staff, Natalie Baker, was meant to be working today?'

'Meant to be?' Elaine's brow furrowed.

'Yes... she called in sick.'

'Really? That's the first I've heard about it.' The woman drummed her fingers on the desk. 'Why didn't the home call us for another staff member? Although I doubt that I'd have been able to do anything at this late stage. And more to the point, why didn't Natalie let me know?'

'Sorry, I can't answer that. We'd like to ask you a few questions about Natalie, if we may.' Lauren pulled out one of the chairs opposite the woman and sat down, leaving the chair next to her for Matt.

He pulled out his notebook and pen.

'Of course. What do you want to know?' The woman sat back in her chair but still maintained eye contact with Lauren.

'How long has Natalie worked for the agency?'

'Not long really. Maybe two or three months. I'll check.' Elaine turned to her computer, tapping a few keys. She appeared more comfortable now, settling into the familiar territory of administrative details. 'Yes, I was right. She joined us on December the first last year.'

Matt's gaze drifted to the certificates lining the wall behind the desk. Most were dated within the last five years so it seemed that the agency was relatively new.

'And at which homes has she worked?' Lauren asked.

Elaine glanced back at the screen. 'She's had several shifts at a care home in St Just, and some in Newlyn but recently she asked if she could work at Silver Fern if a position became available.'

'And you agreed?' Lauren asked.

'Well, yes.' Elaine shrugged. 'I didn't think there was any harm in it. The other homes she's worked at haven't reported any issues with her. And as Silver Fern use us regularly, I thought it would be okay. Mary Collins is also there on a regular basis. Most homes prefer to see a familiar face rather than constantly changing the staff who go there. It's better for the residents. Having said that, I'm not happy that Natalie neglected to inform me that she'd phoned in sick. I'll certainly be looking into it, that's for sure.'

'I see,' Lauren said. 'And what sort of qualifications do your staff have?'

'We don't employ anyone who doesn't at least an NVQ Level 3 in Health and Social Care, or something similar. Why are you asking these questions? Is Natalie a suspect in this death?'

The muffled sounds of Penzance life drifted up from the street below, distracting Matt for a moment. But he turned his attention back to the woman's body language, recognising the subtle signs of someone caught between professional discretion and genuine concern.

'We don't yet have a suspect. We're currently investigating everyone who worked at the home over the relevant time,' Lauren replied. 'What else can you tell us about Natalie? I assume you took out references and did police checks before employing her.'

Elaine drew herself up straighter. 'Oh yes, of course. This is a professional organisation. Plus, it's a legal requirement. We don't do anything underhand and pride ourselves on having good staff who are requested time and time again by homes they work at. It's not in our interest to cut corners.' She paused, her expression clouding. 'But before you mention it, yes Natalie did call in sick at the home, but refrained from letting me know. That is a disciplinary offence.'

'You sounded surprised a moment ago that the home didn't phone you to provide someone else,' Matt said, glancing up from writing his notes. 'Is that what they normally do?'

'Usually. But to be honest it wouldn't have made a difference.' Elaine spread her hands in a helpless gesture. 'Honestly, I could have double the number of staff on the books and still not be able to fulfil the needs of the sector.'

'Are you the only agency in the area?' Matt asked.

'No, there are a few. I'm here in Penzance, and then in St Ives there are several. Land's End has got one, too. But we don't contain ourselves to our discrete areas. We send the staff where the work is.' She smiled wryly. 'There are a lot of care homes around here and plenty of work. People do like to retire to homes in Cornwall. It's hardly surprising, being such a beautiful place.'

Lauren rested her hands on the desk. 'So going back to why Natalie particularly wanted to work at Silver Fern Care Home, did she give you a reason why?'

'Yes, she did.' Elaine seemed to brighten at having information to share. 'Natalie trained as an actress after leaving school, but she couldn't get enough work and so went back to college to train in health and social care. She said the caring profession was her fall-back position. But she wanted to be around people who had been in acting.'

'Why didn't she go for a more permanent position?' Lauren asked.

'She thought agency work would be a good fit because it meant she could take acting jobs in between, if they came along.'

Matt nodded. It made sense.

'Has she had any acting jobs since joining the agency?' Lauren asked.

'No, unfortunately not. They're hard to get at the best of times, even more difficult if you don't live in London.'

Lauren frowned. 'So why would she choose to live here in Cornwall instead of London?'

'Well, it's much cheaper living here, I suppose,' Elaine mused. 'And there are some theatres in this locality, where she might find work. Certainly the competition at auditions wouldn't be so great.'

'I see,' Lauren said. 'Natalie had been informed by the care home manager that we were going to question her and the others today. Do you believe that could be the reason she called in sick?'

'I have no idea. But surely you don't believe she was involved in the death,' Elaine said, repeating her earlier question and expelling a loud breath.

'That's what we need to find out.'

'Natalie's always been reliable and is most personable, but...' Elaine's voice trailed off, leaving the thought unfinished.

'We need her contact details, please. Address and phone number,' Lauren said. 'We'll be visiting her at home. But if she does contact you, please don't tell her that we've been here. If she is at home, we don't want her disappearing again.'

'No. Of course not. But if she is involved then I guess...' Her words hung in the air.

'Please don't jump the gun,' Lauren said, standing. 'Like I said earlier, we're in the early stages of our investigation and Natalie could have a reasonable excuse for not turning up.'

'Okay, understood,' Elaine said, with a slow nod. 'Because I really can't afford to lose her. Good staff aren't easy to come by.' She wrote down Natalie's details and handed them to Lauren.

'Thanks for your help,' Lauren said.

Matt stood and they headed to the door. The familiar tension, when a case started to gain momentum, was building in his shoulders.

Something about Natalie's story wasn't adding up, and in Matt's experience, such inconsistencies usually led somewhere interesting. He was convinced they were about to discover where that was.

FOURTEEN

TUESDAY FEBRUARY 11

The small Victorian terraced house where Natalie Baker lived sat halfway up one of Penzance's steeper hills, offering glimpses of the harbour where fishing boats were bobbing up and down in the water like corks. The front garden was barely more than a handkerchief of space, but someone had made it pretty with wooden planters full of cheerful purple crocus. A recycling bin and a regular bin stood neatly by the gate, the council's logo peeling off in the salty air.

Lauren rang the bell, one of the modern video types that so many people had nowadays, because of the increase in security consciousness everywhere – even the relatively sleepy part of Cornwall they lived in. She approved of this change because it meant additional camera footage for the police should they need it, which seemed to be more and more these days.

After a moment, they heard footsteps clattering down what sounded like an uncarpeted hallway. The woman who opened the door looked to be in her mid-thirties and had the healthy glow of someone who spent a lot of time exercising. She wore leggings and a loose sweatshirt from the new gym that had opened in the town centre a couple of months ago. Her dark hair was pulled back in a messy bun, held together by a silver clip.

'Yes?' she asked, looking from Lauren to Matt.

Lauren held out her warrant card. 'I'm Detective Inspector Pengelly and this is Detective Sergeant Price. We're looking for Natalie Baker, is that you?'

'Oh. No, I'm not Natalie. I'm Sophie Trent, her housemate. Well, landlady I suppose as I own the house and she rents one of my rooms. Sorry, she's not here. She went to London earlier today for an audition. Would you like to come in? It's a bit of a mess, I'm afraid.' She dabbed at her forehead with her sleeve.

'Thank you,' Lauren said.

Stepping inside, the hallway confirmed Lauren's guess about the uncarpeted floors. The original Victorian floorboards were stripped back and varnished, with a faded runner down the middle. The walls were a fashionable shade of sage green, hung with prints of the surrounding areas and some family photos.

'Do you know where in London Natalie is?' Matt asked, his notebook already out.

'Um, yes, actually.' Sophie pulled a phone from the pocket of her leggings. 'She sent me the details in case any post came for her. She's waiting on some scripts. It's at...' She scrolled through her messages. 'The Arcadia Theatre in Southwark. They're casting for a touring production of *The Woman in Black*. Natalie was very excited about landing an audition and thought it might be her big break. She's been doing am-dram at the Acorn locally, but obviously that's not quite the same.'

'Would you mind if we take a look at Natalie's room?' Lauren asked.

Sophie hesitated, pushing a loose strand of hair back into the bun. 'I suppose it's okay. Is she in some kind of trouble? Only she seemed quite chirpy when she left this morning for the early train to Paddington.'

'We need to speak with her as part of an ongoing investigation,' Lauren said carefully, not wanting to alert Sophie.

Natalie's room was at the back of the house, with a bay window overlooking a surprisingly deep garden. Raised vegetable beds and a small greenhouse suggested Sophie was the self-sufficient type. The room itself was tidy, which couldn't have been easy considering it wasn't very large.

A theatrical poster for *The Crucible*, from a production by the National Theatre in the eighties, dominated one wall and the dressing table had stage make-up on one half and a pile of headshots, presumably of Natalie, on the other. A copy of *The Stage* newspaper was on the bedside table.

'How long has Natalie lived here with you?' Lauren asked, as she continued to scan the room.

'About four months?' Sophie leant against the doorframe. 'She answered my ad on a rooming website. I needed someone living here after my divorce because the mortgage is a bit steep for just me to cover. I live here with Lily, my daughter. To be honest, it's nice having another adult in the house. Lily's nine and can be quite a handful,' she added, gesturing to a child's artwork pinned to the cork board in the hallway.

'She's very talented,' Matt said, with a smile.

'Thanks. She does seem to be arty. Gets it from me, I suppose.' Sophie gave a self-deprecating shrug.

'How have you found Natalie as a housemate?' Lauren asked, directing the conversation back to the reason they were there.

Sophie smiled warmly. 'Oh, she's been lovely. She's quiet and pays her rent on time. A perfect tenant. And she's been totally brilliant with Lily recently. She helped her learn lines for the school play. Lily is one of the main characters,' she added proudly.

'What do you know about Natalie?' Lauren asked, wondering whether the woman could really be so perfect. Or whether it was simply an act to ensure her landlady spoke well of her.

'She's been very open with me regarding why she's here. The reason she moved down here from London was to try the regional theatre scene. London's too expensive to live and the auditions are so competitive.'

'And yet she has no problem paying her rent?' Matt said with a frown.

'That's because she's been picking up care work to pay the bills. But she often goes up to London for auditions even though she moved away. I think that's where her heart is. She keeps a spreadsheet of all the casting calls and makes sure to go to all those that might suit her.'

Lauren didn't stop Sophie from explaining despite them knowing much of this, because it corroborated what the agency woman had told them.

'Does she go out much in the evening or during the day when not working?' Lauren asked, studying Sophie's face carefully. They could be closer than the woman had described and she might be providing cover for her.

'It varies really. She does different shifts at the care homes, and she's often out at rehearsals for the local am-dram society she joined. But when she's home, she's often in her room learning her lines or doing these self-tape auditions. She's very serious about her acting.' Sophie paused. 'Although...' Sophie glanced between Lauren and Matt, lowering her voice despite the empty house. 'She's been acting a bit odd lately. I mean, some things I just put down to her being an actress, you know? Like, she's always practising different accents in her room. I can hear her through the walls sometimes, having entire conversations with herself in different voices. Proper method acting stuff.'

Ah... so now they were hearing that Natalie wasn't as perfect as they'd first been led to believe. So what was behind Sophie's initial comments?

Lauren exchanged a look with Matt. 'What else have you noticed?'

'Well...' Sophie wrapped her arms around herself, as if suddenly realising how chilly the landing was. 'She takes a lot of photos whenever she goes out. Not just selfies for her acting portfolio, but of buildings and people. She said it's for character research, but...' She shrugged uncomfortably. 'And she's always making notes about people in the coffee shop or wherever. Really detailed ones. What they're wearing, how they move, their mannerisms. When I asked her why, all she said was that it's acting stuff.'

'So she's not so perfect then,' Lauren stated.

'As a tenant, yes. Like I said. But I remembered some things that I thought were odd, if you know what I mean. Look, I don't want to get her into trouble and then she ends up leaving living here.' Sophie looked from Lauren to Matt as if realising that she could end up without a tenant.

'We understand, and you're not getting her into trouble. Is there anything else strange about Natalie's behaviour you can think of?' Matt prompted gently.

Sophie let out a long sigh. 'Well, she's got this big tote bag which contains different clothes and wigs. I found it when I was cleaning last week. It was poking out from under her bed and I could see into it. When I happened to mention it later, she said it was for different character types for auditions, and...' Sophie paused, grimacing. 'She's really into true crime. Always watching documentaries on her laptop and making notes. I walked past her room the other day and she was listening to a podcast about some famous art heist, scribbling away in that notebook of hers. But honestly, she's really nice.'

Lauren's expression remained neutral, but she could feel her pulse quickening. 'Thanks. We'll take it from here if you'd like to go downstairs.'

Sophie left them but not before glancing over her shoulder, looking worried.

After pulling on disposable gloves, Matt peered under the bed. 'She must have the bag with her because it's not here. That's a shame.'

'Maybe she needed it for her audition,' Lauren mused. 'You take the drawers and I'll look though the wardrobe.'

Flicking through the clothes, Lauren concluded that Natalie had the kind of wardrobe someone builds when they're trying to look successful on a budget. Several sets of scrubs and care home uniforms hung at one end, all neatly pressed. She then headed over to the bed and began feeling under the mattress. Her fingers hit a notebook tucked between the mattress and bed frame which she pulled out. It must be the book Sophie had mentioned. It was a standard spiral-bound. But as she opened it, her pulse quickened.

There were pages of detailed notes about Dawn Cross. Medication schedules, visitor patterns, details about Dawn's jewellery collection including specific pieces: pearl necklace with gold clasp; sapphire engagement ring from late husband; gold charm bracelet; diamond stud earrings. Also noted were door codes for different sections of the home, staff rotations. There was even personal information about Dawn's son.

'Matt,' she said quietly, holding up the notebook.

He came over to look, his expression growing serious as he scanned the pages.

'Wow,' Matt said. 'Surely she couldn't have found out all this from just two sessions at the care home. I've found this.' He held up a scrapbook which he opened and flicked through.

It was filled with newspaper clippings dating back to Dawn's early acting career, and old playbills from Dawn's theatre days, some apparently signed.

'She's clearly obsessed with the woman. All this stuff wouldn't have been easy to find. We need to speak to her, and soon.'

'Agreed,' Matt echoed.

Lauren carefully bagged the notebook and scrapbook as evidence and they went downstairs to find Sophie.

'Do you know when Natalie's due back?' she asked the woman, who was standing in the kitchen staring out of the window.

Sophie turned to face them. 'She said probably tomorrow evening, depending on how the audition goes. She's staying with a friend in Greenwich tonight because London hotel prices are mental these days.' Sophie was looking increasingly worried. 'What's this about?'

'We'll need to speak with her as soon as she returns,' Lauren said, handing Sophie her card. 'Please ask her to contact us immediately.'

They left the house and Matt turned to her. 'Is it wise to wait for Natalie to arrive back here? Shouldn't we try to find her now?'

'Exactly what I was thinking,' Lauren responded, taking hold of her mobile from her pocket. 'I'll contact the Metropolitan Police and get them on the case. We need to send someone to the Arcadia Theatre in Southwark. If she's there, we'll have her brought in. I didn't want Sophie to alert her; that's why I left my card.'

'Wise move, ma'am. I couldn't work out whether they were close or not. Initially I thought so, then she dropped her in it.'

'Yes, that was odd. Contact the care home. I want to know if anything's missing from Dawn's room. Anything at all. We need to get back to the office and start pulling some of this stuff together.'

Lauren started the engine and flicked on the windscreen wipers. The spring sun had disappeared behind clouds, and a fine drizzle was starting to fall, hitting the windscreen.

The notebook sat in its evidence bag on the back seat. The notes Natalie had taken weren't the casual observations of a care worker. They appeared to be the kind of detailed surveillance notes someone would make if they were planning something. But what was it? And if Natalie Baker was responsible for Dawn's murder, then what was her motive?

FIFTEEN

TUESDAY FEBRUARY 11

'Are you sure you're okay to wait for Natalie Baker to get here? Won't your mum be expecting you for dinner?' Lauren asked Matt as they sat in her office waiting for the woman to arrive after being brought in for questioning by the London police. 'I don't mind interviewing her on my own.'

The light was fading outside the window, casting long shadows across the desk between them.

Matt smiled in the direction of his boss. Ever since his dad had been ill, she was always considerate regarding his time. He appreciated it, but there was no need. His dad was doing very well, and almost back to how he'd been prior to the mini stroke. In no small part thanks to his mum taking control over their diet and lifestyle. The majority of what they now ate was unprocessed, and Matt had to admit that he'd never felt so healthy. Although occasionally he longed for the days when his mum would make her legendary cupcakes. She still made cakes, but coconut sugar didn't quite taste the same. Still, if it meant his dad was okay then it was worth it.

Matt nodded, settling back in his chair. 'Yeah, that's fine. I want to be here for the questioning. I've already told Mum to leave my dinner in the oven.'

'How's it going to work when you move?' Lauren asked, looking tired from the long day. The case was already wearing on all of them and they'd hardly started.

'Oh, I think it will be much the same, except we'll be three doors down,' Matt said, considering the forthcoming move. 'And Mum can sit in our house with Dani when I'm at work, or Dani can still go into her old room at their place, which they'll keep for her. I'm looking forward to it. It will be a good move all round.'

'Have you got a completion date?' Lauren asked as she shuffled the papers on her desk into a neat pile.

'No, not yet. I've only just had the survey done. You know what it's like here. I don't expect we'll be in for another few months, even though there's no chain. It's ridiculous how long everything takes. The people I'm buying from are going into a care home. But not Silver Fern,' Matt said with a dry laugh. 'What about your aunt's case? Any closer to the end?'

'They're going through evidence and I don't expect to hear anything for a few days at least. I'll let you know what happens once I do.' Lauren's response was interrupted by the phone on her desk ringing.

'Pengelly,' Lauren answered, her posture straightening. 'Right, okay, we'll be down in a minute.' She ended the call and turned to Matt, her expression becoming professional. 'Natalie Baker's in Interview Room One. Come on, let's go.'

They left her office and walked down the fluorescent-lit corridor to the interview room. When they entered, Natalie Baker was sitting with her arms folded tightly across her chest, staring straight ahead. She was a slender woman with a pixie haircut featuring pink and blue streaks. Matt estimated she was in her mid to late twenties.

'What's going on? Why have I been brought here? And why won't anyone tell me anything?' Natalie demanded.

'I'm going to be recording this interview,' Lauren said firmly, ignoring the questions.

Matt turned on the recorder and went through the preliminaries, noting how Natalie's left leg bounced continually underneath the table.

'Right. Now can you tell me why I'm here?' Natalie's voice dropped an octave as she enunciated each word, her knuckles whitening as she gripped the edge of the table.

'You were meant to meet us at Silver Fern Care Home today,' Lauren began, opening the folder she had in front of her on the table. 'We were there to question staff about the death of Dawn Cross.'

'Yeah, well, I didn't go in. I had an audition.' Natalie's eyes darted between them.

'So we understand,' Matt interjected, keeping his voice level. 'But you phoned in sick and lied to them.'

'I was hardly going to tell the manager that's where I was going, in case it meant I wouldn't get any more work.' A flush crept up Natalie's neck.

'But you also didn't phone the agency and let them know you weren't going in either, did you?' Lauren's tone was sharp.

Natalie stared at them, her painted fingernails digging into her arms. 'Umm, no. I forgot about that. But so what? Surely that doesn't warrant me being dragged back here.'

'How long had you known about the audition? Because you could have refused the shift, and left them time to get a replacement,' Lauren continued.

'It was last minute. I only got the call yesterday. Someone dropped out and they offered me the chance instead. I had no choice but to go. It's my career.'

It seemed genuine enough. But the woman was an actor and Matt knew how effective they could be at misleading people.

Matt tapped his index finger against his chin. 'You've only worked at the care home for two shifts. Is that correct?'

'Yes. Why?'

'And you've been particularly interested in Dawn Cross more than any of the other residents. In fact I'd call it more of an obsession than an interest.' Lauren opened the folder, methodically laying out photographs of items found in Natalie's room.

Natalie's eyes widened at each new piece of evidence: the shrine-like collection of memorabilia spread across her bedroom walls, the scrapbooks filled with newspaper clippings dating back to Dawn's early acting career, and the small notebook containing detailed observations about Dawn and her daily routines at Silver Fern.

'Umm...' was the only sound coming from her.

'We found these things hidden in your room,' Lauren continued, placing down more photos. 'Some of these memorabilia wouldn't have been easy to source.' She paused, letting that sink in. 'The collection of vintage magazines featuring Dawn's interviews. The diary entries about your conversations with her. All related to Dawn. We didn't find anything about the other residents. Why is that?'

Natalie's fingers trembled as she peered at the evidence of her obsession laid out before her. Her confident demeanour cracked as Lauren revealed the final photograph: a candid shot of Dawn at Silver Fern that could only have been taken recently, without the elderly actress's knowledge.

'You've been in my room,' Natalie stated, her voice flat.

'Yes, we went to where you live, and your flatmate allowed us into your room,' Matt explained, watching her reaction carefully. 'That's when we found all this material related to Dawn. Now, you do realise that Dawn's death was not from natural causes? It's being treated as suspicious, and therefore we are interested in anyone who's shown a particular interest in her.'

Natalie's eyes widened, her streaked hair catching the harsh interview room light. 'What? So you're saying Dawn was murdered?'

'That is correct.' Lauren's voice was steady.

'But... but... surely you can't think I'd harm her?' Natalie's voice cracked slightly.

'We're investigating everyone,' Matt said, observing the woman's shaking hands. 'You were fascinated by Dawn. Why?'

Natalie shifted in her chair, her earlier defiance gone. She tucked a short strand of hair behind her ear. 'It's just... I saw a film that she was in from years ago, and it impressed me so much. I loved her style of acting. She wanted me to write her memoir.'

Matt exchanged a quick glance with Lauren, his eyebrows raised slightly. 'And what did you say?'

'I told her that I'd never done anything like it before but she said that didn't matter.' Natalie's hands fidgeted in her lap, twisting a tissue into a tight spiral. 'The fact that I'd shown an interest in her was enough. A lot of what you discovered was given to me by her.'

'But all this in the scrapbook, it doesn't appear to be recently compiled,' Matt said, confused at the timeline. His forehead creased as he tapped his foot against the table leg.

Natalie gave a sigh, her shoulders slumping. 'Look, I visited Dawn a few months ago at the home, before getting a job there. I already knew about her and couldn't believe that she lived so close.' She straightened in her chair, seeming to find her confidence again. 'I went to visit and we got on well. It was then she asked me about writing her memoir.'

'When exactly was this?' Matt asked, his head tilted slightly as he studied her face.

'Just before Christmas.'

'Did you agree to write it?' Matt continued, his gaze remaining fixed on her.

'After getting the agency to send me to Silver Fern I decided that I would. I told Dawn that last week.'

'Did you speak to her on the day of her death?' Lauren asked, leaning in.

'Yes.' Natalie swallowed hard.

'Did you bring her any chocolates?' Lauren asked, in an almost throwaway tone. But Matt knew it was especially meant to sound like that.

'No.' Natalie's response was too quick, too sharp. Her eyes widened slightly, and a flush crept up her neck as she glanced towards the door.

'Are you sure?' Lauren persisted.

'We're not meant to give presents to residents. But okay... yes. I brought her a small bar of milk chocolate. But please don't tell the home or I'll get into trouble.'

Matt exhaled. He'd been hoping she'd given her the tin, but unfortunately not.

'We won't,' Lauren said. 'Did she offer you any of the chocolates from the tin in her bedroom?'

Natalie's fingers twisted together on the table. 'I... I think she did, yes.'

'Did you take one?'

'No. I'm not a sweet lover.' Her voice had grown smaller. 'Why are you asking me about chocolates?' A bead of sweat formed on her temple.

'Because we believe that Dawn was murdered by antifreeze poisoning. It had been put into chocolates in the tin,' Lauren replied, her voice firm.

Natalie's face drained of colour. 'Oh my God.'

'Did you go into her room when she wasn't there? When she was at meals?' Lauren continued.

'Are you accusing me of putting antifreeze into Dawn's chocolate?' Natalie's voice rose hysterically. 'You know she offers them to everybody. Why would anyone put antifreeze in them? Wouldn't that kill whoever took one?'

'Not if you put them into specific ones,' Matt said quietly, watching her reaction.

'I don't... I don't know what you mean.' Natalie's hair trembled as she shook her head.

'Strawberry creams,' Lauren said, laying another photograph on the table, showing the box of chocolates from Dawn's room.

'What about them?' Natalie asked.

'When Dawn offered you a chocolate, did she tell you not to take a strawberry cream?'

'No, she didn't offer me one...' Natalie's voice trailed off as she realised her mistake.

'But you've just said she did,' Matt pointed out, his tone gentle but firm.

'Oh, I don't know. I don't remember.' Natalie pushed back from the table, her chair scraping against the floor. 'Stop accusing me. I didn't do anything.'

'Where were you on Friday between the hours of four and seven?' Lauren's question cut through Natalie's rising panic.

'I was at work. You know that.'

'Which gave you ample time to go into her room and poison the chocolates,' Matt observed.

'But where would I get the antifreeze from?' Natalie's voice had taken on a shrill edge.

'You can pick that up at any hardware shop.' Lauren's response was matter-of-fact.

'This is ridiculous. You're accusing me of something I didn't do.' Natalie's hands were shaking so badly now she had to clasp them together.

'Did you see anybody acting suspiciously when you were on duty on Friday?'

'No, not really. The electrician was there. Have you spoken to her?' Natalie asked, her voice barely above a whisper.

'We will be interviewing everyone present. But you're of particular interest, as I'm sure you understand,' Lauren said firmly.

'I'm not saying anything else,' Natalie declared, crossing her arms. 'Not without a solicitor present. Am I under arrest?'

'No, you're not,' Lauren said, her tone cooling. 'You may go home, but do not attempt to leave the town without asking us first. And I mean anywhere – not for an audition, not for anything.'

They escorted Natalie to the entrance, and as she practically fled from the station.

Matt turned to Lauren. 'Well?'

'I don't know, Matt. I don't know. She was clearly obsessed with Dawn and if it was because of writing her memoir then having all this stuff makes sense. But there's nothing to indicate that she was responsible for her death.'

'Except she first said that Dawn did offer her a chocolate and then changed her mind.'

'True. But maybe she was trying to cover her back, for whatever reason. She's not off the hook yet, though.'

SIXTEEN

WEDNESDAY FEBRUARY 12

'Daddy. Daddy. Watch me play with my zoo,' Dani called out as Matt walked into the lounge. Her small hands were arranging plastic animals in careful rows across the carpet. There were lions next to zebras and elephants beside giraffes. A peaceful kingdom that only made sense in a child's imagination. The morning sun streamed through the bay window, catching the gold highlights in her unruly curls.

Matt paused, warmth flooding through him, his coffee mug in his hands, savouring his daughter's excitement. 'Are you sure you have time for this?' He glanced at his watch, the familiar weight of responsibility settling on his shoulders. 'Aren't you going to nursery today?'

'Yes. Grandma's taking me.' Dani beamed up at him, clutching a plastic giraffe that had lost one ear to an unfortunate encounter when it had been trapped in the door. Her expressive eyes – so like Leigh's – sparkled with excitement. 'I'm ready. I've had my breakfast.' She wiped her hand over the white milk moustache as if to prove it.

His heart tugged. So many of his daughter's mannerisms reminded him of his dead wife. He missed her as much now as he did when it first happened. People, including his mum, hinted at him moving on and finding someone else. But how could he? There would never be another Leigh. It wasn't that he didn't find other women attractive. He did. When he'd first got to know Lauren there had been a spark between them, but that soon changed and they'd become good friends. But they were both careful not to let their friendship interfere with work. He always called her ma'am when on duty. But outside of work she was Lauren. He diverted his attention back to Dani.

'Your face needs washing and what about brushing your hair?' He eyed the wild tangle of curls that seemed to have a life of their own this morning. A smile tugged at his lips despite his attempt at parental sternness. 'You look like you've been in a wind tunnel. Twice.'

'Not yet. Help me play.' She patted her hair, and then the carpet beside her invitingly, shuffling to make space for him in her carefully constructed zoo. 'The lions are having a tea party with the penguins, and you can be the second-in-charge zookeeper.'

'Why can't I be the first in charge?'

'Because I am,' Dani replied adamantly.

Matt's heart softened at her earnest expression. Leaving for work could wait five more minutes; no one was going to mind. 'Okay, but I can only play for a few minutes.' He lowered himself to the floor, his knees cracking in protest, and positioned himself next to her. 'I have to go to work soon.'

'With Lauren?' Dani asked, with a knowing nod.

Lauren and Dani had a special relationship ever since his daughter was kidnapped and his boss was instrumental in rescuing her.

'Yes.'

'So you can be second in charge with her and second in charge with me,' Dani said, pride in her voice.

'That's right. We're very busy but I'm sure Lauren won't mind me spending a little more time with you, as long as we don't—'

His phone rang, shattering the moment. Dani's face fell and her lower lip jutted out in a familiar pout. She knew that ring tone as well as he did. He pulled the phone from his pocket, catching sight of Lauren's number. 'Hang on a minute, sweetheart.' He squeezed Dani's shoulder reassuringly. 'Morning, ma'am.' He knew something had to be wrong because of the early hour of her call.

'Matt, I want you at the care home straight away,' Lauren said, her voice crackling through the speaker, tense and clipped.

The hairs on the back of his neck stood up. 'Why? What's happened?' He glanced at Dani, who was staring directly at him, and then turned away, keeping his voice low, though he could feel his daughter's curious eyes on his back.

'We've just received a call from the home saying that another of the residents has been found dead this morning. He was discovered in his room first thing by one of the carers. By all accounts it's not from natural causes.'

Crap. Just what they didn't need. Two murders to deal with. Did that mean there'd be more if they didn't solve the case quickly?

'Who's the victim?'

'Charlie Cook,' Lauren responded with a sigh.

'What? The stand-up comic?' He remembered Charlie from watching the rehearsal and talking to him. He'd made Matt laugh with his jokes and witty comments.

'Yes, he's the one. If you recall he annoyed Kenneth the director with all those complaints about the play.'

'Yes, I do, but it was only in jest. Why did they phone the police and not the doctor?' Matt moved further into the doorway, away from Dani's earshot.

'According to the desk sergeant, the manager said it all looked odd, whatever that means. So they called us. Henry's already on his way there. I'm heading there now and will see you there so we can check the scene together.'

Matt ran a hand through his hair, going over what he remembered about Charlie Cook from their previous visit to the home. Although they didn't know the man's age, he was certainly on the ball, and quick witted. 'No problem. I'll see you soon.'

He ended the call as his mum walked out of the kitchen and headed towards him.

Her eyes narrowed slightly. 'What is it, love?' she asked, clearly reading the tension in his body.

'I've got to leave for the Silver Fern Care Home.' He walked over to Dani, who was still busy arranging her animals. 'I'm sorry, princess. Daddy's got to go but I promise we'll play zoo soon, okay?'

Dani nodded solemnly, her lower lip trembling slightly. She was too young to understand the nature of his work, but old enough to know it got in the way. 'Promise?'

'Cross my heart.' He leant down and kissed the top of her head, breathing in the sweet smell of her shampoo, trying to hold onto the moment of innocence before stepping back into the darkness that awaited him at the potential murder scene.

'The penguins will wait for you, Daddy,' Dani said softly, holding up the small plastic figure. 'They promise to be good, too.'

The simple statement nearly undid him. He hugged her quickly, not trusting his voice for a moment. 'You be good for Grandma, okay? And maybe tonight she'll let you have pizza for dinner.'

'Can I?' Dani asked excitedly, looking up at her grandmother.

'If you're good,' his mum said with a smile.

'I will be,' Dani replied, returning the smile. She then went back to playing with the zoo.

His mother glanced at him. 'Not another one?' Her face paled slightly.

'It looks like it.' He grabbed his jacket from the back of the chair, checking his pocket for his notebook and pen. 'I've no idea what time I'll be home. Expect me when you see me. Don't worry about dinner; I'll grab something somewhere.'

'Which means you'll forget. I know you. You've got to eat. I'll keep something warm in the oven for you. Now you get going and leave me to sort everything out here.' She touched his arm gently, her eyes worried. The lines around her mouth deepened. 'I do hope this is not going to be the start of another...' She clamped her mouth shut, but Matt realised she was about to say 'serial killer' because that's what seemed to hang around him like a dark cloud. Ever since he'd joined the Penzance force their number had increased ten-fold. He'd been the butt of many a joke at the station because of it, especially from Billy, who often referred to him as a 'serial killer magnet'.

'Thanks, Mum. I don't know what I'd do without you.'

'That's okay then, because I'm not going anywhere. Nor is your dad.' She gave his arm a squeeze and tears threatened to fill his eyes so he hurriedly turned and headed for the front door.

Before he'd even closed it behind him, he could hear his mother already distracting Dani with hair-brushing games, her voice deliberately bright and cheerful. The contrast between his home life and work life had never felt starker. In his living room, plastic animals were having tea parties, while across town, there was another body waiting to tell its story.

A second death at Silver Fern couldn't be a coincidence, and the thought chilled him as he headed down the street to where he'd parked his car. Charlie Cook had been a performer his entire life. What had been his final act? And more importantly, who had made sure it was his last?

SEVENTEEN

WEDNESDAY FEBRUARY 12

'Charlie Cook's room is along here,' Gill Trelawny said, her voice trembling slightly as she led Matt and Lauren up the stairs to the Olivier wing. Her shoulders were tense beneath her navy cardigan. 'The pathologist arrived about ten minutes ago, and I've informed the staff that nobody is to go into the room.'

Early morning sunlight cast ominous long shadows across the green and peach carpet.

'Thank you. The room will be out of bounds until further notice because we'll need forensics to come here after,' Lauren replied.

'Right. I'll let everyone know.'

'Do the residents know yet of Charlie's death?' Lauren asked.

'They know something's wrong but not exactly what. They've been asked to remain in their rooms. We will need to let them know soon, though.'

'Of course, but please keep details to a minimum. We especially don't want them conferring before we've had the chance to speak to them.'

As they made their way to the crime scene, the muffled sounds of residents' televisions could be heard from behind closed doors. It was a shame that they couldn't remain oblivious to what had happened only metres away from where they sat.

The weight of there being another murder pressed down on Matt's shoulders as they followed Gill down the corridor, which was lined with seven identical pale blue doors, decorated with residents' names in cheerful lettering that now seemed inappropriately bright. His mind kept circling back to the first victim, Dawn Cross, wondering whether it was the same killer. Surely it had to be. Two separate killers in such a small place would be beyond the realms of believability.

'We're here,' Gill said, stopping outside a room at the end of the corridor. The nameplate reading 'Charlie Cook' hung slightly askew on the door which was ajar.

'Before we go in, I have a quick question,' Lauren said, turning to face Gill.

'Yes?' Gill replied, sounding a little uneasy.

'I'd like you to run through exactly what occurred leading up to, and during, Charlie's discovery this morning?'

Gill wrapped her arms around herself, as if suddenly cold in the ambient temperature-controlled hallway. Her silver heart-shaped pendant caught the light as she visibly swallowed hard. 'Frank Ellis, one of our care staff, was doing his rounds before handover at eight. He'd worked the night shift.' Her voice wavered. 'He went into Charlie's room and, on seeing him, immediately alerted my assistant manager, who then phoned me. I was already on my way in, and only five minutes away. When I got here, I went straight to Charlie's room. I could see...'

She paused, closing her eyes briefly as if trying to block out the memory. 'It looked as if he'd been strangled. There was a scarf tied tightly around his neck and his eyes...' She grimaced. 'They seemed to be bulging in a weird sort of way. I didn't touch anything in the room, just immediately left and called the police, asking them to send someone straight away. I did say could it be you, because of what had happened to Dawn. Was that okay?'

'Yes, absolutely, that was the right thing to do,' Lauren said softly. 'It must have been a big shock for you.'

'It was. It really was,' Gill replied, exhaling loudly.

Matt's stomach churned as he pictured the scene waiting for them behind the door. But he supposed he should be grateful that there wasn't going to be any blood. Even so, there seemed something particularly disturbing about an unnatural death in a care home. They were places meant to protect society's most vulnerable.

'Charlie was a very big man,' Matt said, frowning as he recalled seeing the victim at the play rehearsal during their previous visit. 'Surely, whoever did this to him must have been very strong because he'd have tried to fight them off. I'm guessing that he weighed at least sixteen or seventeen stone.'

'Ordinarily yes, you'd be right, but Charlie didn't sleep at all well – at least not since his wife passed away a couple of years ago. He always has a sleeping pill at night and it puts him out like a light within twenty minutes of taking it. I guess that means anyone, within reason, could have done this to him.' She glanced down the corridor, as if checking for eavesdroppers. 'Whoever was on duty on this wing would wake Charlie up in the morning, usually at around nine. That was when he liked to get dressed and have his breakfast. He was very particular about his daily routine.'

'So why did the carer go into his room early on instead of waiting until nine?' Matt asked, with a frown.

'It's part of their nightly duties to check on all the residents several times during the shift.'

'Okay, thanks for that,' Lauren said. 'We can take it from here, but we'll come to find you later.'

The manager left them, her footsteps fading quickly down the corridor like a retreating heartbeat. Matt took a deep breath, steeling himself before they walked in.

Lauren pushed open the door revealing Henry, his latex-gloved hands steady as he photographed the scene. The camera's flash illuminated the room in stark bursts, briefly highlighting the horror before them. Charlie's room was neat and organised, with photos lining the walls, most of them of him on stage or with other performers. Smiling faces that now served as unwitting witnesses to his final moments.

'Good morning, Henry,' Lauren said, her voice light despite the grim scene before them. 'What can you tell us?'

Henry lowered his camera, his expression grave, lines of concentration etched around his eyes. 'Until I get him back to the lab, these are just initial findings, as you know.' He gestured towards the victim, who lay partially on his side on the single bed. 'But he does appear to have been strangled. Note that big knot there.'

Matt's gaze followed Henry's pointing finger. Charlie's face was tinged purple and his eyes bulged beneath half-closed lids. A dark blue silk scarf, with a pattern of small white dots, was pulled tightly around his neck, the large knot sitting just below his left ear. The victim's hands lay curled beside him, as if he'd tried to reach for his throat but never made it.

'The body's in a somewhat unnatural position,' Henry continued, moving around the bed to get a better angle for his photographs. 'I assume it's because someone had to wrap the scarf around his neck and pull it tight. He doesn't seem to have put up much of a fight, but I'll check more thoroughly when he's at the mortuary.'

'That's probably because he takes a sleeping pill at night. It must have been a very strong one, though, if it didn't wake him up while this was happening,' Matt said.

'He may have woken but was sufficiently incapacitated that he couldn't do anything to stop it,' Henry added.

Lauren moved closer to the body, her eyes scanning for details. 'What about time of death? Any idea?'

Henry lowered his camera and examined the body's joints. 'Judging by the rigor mortis in the body, I'd say death occurred sometime between three and seven in the morning. But again, I'll let you know for certain once I've done the postmortem.'

Matt's mind raced, connecting patterns as he surveyed the room. A half-empty glass of water sat on the bedside table, likely used to take the sleeping pill. A book, *The Count of Monte Cristo*, lay face-down beside it. Its pages were splayed open as if Charlie had planned to return to it.

'Would a woman be strong enough to do this to him?' Matt asked.

Henry's head snapped up, his eyes sharp behind his glasses. 'It would depend on how strong they were, I guess. Even with the victim incapacitated, it wouldn't have been easy. Why do you ask?'

'Because the first body was poisoned, which we normally associate with a female way of killing. I just thought maybe...' Matt shrugged and walked over to the window, looking out at the care home's well-maintained gardens below. Somewhere out there, a killer was going about their day, perhaps even watching the police activity with false concern.

'Don't start making suppositions, young man,' Henry warned, his voice carrying years of experience. 'Because you and I both know that inevitably leads to a downfall. I've seen too many good detectives led astray by early theories, and I don't wish you to be one of them.'

'Thank you, Henry,' Matt said with a slight smile, though his mind was already mapping possible connections between the two deaths. 'But it was just a question. I can assure you that I'm well aware of the need to always be open-minded.'

'That's good to know,' Henry said gruffly, with a sharp nod.

Lauren cleared her throat. 'Right, okay, we're going to leave you to it, Henry. We need to speak to the manager, staff and residents. At least we have a captive audience, so to speak.' She turned to Matt, her expression determined. 'Somebody must have seen or heard something. This is the second murder here, and in a place this small, secrets don't stay buried forever. We need to search them out.'

'Good luck,' Henry said. 'I hope to have something for you later in the day.'

'Thanks, Henry,' Lauren said, turning and heading towards the door.

As they left the room, the care home's quiet hallways suddenly seemed more menacing than peaceful, each closed door potentially hiding witnesses – or suspects. Matt paused briefly, looking back at Charlie's room where Henry continued his methodical documentation.

These two deaths were connected by more than just location. No way could it be a coincidence, not in a place like this.

EIGHTEEN

WEDNESDAY FEBRUARY 12

Lauren walked downstairs with Matt, her mind still processing the grim scene in Charlie Cook's room and wondering how it linked to the death of Dawn Cross. It certainly wasn't the mode of killing, so it had to be something else.

At the bottom of the stairs, she spotted Gill Trelawny talking to one of her staff in hushed tones.

She approached them purposefully. 'Excuse me, we really need to have a chat with you, Gill.'

'Of course. Shall we go to my office, where it's private?' Gill replied.

'Yes, that's a good idea,' Lauren replied.

'I'll catch up with you later,' the staff member said, hurrying away.

They walked to Gill's office in silence and once inside and the door closed behind them, they sat around the desk.

'What do you want to know?' Gill asked.

'Are the staff on duty last night still here?' Lauren asked, hoping they would be, despite their shifts probably being over.

'Yes, they are. I asked them to stay. After our last death, I knew you'd want to speak to them,' Gill explained, settling into her chair.

'There were two staff on Charlie's wing, plus our assistant manager, who floated around the whole place.'

'And what about the other three wings?'

'We had two staff on each.'

Lauren leant forward. 'So that's nine staff in total. Do the staff visit each other's wings?'

'Not really. They're usually too busy doing the checks and sorting things out. The wings are pretty much self-contained, including for the meals. As you know, they eat in four separate dining areas. The only time the residents come together is during activities or play rehearsals.'

'Thanks. First, we'll speak to the two staff working on Charlie's wing and then we'll have a word with the residents. Are they all in their rooms?'

'Actually a few moments ago I instructed my staff to go into each of the residents' rooms and ask them to congregate in the ball-room,' Gill said, fidgeting with her pendant. 'They obviously know that there's something amiss, although they don't exactly know what it is. I was going to break the news to them. They should all be there by now.'

'Okay, I'll come with you,' Lauren said. She turned to Matt. 'You can start questioning the carers. Who else was on duty with Frank?'

'Lynn Tremaine.'

'We've spoken to Lynn before, haven't we?' Lauren asked, recalling their previous interviews.

'Yes, that's correct. They're both full-time carers,' Gill confirmed. 'You'll find them somewhere on the wing, I expect,' she added, addressing her comment to Matt.

'Thanks,' Matt replied.

'What about agency staff?' Lauren asked.

'There were some working last night, but none on that wing.'

'Okay. What about your assistant manager?'

'Ali Penrose. I've asked her to wait in the ballroom with the residents so we could deliver the news together and be there to support them.'

'We'll need to speak to her, too. I'll do that after we've seen the residents. Okay, let's go.'

Lauren straightened her jacket, preparing herself for what would undoubtedly be a difficult and upsetting conversation. They left the office and Matt headed back towards the stairs leading to the Gielgud wing, while she walked to the ballroom with Gill. As they entered the large room, the chatting came to an immediate halt and worried faces turned expectantly towards them.

'Can I have your attention please, everyone?' Gill called out, albeit unnecessarily because she already had it, her voice carrying across the quiet room.

'What's going on?' Fred asked, his weathered hands gripping his walking stick.

'Because we know *something* is,' Kenneth added.

Lauren observed the room carefully as Gill continued, 'Unfortunately, I do have some very bad news. We've had another death in the home, again not from natural causes and this time it's Charlie Cook.'

A collective gasp rippled through the room. Lauren noticed several residents reaching for each other's hands, while others sat in stunned silence.

'Charlie?' Kenneth said, his eyes wide with shock. 'That's impossible. He's here in the ballroom, I saw him a few minutes ago. Didn't I?' He turned and slowly scanned the room. 'Where is he? I saw him, I did. I know it.'

'I'm sorry, Kenneth, you can't have because he wasn't here. Charlie died sometime during the night,' Gill said, kindly, walking towards him and placing a steadying hand on his arm.

'No. This is ridiculous. I refuse to believe it,' Kenneth responded, shaking off Gill's hand.

Was he protesting too much, or was his confusion and shock genuine? It was hard to tell considering he was an actor.

'What happened to him?' one of the women standing at the back of the room asked.

'The pathologist is here and we won't know that until he's completed his postmortem,' Gill said, before Lauren had a chance to respond. 'Detective Pengelly is here, and she would like to have a chat with you all.'

Lauren stepped forward, conscious of the emotional weight in the room. 'Thank you. I'm very sorry to all of you for your loss and appreciate how hard this is. To confirm what Gill said, we're treating Charlie's death as suspicious, in the same way as Dawn's.'

'So he was poisoned with antifreeze?' Kenneth called out sharply, appearing to have regained some of his composure.

Lauren tried to hide her grimace, her mind racing. They hadn't officially announced that detail about Dawn's death. Someone had been talking – or someone knew more than they should. 'No, we don't believe that to be the case, but until the pathologist has completed his work and we have the report, we won't know for certain.' She watched Kenneth's face carefully, noting his reaction. 'I'd like to ask, have any of you known Charlie a long time?'

'Me,' Kenneth said, raising his hand slightly. 'We've known each other since the 1960s.'

Lauren tried to hide her surprise, considering Kenneth was an RSC actor and Charlie a stand-up comic. 'I see. In that case, if you don't mind, I'd like to sit down with you over there so we can have a few words on our own,' Lauren suggested, nodding to the rear of the room, after noticing the other residents straining to hear. 'The rest of you please stay here because I may wish to speak to you further.'

She glanced across and saw Gill talking quietly to a member of staff, who Lauren assumed was Ali Penrose. Lauren quickly strode over to them. 'Please stay here with the residents, who are likely to be in shock, while I have a word with Kenneth. After which I'll catch up with Matt and interview the staff. I don't have time to speak to the residents individually now – keep them here for a little while, for support. Then after that they can return to their rooms.'

Lauren walked over to Kenneth, who was standing unnaturally still, and guided him over to the corner of the ballroom where they sat facing one another.

'I'm very sorry for your loss,' she repeated to Kenneth, studying his face for any signs of his responses being an act.

'Thank you,' he replied, his hands clasped tightly in his lap.

'Can you explain to me: you said you'd known each other since the 1960s, but Charlie was a stand-up comic and you're an actor. How did you know each other?' Lauren clasped her hands together in her lap.

Kenneth shifted in his seat. 'Charlie wasn't just a comedian. He was also an actor. We trained together at RADA, but his real love was comedy and he had an amazing talent for it. He could have gone far as an actor but he was a bit out of place at RADA because of his accent. Despite me trying to persuade him, he refused to change it, like others did in those days. Part of our training was for us to all speak in received English. Charlie refused and that meant he struggled to get any decent parts. So he went into stand-up comedy. It was such a waste of his talent. He could play both straight and comedy.' His wistful tone took Lauren by surprise.

'I was under the impression you didn't get on, but you're making it sound as if you did,' Lauren said, watching his expression carefully.

Kenneth paused as if trying to work out what to say. 'A long time ago when we were young, we were friends. But not now. In fact, since we've been living here, he went out of his way to undermine me, especially when I'm directing the productions. But that doesn't mean I wanted him dead. We were just incompatible as friends.'

Lauren nodded slowly. 'Can you think of anyone who might have wanted him dead?'

'Well, he did rub a lot of people the wrong way with his constant quips, and very often they were at the expense of someone. Behind that smile of his, he could be quite hurtful. But as for someone wanting to kill him... no. People accepted him for who he was.' Kenneth's eyes darted around the room nervously.

Was he telling her everything?

'I see. Do you know anything about Charlie's family? Did he have many visitors?'

'I'm not sure he has any family left. His wife died a couple of years ago. She was in the home here with us. She was a singer and could have given Maria Callas a run for her money, if only she'd had the opportunity. An amazing talent.' Kenneth straightened in his chair, his actor's training evident in his posture. 'Whatever you think of mine and Charlie's tricky relationship, I can promise you I had nothing to do with his death. Despite everything between us, I'm going to miss him.' Tears filled his eyes, and he took out a pristine white handkerchief from his pocket and wiped them, giving a sniff. 'Sorry,' he muttered.

'No need to apologise, this is most distressing. Thank you for your honesty.' Lauren studied him for a moment, noting the slight tremor in his hands. 'If you do think of anything else that might be relevant, please let me know. Gill has my details and can contact me.'

'With two residents dead, are the rest of us at risk?' Kenneth asked, as they both stood.

'I sincerely hope not, but everyone needs to be on their guard.'

As they headed back to where the other residents were, Lauren couldn't shake the feeling that beneath the surface of this seemingly peaceful care home lay a web of old grudges and hidden resentments. Two deaths in such quick succession couldn't be a coincidence. The killer was here, perhaps watching her question Kenneth right now, and she was determined to uncover the truth hiding behind these theatrical facades.

'Ma'am,' Matt called out, quickening his pace as he spotted Lauren leaving the ballroom.

Lauren turned, her expression questioning. There were dark circles under her eyes. Having to deal with two murders in a short number of days, on top of her aunt's case, was clearly wearing on her.

'I've just been with Lynn Tremaine and Frank Ellis,' he reported, falling into step beside her. 'They're both shocked by Charlie Cook's death but according to them, they didn't see anybody who shouldn't be around acting suspiciously throughout the night.'

The receptionist walked past them and they paused their conversation until she was out of earshot.

'Which points to it being an inside job,' Lauren said.

'My thoughts exactly. Frank Ellis was particularly upset by it all,' Matt added, remembering the carer's constant fidgeting during their interview. 'But he was the one to find the body. He said he'd worked here for twelve years and nothing like this has ever happened before Dawn's death.'

'Murders in care homes aren't a regular occurrence, anyway, so I'm not sure that's relevant,' Lauren replied, with a frown.

'I don't believe he meant murders, ma'am. More that nothing out of the ordinary happened at the home.' Matt pulled out his notebook and opened it, scanning his hastily scribbled notes. 'I asked them both for a run-down of what they did during their shifts and it seems they're kept quite busy with admin when they're not checking residents in their rooms. Part of their job is to write daily reports on each resident regarding their physical and mental health. This means they're not keeping an eye on the comings and goings on their respective wings one hundred percent of the time.'

'And I'm betting admin isn't their favourite part of the job,' Lauren mused. 'Did you ask them about Charlie's demeanour recently, and whether anything had changed?' She stopped by a window that overlooked the care home's delightful garden and glanced out. A few early birds were pecking at the bird feeders, oblivious to the drama unfolding inside. And a gardener was trimming the hedges, the gentle whirr of his electric trimmer just about audible through the double-glazing.

'Yes, and according to Frank, who was responsible for Charlie's report yesterday, he was the same as usual,' Matt replied, leaning against the windowsill. 'Cracking jokes, some of them not PC, but seeming to get away with it. I sensed from Frank's uncomfortable expression when describing Charlie's humour that he wasn't particularly impressed.'

'So Frank wasn't a fan of Charlie then?'

'He didn't say anything against the man, but like I said, he was clearly not happy with the jokes. But Charlie was a product of his time and that sort of humour was acceptable then. Lynn also mentioned that Charlie had been telling jokes about the local vicar just yesterday evening. Something about confession and whisky... she couldn't remember exactly, but she said everyone was laughing. Well, almost everyone.'

'Was there anyone notably not laughing?'

Matt consulted his notes again. 'Kenneth apparently left the room during the joke, muttering something about "tasteless humour" on his way out. But, again, nothing out of the ordinary because, according to Lynn, Kenneth often complained about Charlie's so-called humour.'

'When I spoke to Kenneth a few minutes ago, he didn't mention anything about this. He said he'd known Charlie since the 1960s and they were once friends but not now.'

'Maybe the humour was part of the reason he wasn't friends with Charlie,' Matt suggested.

'Possibly. Is there anything else from your interviews?'

'Yes. Frank mentioned that a few days ago in the garden he overheard Charlie arguing with someone on the phone. He couldn't make out what it was about, but he said Charlie seemed upset afterwards. Didn't even make his usual jokes at dinner.'

Lauren's eyebrows arched. 'And he had no idea what it was about?'

'No.' Matt shook his head. 'But supposedly the next day he was back to his usual self.'

Lauren's eyes brightened. 'Let's pop back to his room to see if his phone is there.'

When they reached Charlie's room, Matt pushed open the door with his shoulder, careful not to touch the handle with his bare hands. Henry was still there and he glanced up at them, his gloved hands pausing over an evidence marker.

'I've almost finished in here.' He stood up from his crouched position, rolling his shoulders. 'Is there something you want?'

'Did you come across a mobile phone, by any chance?' Lauren asked, scanning the room.

'Yes, it's on the bedside table.' Henry nodded to where it was sitting.

'Thanks. Are you okay for us to take it?' Lauren asked, already pulling gloves from her pocket.

'Be my guest. I've already photographed it.' Henry waved dismissively, returning his attention to his work.

Lauren carefully placed the phone in an evidence bag and they left the room and headed back down the stairs.

'Back to Frank,' Lauren said, turning to Matt while they were walking. 'What else did he say about last night?'

Matt retrieved his notebook and flipped through the pages. 'Charlie had his sleeping pill at his usual time, when he went to bed, and they didn't hear a peep from him after that. Again, nothing out of the ordinary.'

'Did Frank give you an account of when he found the body?'

'Yes,' Matt said, recalling the carer's pale face during the interview. 'He was doing the morning checks and he knocked first on the door – they always do, apparently, even if they expect the resident to be asleep. He then opened the door and went in.' Matt's voice dropped lower. 'Frank said he knew something was wrong straight away because Charlie was lying in such a strange position. He moved forwards to take a better look.'

Matt ran a hand through his hair, remembering Frank's distress. 'After seeing the body he ran out of the room to find the assistant manager who was on duty. She called Gill Trelawny in. He didn't return to the room after that.' Matt hesitated, before adding, 'Oh yes, although I doubt this is relevant, according to Frank, Charlie had a wife who died a couple of years ago?'

'Yes, I already know that from Kenneth.' Lauren nodded, pulling out her phone to check something.

'Do you think he had anything to do with Charlie's death?' Matt asked, lowering his voice as another staff member walked by them.

'My gut says no. They've known each other for years and years. They trained together at RADA.'

Matt frowned, his forehead creasing. 'But he was a stand-up comic?'

'Yes, but he was an actor first and fell into comedy later,' Lauren explained, checking her phone briefly. 'I wouldn't say there was a lot of love lost between them because they were very different, but Kenneth seemed genuinely shocked by what had happened.'

A door slammed somewhere down the corridor, making them both start slightly.

'Lynn mentioned something else,' Matt added, flipping back a page in his notebook, suddenly remembering. 'Apparently, Charlie had been working on his memoirs and—'

'What? Him too? That's what Dawn Cross was doing,' Lauren interrupted.

'Do you think that could be our link between the two deaths? Lynn said Charlie had been asking residents and staff about their memories of his old performances. Some people found it annoying. He'd corner them in the TV lounge and demand to know if they remembered specific shows he'd done. If they said they didn't, he'd do some of the act for them. He must have had an amazing memory to be able to do that.'

'That's definitely something we need to investigate,' Lauren said. 'Did they have any idea where his memoirs might be?'

Matt shook his head. 'I don't know whether he'd begun writing them, or whether he was collecting material. I hope you don't mind, but I've said Lynn and Frank can go home. They've already worked a twelve-hour shift and need some sleep. I explained that we might want to speak to them later.'

'That's fine, providing we have their contact details.'

'I do. What do you want to do now?'

Lauren glanced around the corridor before responding. 'We need to wait until we've got the report from Henry, although it's clearly murder. Let's go back to the office and get the team looking into the residents and the staff in more detail.' She lowered her voice. 'I want to interview the other care staff at the station rather than here. That way we can record the interviews properly and they can speak freely.'

'And what about Natalie Baker?' Matt asked, replacing his notebook into his jacket pocket.

'We'll question her again, to find out where she was last night.'

An elderly resident shuffled past with a walker, accompanied by a carer, heading to the toilets on the ground floor. The normality of the scene felt surreal against the backdrop of two murders.

'What did Frank and Lynn say about the night rounds?' Lauren asked, starting to walk towards the entrance.

Matt fell into step beside her, consulting his notes again. 'They do checks every three hours. Last night's rounds were at ten pm, one am, and four am. Then they check before handing over.'

'And nothing seemed out of place?'

'Not according to them. Though Lynn mentioned that during one of her checks, she thought she heard voices from the direction of the TV lounge, but when she looked in, it was empty. Just the television left on. Do you want us to interview the rest of the residents?'

The sound of a door closing somewhere down the corridor made them both turn. In a place like this everyone was both a potential witness and a potential suspect. The killer could be anyone... staff, resident, or visitor... and they needed to move quickly before they struck again.

'Definitely.'

'Shall we bring in more officers?' Matt suggested. 'We could use some help interviewing them all and there might be connections we're not seeing yet.'

'That's an excellent idea.'

'Okay, I'll sort that out when we get back to the office. On the way out I'll ask the receptionist to forward the CCTV footage from yesterday and—'

Matt was interrupted by some carers passing them.

Through a nearby doorway, residents were gathering for breakfast, their faces drawn with concern as they whispered among themselves.

Lauren checked her watch. 'Let's get a move on. I want to start building a timeline and to check Charlie's phone records to find out who he was arguing with yesterday.'

After stopping to speak to the receptionist, they headed out to the car. The morning sun had risen higher now, streaming through the trees and illuminating the care home's grounds in harsh clarity. Matt suspected that somewhere close by was a killer who was perhaps watching them right now. They needed to move quickly, before anyone else ended up like Charlie.

TWENTY

WEDNESDAY FEBRUARY 12

Lauren strode into the office, her shoulders tense with the weight of the two unsolved murders, and, although she hardly dared think about it, potentially more to come. She marched over to the whiteboard, uncapping a marker with determined precision.

'Right, everyone,' she called, her voice cutting through the morning chatter. 'We need to focus. We have two deaths on our hands, both with different MOs and no clear motive.'

Billy looked up from his computer screen. 'The timing's what's getting me. Two murders in one care home within days of each other? That can't be coincidence.'

'Agreed,' Lauren said, adding Charlie Cook's name to the whiteboard in bold letters, beside Dawn's. She underlined both names twice. 'Different methods, different locations within the home, but something, or someone, connects them.' She added more details to the board. 'Let's break down what we know. Thirty residents in the home, separated into four wings, each named after a famous actor. Olivier, Gielgud, Plowright and Richardson.' She drew a quick diagram. 'Staff tend to stick to their assigned wings.'

'How many staff per wing?' Billy asked, taking notes.

'Two at any given time, operating on a twelve-hour shift,' Lauren replied. 'Plus the manager and deputy manager floating between areas. Some are full time, others part time and when necessary, they use agency staff. They have eleven staff currently on their books.' She turned back to the board, adding staff numbers.

Clem whistled low. 'Seems understaffed for thirty residents.'

'That's where the agency workers come in,' Lauren explained. 'Four regulars: Natalie Baker, Mary Collins, Rose White and Dylan Harper.' She wrote each name carefully. 'Baker's only worked a couple of shifts, but the others are there frequently.'

'Yes, but two per wing still seems low. What happens if a resident needs the commode, for example, and the two staff are busy lifting another one?' Clem asked. 'There are strict protocols involved in this to protect from back injuries.'

'They have to wait until there's someone free,' Lauren replied with a shrug.

'Or have an accident,' Billy added, with a smirk. 'Anyway, how do you know so much about this? Oh wait, stupid question. You've no doubt researched it for some reason or another.'

'Billy, you may choose to limit your knowledge base, but I don't,' Clem said, rolling his eyes.

'Focus, please. I've been assured that they stick to government guidelines. But that's not our worry. We have other things to consider,' Lauren added, wanting to bring them back on track.

'Was there any overlap between the carers' shifts and both murders?' Jenna asked, pulling out her tablet.

Lauren shrugged. 'That's what we need to find out. Matt interviewed Lynn Tremaine, and Frank Ellis, but we still need to talk to Melody Wright and Di Patel, plus Rose White and Dylan Harper from the agency. Brian Carson was interviewed regarding Dawn's death.'

'Any red flags?' Billy asked.

'Nothing obvious,' Lauren replied, unable to hide her frustration. 'Tremaine and Ellis were working Gielgud wing during Charlie's estimated time of death but they didn't see anything unusual during their shift.'

'What we have learnt is that Kenneth, Charlie and Dawn went way back. They'd known each other for years before ending up in the same care home,' Matt added.

Jenna perked up. 'Well, that surely can't be coincidence, can it? Did they all choose this home specifically to be with each other?'

'Good question,' Lauren said, adding it to the board. 'We also know that Charlie and Dawn were both planning to write their memoirs.'

Jenna's eyebrows shot up. 'Were they focusing on anything in particular? Because that could certainly provide a motive.'

'Again, that's what we need to find out,' Lauren said. 'There could be something in their pasts that someone else wanted kept hidden. At least now we have something to go on.'

Clem pulled his keyboard closer. 'I'll start digging into their histories. Three elderly people who have known each other for years end up in the same care home, and then two of them turn up dead... There's got to be a story in there somewhere, and we'll find it.'

'Jenna, you can assist,' Lauren instructed. 'I want you both looking into all thirty residents, not just Kenneth, Charlie and Dawn. Even if the other residents aren't connected to our victims in the past, we need to rule everyone out.'

'Thirty background checks?' Jenna groaned. 'That's going to take forever.'

'Split them fifteen each,' Lauren suggested. 'Focus on any connections to our victims first, then dig deeper into their pasts. Pay special attention to any overlapping timelines or locations.'

Billy cleared his throat. 'What about staff backgrounds?'

'That's for you and Tamsin,' Lauren said. 'Start with the permanent staff, then move on to the agency workers. I want to know everything: previous employments, references, any complaints or incidents, however inconsequential it might seem.'

'We're on it, ma'am,' Billy replied, his previous flippancy gone.

'I also want someone to contact Hazel Dunston, the electrician, and find out where she was last night. She was definitely on edge when we interviewed her. Whether that was simply because of the situation or because she knows something, we need to find out.'

'I'll do it, ma'am,' Tamsin said.

'What about Kenneth?' Clem asked suddenly, worry lines appearing on his forehead. 'He's still alive, and if he knew both victims, surely it's not beyond the realms of possibility for him to be next...' His words hung in the air.

Lauren nodded grimly. 'Good point. I spoke to him earlier, and he's in shock. But we need to be careful. If he is involved, we don't want to tip our hand. But, equally, if he's not, he could very well be the next target.'

'Shouldn't we put protection on him in that case?' Jenna suggested.

Lauren turned to Matt. 'Contact the manager and ask her to increase checks on him. Ask her not to tell him, though. We don't want to either alert or worry him.'

'But if the murderer is one of the staff, that could give them a chance to get Kenneth,' Matt said, frowning.

'We don't have a choice. But I'm working on the premise that the killer won't do anything to implicate themselves, and if they've been asked to watch Kenneth that's what they'll do.' She stepped back from the board, now covered in names, timelines, and questions. 'Something else that's bothering me is the different methods used. Killers frequently use the same method to kill each time. So why was Charlie's murder different? Would it have been impossible to poison him? Also, strangulation is personal... up close. Whereas poisoning... it's almost a step back, if you get what I mean.'

'It could be two different killers working together,' Billy suggested.

'Or one killer adapting to circumstances,' Clem countered. 'Maybe they found poisoning Charlie too risky in case of the wrong person dying. Unlike Dawn, who was very precious over her strawberry cream chocolates. So they switched tactics.'

Lauren tapped the marker against her palm, thinking. 'Yes, that could be the reason. We need to find out if any staff member or resident has medical knowledge. They need enough to know about how to effectively murder using antifreeze. Although, of course, carers will have some. Even so, add that to your background checks.'

'Back to the memoirs,' Jenna said. 'Did the victims leave behind any notes, drafts, or recordings? Anything that would give us a heads up on what they know.'

'Nothing was found in their rooms,' Lauren said. 'But that doesn't mean they didn't store information elsewhere, or that the killer stole it. Clem, when you're doing the background checks, look for any safety deposit boxes, storage units, anything like that.' Lauren sighed, running a hand through her hair. 'We need to move fast. Two murders in one care home with ex-famous people as residents: the media is going to be all over this soon, if they're not already. We're going to interview the staff today, but not on site. They're coming in here. We'll start with anyone who was working during Charlie's strangulation, since we have a more specific timeline for that.'

'And Dawn's murder?' Clem prompted.

'The poisoning makes it trickier,' Lauren admitted. 'Not because we don't know when she died, but we don't yet have any idea of the time, or how the chocolates were contaminated.'

'Do all the staff have access to both victims?' Clem asked.

'Staff tend to stick to their wings while working but that doesn't mean they don't visit the other wings if there's a problem or maybe to chat with one of the residents. It's not a prison. We'll be questioning them about it though,' Lauren replied.

Jenna raised her hand slightly. 'What about interviewing the other residents, ma'am; who's going to do that?'

'I've already asked the desk sergeant to arrange for some uniformed officers to visit the home and take statements. I emphasised that they must be gentle. Some of them might be confused and others scared. We don't want to cause a mass panic because that won't help the investigation. I also don't want them informing their families, if that's possible, although I suspect they might. Kenneth mentioned Dawn being poisoned, and that isn't meant to be public knowledge.'

'And it could tip off our killer,' Billy added grimly, pulling a face. 'Although surely they'd be expecting us to question everyone there. But if it is a member of staff or a resident, they're going to have to be careful not to drop themselves in it.'

'If the killer was able to undertake both a poisoning and a strangulation without being spotted, then being questioned by the police isn't going to worry them,' Clem said, with a sigh.

'It depends on who's doing the interviewing,' Billy replied.

Lauren nodded, checking her watch. 'I'm sure that whoever interviews will be on the ball. Right, let's get moving. I'm going to update the DCI while waiting for some staff members to arrive.' She paused, looking at each team member in turn. 'Keep in constant contact. If anyone finds anything, even if it seems small, I want to know immediately. Don't worry about interrupting me.'

'I'll contact Gill Trelawny regarding keeping an eye on Kenneth and then give the team a hand while we're waiting, ma'am,' Matt said, heading over to his desk, his phone already in his hand.

The rest of the team dispersed to their tasks, the weight of urgency heavy in the air. Two murders, thirty residents, eleven staff members and countless questions. Lauren took one last look at the board before leaving, hoping they'd find the connection before anyone else died.

TWENTY-ONE

WEDNESDAY FEBRUARY 12

'Ma'am,' Matt said, knocking on Lauren's slightly open door, and stepping into her office. 'Di Patel and Melody Wright are here for an interview. They've been put in the visitors' suite.'

'Thanks, Matt. We'll interview them separately.' Lauren glanced up from her computer screen.

'Also, it turns out Hazel Dunston has a solid alibi for last night. She was in St Ives with her sister and stayed over, after they'd been drinking at the local pub. Tamsin phoned the pub to further verify and they also confirmed it.'

'Maybe it was just nerves then when we interviewed her. At least we can now eliminate her.'

Lauren pushed back her chair and stood, grabbing her jacket from the back of the chair and putting it on. They left through the door straight onto the corridor and headed downstairs, making a right turn at the bottom towards the visitors' suite. When they reached the room, Lauren opened the door.

'Di, can you come with us please?'

A woman of medium height in her mid-forties, with long bleach-blonde hair pulled back into a severe ponytail, stood up. Her care home uniform looked slightly rumpled, and there was a coffee stain on the sleeve.

'What about me?' asked the other woman, who was slighter than her colleague and appeared to be at least a decade younger.

'Please wait here and someone will collect you when we're ready. Help yourself to a drink.' Lauren nodded to the drinks machine in the corner.

Matt moved out of the way to allow Di Patel to leave the room and they walked in silence to of the interview rooms.

'Please take a seat,' Lauren said once they were inside, gesturing to the chair opposite them. The legs scraped against the floor as the care assistant pulled it out. 'We'll be recording this.'

Di's forehead creased with concern, fine lines appearing between her carefully plucked eyebrows. 'Why?'

'It saves us having to take notes.' Lauren's tone was deliberately casual, but Matt could sense her keen attention to the woman's reactions.

'Were you on duty last night?' Matt asked, after setting up the recording equipment.

Di's hand moved to her neck, a classic tell of discomfort.

'No, I was on duty during the day. I finished at eight o'clock after the handover and then left. I'm meant to be on duty now, but Gill told me to come here instead.' She fidgeted with the hem of her top, picking at a loose thread that seemed to fascinate her.

'What wing are you on?' Lauren's fingers drummed lightly on the manila folder she had placed on the table.

'I'm on the Olivier wing. We have four wings: Olivier, Gielgud, Plowright and Richardson.' Di seemed to relax slightly when talking about the building's layout, her shoulders dropping from their defensive hunch.

Even though they were aware of the home's set-up, Lauren let the woman continue. Matt assumed this was to help Di relax because that would be the time when useful information might be imparted.

'So all your wings are named after famous actors? But I thought this was an entertainment home for all disciplines,' Matt said. The peculiarity of the naming convention had been bothering him since he'd first visited the crime scene.

'Well, yes,' Di explained, seeming comfortable with this topic. Her hands stilled in her lap. 'But the person who set up the home all those years ago was an actor and named it after famous actors of the day. A bit pretentious if you ask me,' she added, then looked immediately regretful at her unprofessional comment.

'Is the Olivier wing close to Plowright or Gielgud where Dawn and Charlie were?' Matt asked, despite already know the answer – he wanted the woman to continue opening up.

'Olivier and Plowright are both upstairs and the other two downstairs,' Di replied, shifting in her chair, her words coming faster now, almost running together.

'Were you there last Friday, when Dawn died?' Matt asked.

'I was off duty that day. It was my silver wedding anniversary and we had a big party.' A smile played on her lips. 'Who'd have thought we'd have lasted this long.'

That gave her an alibi which would easily be proved.

'Yesterday, who did you hand over to?' Matt asked, watching her face carefully and noting the slight twitch at the corner of her mouth.

'Melody. She was working with one of the agency staff.' Something in her tone when she mentioned the agency staff caught Matt's attention. Was it because she didn't like agency carers for some reason?

'Was that a problem?' he asked.

'No. We're used to working with them. It's just... well, you know... they're not so familiar with the way we do things, that's all.'

'Do you recall seeing anybody strange hanging around the home recently? Someone who shouldn't have been there?' Lauren asked.

Di was silent for a few seconds, as if running through the various shifts she'd worked. 'Ummm. No. I don't think so.' She shook her head emphatically, her ponytail swishing against her collar. 'I mean, during the day visitors come and go. Not that our residents have many. And then we get deliveries, and maintenance work done. But nothing that made me think, *what are you doing here?*'

'Do you know if anyone visited Charlie while you were on duty yesterday?' Lauren asked.

'Not that I know of, but as I said, I wasn't on his wing. Anyway, he hardly ever gets any visitors. So I wouldn't have thought so.' Di shrugged and a small sigh escaped her lips, as if she felt sorry for the man.

'What about people who you expect to see in the home. Were any of them not in the places they were meant to be?' Matt asked, trying to piece together in his mind how what had happened was able to go unnoticed.

Di's expression remained steady, but her fingers returned to the loose thread on her uniform. 'No, honestly, everything seemed as normal. I'm sorry I can't help you, but certainly up until I left, there was nothing out of the ordinary.' The thread finally broke under her nervous picking.

'Okay, well, thank you for your help,' Lauren said, her tone warming slightly. 'You can wait for Melody in the visitor suite, unless you want to go.'

'I will go, if that's okay, because I'm meant to be at work and they'll be short staffed until I get there.' Di stood up quickly, clearly eager to leave, her chair scraping against the floor in her haste.

After escorting Di Patel to the front entrance, Matt went to the visitors' suite to collect Melody, who was sitting with her head bowed, quietly staring at her phone.

'Melody, if you can please come with me?'

The woman glanced up, giving a tense smile, and her phone disappeared into her pocket with fumbling movements. 'How long will this take? Because I've got a dentist appointment in an hour.'

'You won't be late, I promise,' Matt said softly, wanting to make her feel more at ease.

They walked into the interview room where Lauren was still waiting, the air heavy with unasked questions. Melody sat opposite them and Matt pressed the recording button, the small red light blinking like a watching eye.

'Melody, perhaps we can start by asking how long you've worked at the home,' Lauren said gently.

'Umm... it must be around eighteen months now,' she replied, twisting her hands in her lap, her fingers interlacing and separating.

'And do you enjoy working there?'

The woman's eyes lit up, her nervousness appearing to disappear. 'Oh yes, I really do. I know some of them can be a bit difficult. But you find that in any care home.'

'Gill Trelawny mentioned that you helped Bertha with her lines, when she was understudying Dawn. Is that something you often do?' Matt asked, suddenly remembering the conversation they'd had with the manager.

'I'll help if any of them ask. I'm also responsible for arranging activities for the residents, aside from when they're rehearsing. Especially for those not involved in the play. We draw or play bingo. Sometimes we invite in outside entertainers.'

'I'm sure they must enjoy that,' Matt said. 'I understand you work with Di Patel on the Olivier wing?'

'Yes, that's right. Sometimes I work on the other wings, but that's the main place I am. It depends on whether anyone's off sick or on holiday.'

'And you took over from Di last night at eight o'clock?'

'Yes, I did the night shift.' Melody's eyes kept darting to the recording device, its red light reflecting in her pupils.

Lauren leant forward, her chair creaking slightly. 'Did you notice anything out of the ordinary happening at all? I know you're on a different wing from where Charlie was, but did you see anyone who shouldn't have been there?'

'No, I don't think so.' Melody's voice wavered slightly. 'There are no visitors at that time of night. It was quiet, apart from a couple on my wing who have dementia – they can be a bit loud, often shouting about nothing we can work out.' She paused, her shoulders tensing, as if bracing for impact.

'What is it?' Matt prompted gently, recognising the look of someone who wanted to say more but was afraid of the consequences.

'Well, I'm not sure if it means anything, but...' Melody wet her lips nervously, leaving a smudge of pink lipstick on her front teeth. 'When I came out of Nessa's room, which is near the stairs and the corridor leading to the other wing, I saw Rita Bird, one of the residents, walking along the corridor.'

Matt's interest piqued, the familiar surge of adrenaline that came with a potential lead coursing through him. 'What time was this?'

'I can't remember. But definitely after eleven.'

'Is it unusual for someone to be walking around at that time?'

'No, I suppose not, I mean it's not like they're not allowed to leave their room. But she was heading in the direction of Charlie's room, which was right at the end.' Melody's voice had dropped to almost a whisper, as if she was sharing a secret she wasn't sure she should know.

'Did she see you?'

'No, I don't think so. All I saw was her back. But I don't know if it means anything. Does it?' Her fingers had moved to her collar now, tugging at it like it was too tight around her neck.

Matt exchanged a glance with Lauren, whose mouth had dropped open slightly. She was clearly thinking the same as he was.

'Were Rita and Charlie friends?' he asked.

'The residents are all quite friendly with each other.' She paused. 'Apart from when they're arguing.'

There was a universe of meaning in that pause, in the way Melody's eyes skittered away from their faces.

There was definitely more to this than she was letting on.

'Do they argue a lot?' Matt asked.

Melody sighed. 'Some of them are really full of themselves and still think they're famous. And...' She flushed bright red.

'And what?' Matt pushed, his arms tense as they rested on the table.

They were about to learn something, he was sure of it.

'Nothing. I shouldn't have said that about the residents. They're a great bunch really. I love working with them. They're no different than the residents in other places I've worked.'

Did she really mean that? Or was she being tactful?

'Back to Rita and Charlie. Did they argue more than some of the others did?' Matt asked.

'Rita wasn't keen on his constant jokes. She took offence at them.' Melody glanced down. 'I don't blame her, because sometimes he did push it too far. She wasn't the only one who didn't like it. But she was the one who moaned about it the most. But that doesn't mean she killed him. I mean... to do that... no way.'

'How did Rita get on with Dawn?' Lauren asked, jotting something down in her notebook that was resting on the table.

Melody looked up at the ceiling and closed her eyes for a second. 'This is really hard,' she muttered.

'Nothing you say will go any further, if that's what you're worried about,' Matt said, hoping that would loosen the woman's tongue.

'Okay, but this is only my view. It's not something I've discussed with anyone else. I think Rita was jealous of Dawn because she was still in the public eye with the magazine she wrote for. Rita often made sarcastic comments about her.'

Finally they had someone to question.

'What sort of comments?' Lauren asked, tilting her head to one side.

'You know... that she has someone to write the column for her because she's not clever enough. And that she paid the magazine to let her have the column. Rita also said that Dawn shouldn't have had a main role in the play they're doing because she's not talented enough... That sort of thing.'

'And were these comments made directly to you?'

'Some of them. Or I overheard her moaning to other residents.'

'We've been told that Dawn was well liked by staff and residents. Are you saying that's not the case?' Lauren asked, resting her hands on the table.

'Dawn is— I mean, was lovely. Mostly everyone did like her. But there a couple who didn't. Rita being one and—' Melody glanced at her watch. 'I've really got to go now... for the dentist.'

'Of course. You mentioned another person who didn't like Dawn.'

'Margot and Dawn had issues,' Melody replied.

Something they already knew.

'What about Margot and Charlie? Were there any issues between the two of them?'

'Not that I've witnessed.'

'Well, thank you for your time and honesty. You can go now. But if you do think of anything else, please let us know. Or let Gill know and she'll contact us.'

After walking Melody to the entrance, Matt turned to Lauren. 'Well?'

Lauren's lips pressed into a thin line. 'We need to interview Rita Bird.'

'Yes,' Matt agreed. 'Even if she's innocent she could've witnessed something.'

'But not straight away. It can wait until tomorrow. It's not like she's going anywhere. Let's get the other staff interviews done first and see how the team's research is getting on. I'd rather make sure we have as much information as we can before approaching her.'

TWENTY-TWO

THURSDAY FEBRUARY 13

Lauren pulled out her phone as she strode towards the imposing limestone courthouse, its stone facade looming against the grey morning sky, a persistent drizzle misting the air, and pressed speed dial.

'Hi, Matt, it's me,' she said after he'd answered, trying to keep her voice steady despite her racing heart. 'Look, I'm in Truro. The jury were sent out yesterday afternoon, and it looks like they've reached a verdict very quickly. It's going to be delivered first thing this morning so I'm not sure when I'll be back. It all depends on the outcome.'

She'd heard last night about the jury coming to a decision quickly but had decided not to bother him because it wasn't going to change anything and he deserved some time with his family, without having to worry about her aunt's trial.

'Oh right. That was quick. Don't worry, I'll deal with everything. Fingers crossed it goes okay,' Matt replied. 'Now, what about interviewing Rita Bird? Would you like me to go on my own or take one of the others with me? Maybe Jenna?'

Lauren paused at the courthouse steps, watching as barristers in their flowing black robes hurried past her. 'No, wait for me to get back and we'll go together,' Lauren insisted, her free hand fidgeting with her jacket button. 'Just keep an eye on the rest of the team, see if they've found out anything useful that we need to act on. I think Rita Bird is potentially a great lead and I'd rather we tackled her together.'

She had no doubt that Matt was perfectly capable of leading the interview – it was something he'd done in the past. But with so much on the line, she wanted to be in the thick of it and not having to rely on second-hand accounts.

'Yeah, no problem. I totally get it. It won't matter if we wait a little longer to interview her. Good luck.'

Lauren's throat tightened. 'Thanks, but I don't know about needing good luck. We need the jury to see sense and realise that Aunt Julia made a tragic mistake, or otherwise...' She left the sentence unfinished, her voice cracking. 'Going in now.' She ended the call abruptly.

After reaching the entrance, she pushed through the heavy wooden doors into the courthouse.

The marble-floored corridor echoed with her footsteps as she made her way to Courtroom Three and the scent of old wood and leather files filled her nostrils. Through the corner of her eye, she spotted the two barristers – prosecution and defence – standing together, sharing a quiet laugh.

If only the public knew that most of the time, despite whatever they saw going on in court, either side having a go at one another and trying to put the other one down, they were actually good friends and hung out together outside of work.

Lauren headed into the courtroom where the overhead fluorescents cast a harsh light on the rows of empty seats, making the empty jury box appear stark and expectant. She slipped into a seat at the back of the gallery, the wooden bench creaking softly beneath her.

As other spectators began filtering in, a familiar voice cut through the quiet murmur of the room. 'Well, look who it isn't.'

Lauren's muscles tensed as she glanced up to see her cousin Clint's sneering face. He stood at the end of her row with his brother, Connor, both wearing expressions of mock surprise. She fixed her gaze straight ahead, squeezing her hands together tightly in her lap, hoping they'd take the hint to leave her alone.

Clint, however, had other ideas. He walked along the row until he was closer to her. 'What's the matter? Too embarrassed to be seen with us, *Detective Inspector?*' His voice dripped with contempt.

Something snapped inside her. Probably years of childhood torment crystallising into cold fury. She rose slowly to her feet, drawing herself up to her full height, and met his gaze with steel in her eyes.

'Sit away from me, or else,' she commanded, her voice low but carrying the full weight of her authority.

Clint took an involuntary step backward, and for a moment, Lauren saw a flash of the same uncertainty she'd felt as a child living under their reign of terror. But now, she was the one with power and never again would they be able to get the better of her.

'Is that a threat?' Clint attempted to recover his bravado. 'Are you going to arrest us?'

Lauren's lips curved into a dangerous smile. 'I have a team of detectives at my disposal. Do you really want me to get them to start looking into what you're up to? Because I can, with pleasure.'

Connor and Clint exchanged worried glances, the old dynamic crumbling before her eyes. As they backed away, Connor, not able to look Lauren in the eye, said, 'It was just a bit of fun.'

'Yeah, well you can keep your fun. And remember,' Lauren added, unable to resist a parting shot. 'Don't push me because you'll lose big time.'

Sitting down, her jaw was rock solid and satisfaction coursed through her veins as her cousins retreated to a different row, occasionally throwing impotent glares over their shoulders.

She didn't have time to dwell on dealing with them: the tension in the room suddenly shifted as the door leading down to the holding cells opened. Aunt Julia was led in, and Lauren's heart clenched at the sight of her. The woman who had once been her protector now looked frighteningly fragile, her floral dress hanging loose on her. Julia's skin had taken on the pallor of someone who'd hardly seen any sunlight in months, and her eyes had a haunted expression that overshadowed her gaunt face.

'All rise.'

The clerk's voice rang out as the judge entered. Everyone stood, the rustle of clothing and scraping of feet filling the courtroom. Lauren's heart pounded so hard she could feel it in her throat.

The judge, a stern-faced woman with silver hair, settled into her high-backed chair, and then everyone else sat down.

'Bring in the jury,' the judge said, nodding to the clerk.

Twelve men and women filed in, their faces unreadable. Lauren searched for any hint of their decision in their body language, but they were carefully composed and gave nothing away.

'Will the foreperson please stand,' the clerk of the court instructed, also standing. 'Have you reached a verdict?'

'Yes.' The foreperson's voice was clear and steady.

Lauren reached for the bench in front of her, and clutched it tight, her knuckles white with tension.

'On the charge of murder, how do you find the defendant?' the clerk asked.

A pause followed that seemed to stretch for an eternity.

'Not guilty.'

A collective gasp was heard around the courtroom and Lauren's breath rushed out in a silent prayer of thanks.

But that didn't mean her aunt had escaped punishment. It just meant the jury didn't believe the death of Roy to be pre-meditated. There were other charges to consider.

'On the charge of manslaughter, how do you find the defendant?' the clerk asked.

'Guilty of involuntary manslaughter.'

Lauren stifled a gasp of relief. It wasn't perfect, but given the circumstances, it was probably the best possible outcome. After all, that was what had happened. It was a tragic accident born of desperation gone wrong.

The judge's voice cut through Lauren's thoughts. 'Julia Cave, you have been found guilty of involuntary manslaughter. However, considering the time you have already served in custody and the circumstances of this case, I am giving you a suspended sentence of two years. You are free to go.'

Aunt Julia turned in the dock, her eyes finding Lauren's through a veil of tears. Lauren hurried towards her aunt, pushing through the gate that separated the gallery from the actual court. She wrapped her arms around her, wincing as she felt the bones beneath her clothing.

'It's okay,' she whispered to her aunt. 'Come on, let's get you out of here.'

They made their way slowly towards the exit, Lauren supporting her aunt's trembling form. The courthouse steps were crowded with reporters, their cameras at the ready, but Lauren knew how to handle them. She guided Julia through a side door, heading for the car park. Luckily her cousins hadn't tried to come over to see their mother. Which said it all. They didn't really care about her, despite the times Julia had bailed them out.

The rain had stopped and the morning air had warmed slightly, but Julia shivered anyway. They were almost at Lauren's car which was parked in a side street when her phone rang. The screen showed Matt's number.

'Sorry, I've got to get this,' Lauren said apologetically, keeping one hand on Julia's elbow. 'I won't be long.' She answered the call. 'Matt, I'm about to take my aunt Julia home. She's got a suspended sentence.'

'That's fantastic, I'm so pleased for you,' Matt replied, but his tone put Lauren on alert. Something was wrong. 'I'm sorry to have to call you, but there's been a third incident at Silver Fern Care Home.'

Lauren's blood ran cold. 'Not another murder?'

'*Attempted* murder,' Matt said grimly. 'Of Kenneth Blencoe. He's at the hospital.'

Lauren breathed a sigh of relief that the man was still alive, but that didn't change the fact that she couldn't stay with her aunt – or even take her home. This was too important to leave.

'How serious is he?'

'I don't know,' Matt replied, sucking in a breath.

'Right, okay. Meet me at the care home. I'll be as quick as I can.' Lauren ended the call and turned to her aunt. 'I'm really sorry, Aunt Julia, but I can't take you home to Bodmin right now; something urgent has come up at work. I'll arrange for somebody to take you.'

Guilt coursed through her. But as much as she wanted to drive Julia back to Bodmin, it was in the opposite direction to Marazion and would end up adding well over an hour, if not more, to her journey.

'Don't worry about me, I can get the bus—'

'No,' Lauren cut her off firmly. 'I'm not letting you go home alone. I'll get someone.' After arranging for someone from the local police force to collect Julia, she guided her aunt back towards the courthouse and took her to a quiet spot in the hall where she could sit. Lauren glanced around. Luckily her cousins had gone. So, too, any reporters. 'I want you to stay here and a police officer will find you and drive you home. I'll be in touch and we can celebrate together – well, not celebrate but—'

'I understand what you mean,' Julia said, resting her hand on Lauren's arm, giving a watery smile. 'Now you must get going. I can't thank you enough for everything you've done.'

Lauren leant in and gave her aunt a hug. 'It's me who owes you. Take care, and I'll see you soon.'

Lauren turned into the care home's driveway and drove to the entrance, the gravel spraying out from under her tyres as she came to a halt. Matt's familiar figure stood waiting by the front door, his shoulders hunched as he paced back and forth.

'I take it you're waiting for me,' Lauren called as she stepped out of her car, grabbing her jacket from the passenger seat and hurriedly pulling it on, shivering in the cold breeze.

Matt smiled in acknowledgement. 'Yes, ma'am. I didn't want to go in without you.' 'But I did speak to the woman on reception, and she told me what had happened. It seems they were rehearsing the play and Kenneth was shot with a gun that was meant to have been a replica.'

Lauren's stomach tightened. 'Bloody hell. Has the ballroom been cleared?'

'Yes. Forensics are already in there. Shall we take a look before speaking to the residents about the incident?'

'Yes, I'd like to see the scene. Did the receptionist say how Kenneth is doing?'

'There was a lot of bleeding, but he was conscious and dictating to the paramedics what to do.' Matt's lips quirked into a slight smile. 'It seems he once did a first aid course and of course knew better than them.'

'That sounds like him, and hopefully means that he's not too badly injured,' Lauren said, unable to suppress a wry smile despite the gravity of the situation. 'I assume he's gone to the hospital?'

'Yes.'

'Good, we'll phone for an update later.' Lauren's mind was already racing ahead, deciding on next steps. 'In the meantime, let's see the crime scene first, then we'll speak to the residents who were present, in particular the person who actually did the shooting, and then we'll find Rita Bird.'

They entered the care home's reception, their footsteps echoing on the polished floor, and the receptionist let them through. When they reached the ballroom, three forensics personnel in white suits were methodically working their way through it, the flash of their cameras creating brief bursts of light.

'Morning, Eve,' Lauren said to the woman closest to the door, whom she knew from previous cases. 'Have you found anything useful yet?' she added, even though it was early in the investigation.

The woman straightened up from where she'd been dusting for prints. 'We've found nothing conclusive yet, but we haven't been here long. The gun's been bagged for forensic examination at the lab.' Eve gestured towards her colleague who was carefully documenting the scene on the stage. 'There are several fingerprints on the weapon and, of course, all round the room.'

Lauren surveyed the space, taking in the scattered chairs and the small stage area where the residents had been rehearsing. A script lay abandoned on one of the seats, its pages fluttering in the draught from the doorway. 'Do you know where the residents who witnessed the event are?'

'They're in the Plowright dayroom,' Matt interrupted.

Lauren nodded briskly. 'Okay, let's go there.'

The dayroom, when they reached it, was thick with tension. About fifteen elderly residents sat in various poses of distress and shock, some staring into space, others fidgeting with their clothes or hankies. The usual cheerful chatter of the care home was notably absent.

Two carers stood close to the entrance, muttering to one another. Lauren glanced in their direction. Shouldn't they be comforting the residents? And where was Gill Trelawny?

'Good morning,' Lauren said, cutting through the tension, her voice gentle but authoritative.

Fifteen pairs of eyes turned towards her, some fearful, others clearly relieved to see the police finally arrive.

'I understand you all witnessed the shooting this morning,' Lauren said, scanning them all.

A murmur of assent rippled through the room, accompanied by slow nods.

'Who actually pulled the trigger?'

'I did.' A woman with striking short red hair and unusually pale skin raised her hand, her voice shaky. 'But I didn't know it was a real gun. I had to do it as part of the play. I didn't know...'

Lauren kept her expression neutral. 'Yes, I understand. What's your name?'

'Rita Bird.'

Lauren and Matt exchanged a meaningful glance. This was the woman they'd been planning to interview next. The coincidence sent shivers down Lauren's spine. Surely it meant they were getting closer to solving the case.

'Rita, if you'd like to come with us, we'll find somewhere quiet to have a chat,' Lauren said, the irony of seeking quiet when the room was already as silent as a tomb not lost on her.

An elderly man in a beige cardigan over a checked shirt cleared his throat. 'Excuse me. What do you want us to do? It's nearly time for my quiz on telly.'

Lauren softened her expression. 'There's no need for you to remain here. You can all go back to your rooms. One of my officers will take a statement from each of you at some time during the day.'

'Thank you,' the man said, taking his dark wood walking stick from against the side of the chair, and hurried off – remarkedly sprightly considering he used a walking aid.

As the rest of the residents began to shuffle out, aided by the carers, Lauren turned to Matt, keeping her voice low. 'Can you ask Jenna and Billy to come here now and take statements from the residents? I'll be in the dining room in this wing questioning Rita. Join us when you've sorted it.'

Matt nodded efficiently. 'Okay, ma'am. I'll be along shortly.'

Lauren led Rita to the dining room, selecting two chairs leaning against the wall. She pulled hers out until she was facing the older woman, noting how Rita's hands trembled slightly as she settled into her seat. Fear was etched across the elderly woman's lined face.

'What do you want to know?' Rita asked, her voice thin and reedy. What little colour there was had drained from her face, leaving her looking almost ghostly in the morning light. Her fingers were twisting a tissue into shreds in her lap.

Lauren leant forwards slightly, wanting to put the woman at ease to ensure she didn't clam up. 'How are you feeling? It must have been a terrible shock.'

'I still can't quite believe it. We were just rehearsing as normal and then this happened.' She bowed her head.

'I'd like to ask you more about the gun, if you're up to it?' Lauren prodded, gently.

'Okay,' Rita said, nodding.

'Where is the gun normally kept?'

'In the cupboard in a box with other props. It's only a replica so doesn't need to be kept locked up or anything.'

'Except it wasn't a replica. Did it look and feel different from the last time you held it?' Lauren asked, trying to piece together how someone had managed to replace the replica with a real gun and it not be noticed by the woman.

'This was the first time I'd used it, so I don't know.' Rita's shoulders hunched defensively.

Would the assailant have known that? If so, it was looking more and more like an inside job.

'Did everyone in the play know that you'd be using the props for this particular rehearsal?'

Rita sucked in a breath. 'Yes, I think so. Kenneth wanted us to move away from reading off our scripts and to do the acting properly.'

The tissue in Rita's hands was now completely shredded and Lauren studied the older woman's face carefully, looking for any tell-tale signs of deception. 'Have you ever shot a gun before?'

Rita's hands stilled for a moment. 'Years ago I did, but that was at a rifle range. My father took me.'

'Were you close to Kenneth?' Lauren asked.

The question seemed to strike a nerve, and Rita glanced away, a flush of pink creeping up her neck and into her cheeks. 'Not really,' she muttered, her voice barely audible. 'He was mean and used to criticise my acting, even though there was nothing wrong with it. But he's always been like that to everyone, so it's not like he singled me out. He's been the same his whole career.'

Lauren sat up straighter, sensing they were approaching something important. 'Oh... so have you known him a long time then?'

'Years. When I was in rep in the 1960s, he was too. We were often in the same productions.'

'With Dawn Cross?'

'Yes, Dawn was one of us.' Rita's voice took on a distant quality, as if she were remembering all those years ago.

'And what about Charlie?'

'I knew him, too. He trained at RADA but then went into comedy.' Rita's expression softened momentarily, then hardened again.

'And what did you think of Charlie?'

A flash of something – regret? bitterness? – crossed Rita's face. 'In my twenties I used to have a thing for him, but then he met Cherry, his wife.' Rita shrugged, trying to appear nonchalant. 'But he was okay, I suppose. His jokes could be cruel, especially if you were the butt of them.'

Lauren paused, then decided to push harder. 'We understand that you were in the corridor on Tuesday evening, the night Charlie was murdered. Were you on your way to see him?'

Rita's head snapped up, her eyes wide with alarm. 'Who said that?' she demanded, attempting indignation in her tone but achieving only fear.

'You were seen by one of the carers.'

'Oh.' Rita seemed to deflate slightly. 'Well, yes, I did think about going to see him. I was upset about Dawn and I knew he was too. But...' Her voice trailed off into silence.

'But what?' Lauren pressed, sensing Rita was holding something back.

'I changed my mind halfway there and returned to my room. That's all. How long do you need me here? I'm due to take my insulin soon,' Rita said, staring down at her watch.

'Not much longer. When you were in the corridor, did you see anyone acting suspicious in the vicinity of Charlie's room?' Lauren kept her gaze steady, determined to assess every little tell on her face, however small.

'No. There was no one around.' Rita shook her head emphatically. 'I didn't even see the carer who you said saw me.'

'Can you think of anyone who might have it in for Dawn, Charlie and Kenneth? I know you all went way back – could it be something to do with that?'

'I don't know,' Rita said, suddenly looking even paler. Her eyes widened with fresh fear. 'But if it is... do you think my life is in danger?'

Before Lauren could respond, Matt appeared in the doorway.

'Is everything okay?' Lauren asked, turning to him.

'Yes,' Matt replied, his notebook in hand. 'Jenna and Billy are on their way. I just popped back to the reception desk and asked them to send the CCTV footage from today and yesterday to Tamsin, so she could start analysing it. Jenna also mentioned that

Henry had been in touch, so I phoned him. I'll explain everything shortly.'

Rita suddenly straightened in her chair. 'I've just thought of something.'

Lauren and Matt both turned to her, their attention sharpening. 'Yes?' Lauren encouraged.

'Whoever changed the gun must have done it after five yesterday afternoon because I was with Bertha and looking at the props then.' Rita's voice grew stronger, more confident. 'She picked up the gun and gave it to me. I held it up and pressed the trigger.' She leant back in her chair, looking pleased with herself.

Finally, a concrete timeline.

'But you told me that today was the first time you'd seen, or held it,' Lauren said, exchanging a quick glance with Matt.

'Sorry. I forgot,' Rita said, bowing her head.

Was that the truth? Or was the woman relying on getting away with it because they viewed her as elderly and confused?

'That's okay. There's a lot going on. Can you think back whether it felt different then from when you held it this morning?' Lauren asked, refraining from shaking her head in annoyance.

'I don't know. Sorry. It's a gun, that's all,' Rita replied, suddenly sounding all pathetic.

Lauren wasn't buying it, but she wasn't going to let on to the woman.

'Are you sure that you didn't return to the props cupboard at all? Maybe you went to check on the gun before the rehearsal.'

'Umm... I don't think so. Now I'm not sure.' Rita pulled a face.

'Who brought out all the props from the cupboard at the start of the rehearsal? Do you remember?' Lauren asked, struggling to keep her tone even.

'That was... um... I think one of the carers did it with Kenneth. One of the agency people. I think her name was Roz. But I'm not sure. Kenneth told her what props we needed.'

'Okay. Well, thank you for your help. You can go back to your room to take your insulin and we'll be in touch again if we need to ask you anything further.'

After Rita had hurried out, Lauren turned to Matt. 'Something isn't sitting right with that woman. But if what she said is true about going to the props cupboard with Bertha at five in the afternoon, it gives us a timeline to work from. But if Kenneth was at the props cupboard with the carer, why didn't he notice the gun had changed? We'll have to ask him. What did Henry say?'

'He's had confirmation that the strawberry creams were the only chocolates poisoned. He examined all the chocolates in the tin and there were three strawberry creams left and they all contained antifreeze. None of the others did.'

'So whoever poisoned Dawn knew that no one was allowed to take the strawberry creams. We'll go back to the office, now, and contact the hospital.' She gathered her things, already thinking about the next steps. 'We'll visit Kenneth tomorrow. I doubt he'll be up to talking yet.'

As they walked back through the care home's corridors, Lauren replayed Rita's interview in her mind. She was most definitely hiding something. But what was it – and why?

TWENTY-FOUR

FRIDAY FEBRUARY 14

Matt and Lauren walked down the sterile corridor leading to the ward where Kenneth Blencoe was recuperating. The antiseptic smell that permeated all hospitals made Matt's nose wrinkle. He'd never get used to it.

'I hope he'll be well enough to speak to us,' Matt said, keeping his voice low.

His eyes darted around, taking in the busy medical staff hurrying past them.

Lauren nodded. 'Ditto.'

They carried on into the ward, their footsteps echoing on the polished floor. At the reception desk, a nurse with tired eyes but a kind smile looked up at them.

'Kenneth Blencoe?' Lauren asked, flashing her identification.

The nurse grimaced slightly. 'He's in a private room on the right-hand side.' She pointed down the corridor.

Was he giving them trouble? He was, if the look on the nurse's face was anything to go by. They continued walking and after only a few seconds a voice boomed out from one of the rooms.

'Don't put it there.' The voice thundered with surprising strength. 'How am I meant to reach it?'

Matt glanced at Lauren, his eyebrows raised. 'I think it's safe to assume that our victim is able to talk to us.'

A small smile tugged at the corner of Lauren's mouth as she nodded in agreement.

They approached the window of the private room and peered in. Through the glass, they could see a nurse standing by the bed, where Kenneth sat upright, his face flushed. Various medical equipment surrounded his bed.

Lauren tapped gently on the window and then pushed the door open. Matt followed close behind.

'Good morning, Kenneth,' Lauren said, her voice warm and friendly. 'How are you feeling?'

Kenneth's eyes darted between them, recognition and irritation battling on his face. 'I'd be a lot better if people around me made things easy,' he huffed. 'How am I expected to reach the jug of water when it's on the trolley over there?'

Even injured, he was still commanding the room like he was directing a play.

Matt glanced at the jug in question, which was indeed placed out of comfortable reach for someone confined to bed.

'I'll put it back, shortly,' the nurse said, her patience clearly tested. 'I moved it there while doing your obs. You wouldn't be happy if it tipped over, would you?'

'We're here to have a quick chat with Kenneth,' Lauren said, holding out her ID, before Kenneth had time to answer.

'Well, please don't be too long,' the nurse said, moving the water to beside the bed and within reach. 'Despite outward appearances, he needs his rest.' With one last glance at Kenneth, she left them, closing the door softly behind her.

Matt stepped closer to the bed, taking in the man's appearance. Despite his obvious discomfort, the theatre director looked remarkably well for someone in his condition.

'So, how are you?' Matt asked, pulling out his notebook.

Kenneth's eyes narrowed. 'How do you think?' he snapped. 'I was shot. I could have been killed.'

Matt nodded sympathetically. 'You were very lucky that the bullet missed your vital organs.'

'Yes, indeed,' Kenneth said, his voice dropping to a quieter, more reflective tone. He adjusted himself slightly in the bed, wincing. 'According to the doctors it could have been much worse.'

'Are you up to answering a few questions?' Lauren asked, standing at the foot of the bed.

'I most certainly am. You must catch whoever did this to me.' He leant back against his pillow and exhaled loudly, gasping as he did.

'The shot came from a gun that was put in the props cupboard, to replace the replica one you have.' Her eyes watched Kenneth carefully. 'Who has access to the props?'

Kenneth sighed, his hand unconsciously moving to his bandaged chest which was showing through his open pyjama top. 'Well, everyone does,' he admitted. 'I mean, we all know where they are. They're not kept locked up. Nothing in there is dangerous.'

'Did you or anyone else check the gun when it was brought out of the cupboard and spot that it was different from the usual one?' Matt asked.

'What a ridiculous question,' Kenneth replied indignantly. 'For a start, why would we? It's not like it's happened before. *And* if someone did notice it was a different weapon then we'd have inspected it and realised that the gun was real...' For a moment, his confident facade cracked, revealing genuine fear.

'I'm sorry,' Matt said. 'We just need to get a clear picture of everything that occurred.'

'Okay,' Kenneth responded gruffly. 'I was with one of the carers and instructed her on what props we needed. She brought them through.'

'And were you with her and the props the whole time?' Matt asked, wondering if the carer had time to replace the replica gun with a real one.

'Yes. It only took a few minutes to collect everything,' Kenneth confirmed.

'Where did the prop gun come from in the first place?' Lauren asked.

Kenneth's brow furrowed in concentration. 'I've no idea. When I moved into the home, it was already there with all the props.' His hands gestured vaguely. 'We have boxes and boxes of props in the cupboard that we use at various times, depending on the show.'

Boxes of uncatalogued items would give the perfect opportunity for someone to slip in a loaded weapon. Matt suspected it would be a nightmare to trace where the gun came from.

'Has the replica gun been used in other shows?' Lauren pressed.

'Not in any I've been involved with,' Kenneth said, his voice growing weaker as fatigue began to show. 'But why does it matter if it wasn't the prop gun that was used by Rita to shoot me?'

'It helps us ascertain who knew of its existence and then how it could be swapped with a real gun.'

Kenneth stared directly at them, his eyes intense. 'Do you have any idea who did this to me?'

Matt met his gaze steadily. 'That's what we're investigating, but we believe it's most likely the same person who murdered Dawn and Charlie.'

'They weren't as lucky as me,' Kenneth acknowledged with a sigh, wincing as he shifted position. 'Why us?'

'One thing you have in common is that you worked together for many years before you came to the home. Can you think of anything that occurred over the years you were together that might have led to this?' Matt asked.

'We weren't together all the time.' Kenneth's face contorted with pain briefly before he regained his composure. 'And lots of things *occurred* during our careers, but nothing to warrant killing us. That's crazy.'

'Did you know that both Dawn and Charlie were writing their memoirs?' Matt asked, drumming his pen lightly on his notebook.

'Yes, but so what?' Kenneth snapped, pressing his palm against his temple as though fighting a headache.

'Could there be something in them that someone wanted to keep quiet?'

Kenneth shrugged. 'Maybe. I don't know. But then why shoot me, because I've got no plans to write mine. Although if I did, mark my words... it would be a bestseller.'

'Have you ever mentioned that it's something you're considering?' Matt continued, desperate for them to find a connection.

'Possibly.' Kenneth straightened up despite the obvious discomfort, his demeanour suddenly changing. A self-satisfied smile spread across his face as he smoothed down the hospital gown with a theatrical flourish. 'I do sometimes say that my life would make a great movie, if anyone wanted to write it.'

'I'm sure it would,' Matt agreed, to placate the man.

'We'll leave you now,' Lauren said. 'We don't want to tire you out. You take your time and get better. You're in the best place here.'

A stubborn expression crossed Kenneth's face. 'I'm coming home today, or at least tomorrow,' he declared. 'The doctors want me to stay, but I need to get back to rehearsals. I'm not having anyone else take over and ruin it.' His voice grew more animated, colour returning to his cheeks. 'I mean, can you imagine what would happen? I'm the only person who knows the play properly.'

Matt let out a frustrated sigh. The old man was putting himself at risk. 'Maybe you should think about putting the play on hold,' he suggested carefully.

'No way.' Kenneth's reaction was immediate and forceful. He sat up straighter, ignoring the pain it clearly caused him, judging by the way he flinched. 'Absolutely not.'

His eyes flashed with determination. 'No one's going to get the better of us. This play's going on – over my dead body.'

Matt glanced at Lauren. His concern was mirrored in her eyes. The man was making himself a target.

TWENTY-FIVE
FRIDAY FEBRUARY 14

Matt hung his jacket up on the coat stand, smoothing out a wrinkle with distracted fingers. The fabric was damp from the light rain that had started. He headed to the front of the room where Lauren was standing beside the whiteboard with, as usual, a marker in her hand.

'Okay, attention please,' Lauren said, her voice cutting through the murmurs of conversation.

The room fell silent, all eyes turning towards her. Matt leant against the edge of a desk, crossing his arms as he surveyed the faces of the team.

'We've just got back from the hospital,' Lauren continued, drawing a line under Kenneth Blencoe's name on the board. 'Our victim is very lucky to be alive. The bullet narrowly missed his vital organs, but that was pure luck.'

She turned to face the team, her expression grave. 'We need to catch this murderer before they try again and are successful.'

Matt nodded in silent agreement. Kenneth's stubborn insistence on returning to the play echoed in his mind. The old man had no idea how much danger he was still in.

'Where are we on the research into the care home residents, staff and CCTV footage?' Lauren asked, scanning the room.

'None of Silver Fern's staff, including those who are agency, worked at any of those homes who had reported the petty thefts,' Jenna said. 'I'm not particularly surprised, because it was a tenuous connection at best.'

'Well, it's good to eliminate it, anyway,' Lauren said. 'Now what about—'

'Ma'am,' Clem interrupted, raising his hand.

Lauren paused, the marker suspended in mid-air between her fingers. 'Yes, Clem?'

'Something's just occurred to me,' Clem said, adjusting his glasses.

'Oh no, here we go,' Billy muttered from the back of the room, rolling his eyes dramatically. 'Clemipedia strikes again...'

'Billy, enough,' Lauren snapped. 'This is serious.'

Matt noted the flush of anger on Lauren's cheeks and the tight set of her jaw. Their lack of progress was clearly beginning to get to her.

'Sorry, ma'am. I didn't mean anything by it,' Billy said, his face pink.

'It's fine,' Lauren responded, sounding less angry. 'Continue, Clem.'

Clem cleared his throat, sitting a little straighter. 'I don't know if this is relevant or just a strange coincidence, but so far, the attacks have all occurred in the same sequence as the murders in the Genevieve Hartwell play *The Last Guest*.'

A heavy silence fell over the room and a chill ran down Matt's spine as the implications of this revelation crystallised. If there were more than three deaths in the play then it didn't bode well for the other residents.

'I don't know it,' Lauren said slowly, her eyes narrowing. She looked around the room. 'Does anyone?'

The rest of the team muttered no and shook their heads.

'I haven't seen it, but know what it's about,' Clem said. 'That's why it came to me. It's set in a remote country lodge.' He gestured with his hands as he spoke. 'The guests are invited by the mysterious Mrs Blackwood for a weekend gathering but when they arrive their host is nowhere to be found. All they have is a gramophone recording of her voice saying that each guest harbours a deadly secret. They're trapped in the house because of a bad storm and while they're there, they're systematically killed off by an unknown murderer. It turns out the killer is Mrs Blackwood, who's seeking revenge on all these people for causing the deaths of members of her family. The mode of death for each person is different and relates in some way to the way in which the family member had died.'

Matt pulled out his notebook, flipping to a fresh page as he began taking notes, his pulse quickening. After days of dead ends, this could be the breakthrough they'd been waiting for.

'I take it you know the order of these deaths?' Lauren asked, leaning against the side of the whiteboard.

'Yes, ma'am. It goes poisoning, strangulation, gunshot, blunt force trauma, drowning and stabbing,' Clem continued, ticking them off on his fingers.

'Oh,' Billy exclaimed, sitting up straight, his earlier scepticism vanishing. 'So Dawn Cross was poisoned, Charlie Cook strangled and Kenneth Blencoe shot. Except the murderer didn't succeed in the shooting.' He frowned. 'Does that mean Kenneth is still at risk? Will the murderer try to finish him off?'

The thought had hit Matt at the same time Billy uttered the words.

Clem nodded solemnly. 'Yes, I think he could be, if the killer's going to stick religiously to the play.'

'Kenneth insisted he was going back to the care home today or tomorrow,' Matt said urgently. 'He's determined to continue with the play. We can't let that happen.'

He turned to Lauren for her to back him up.

'Agreed,' Lauren said, her expression hardening with resolve. 'We need to arrange security for him immediately. Jenna, phone downstairs and ask for a uniformed officer to be put outside his hospital room.'

'Yes, ma'am,' Jenna replied, nodding, and reaching for her phone.

'Luckily, he's already in a room of his own. We need to make sure he stays there. Clem, phone the hospital and explain what's going to happen.'

'Okay, ma'am.'

'Tell them he needs to stay put, and they're not to allow him home, however much he insists.'

'Yes, ma'am.'

Lauren turned back to the whiteboard. 'This puts a different picture on it entirely.' She wrote the sequence of murders from the play on the board, drawing arrows to connect them with their current victims. The pattern was undeniable. 'We should check if anyone in the home has ever been in this play,' Lauren said, underlining *The Last Guest* twice. 'Let's see if this is the link.' She turned to face the team, her expression intense. 'Look at all the residents and find out if in their past – however long ago, it doesn't matter – anyone appeared in this Genevieve Hartwell play.'

The room's energy transformed from resignation to focused determination. Finally, they had something concrete to work with. Kenneth's defiant words at the hospital of 'over my dead body' now carried an ominous weight.

'I'll come at it from the opposite direction,' Clem said. 'And check theatre records for anywhere that might have put on *The Last Guest* in the last fifty years.'

'Good plan.' Lauren nodded approvingly. 'I want further checks into everyone at the care home: staff and residents. Whoever's doing this knows the play intimately. But we can't just focus on this, in case we've got it wrong. I still want you to continue looking into everyone. Where are we on Dawn Cross's son Quentin?'

'I'm just checking something regarding him, ma'am,' Tamsin said. 'Leave it with me.'

The team dispersed to their tasks with renewed purpose. Matt lingered by the whiteboard, studying the sequence of murders.

Poisoning, strangulation, gunshot... His finger traced the next method in the sequence. Blunt force trauma.

If they were right about this pattern, and if the killer was indeed following the play, then they now knew not only that Kenneth was still in danger, but exactly what form the next attack would take. But, as much as that mattered, more important was to find out the motive because that would, hopefully, lead them to the killer.

TWENTY-SIX

FRIDAY FEBRUARY 14

A sharp rap on the door broke the silence and Lauren rubbed her temples, the echoes of DCI Mistry's voice still ringing in her ears after their lengthy phone call about the investigation's latest developments.

Without waiting for permission to enter, Matt popped his head round, his eyes wide and bright with an unmistakable energy. She raised an eyebrow, setting down her pen.

'Yes?' she asked, curious what could have triggered such obvious enthusiasm in her colleague.

'Ma'am, you'd better come through. We've got some information.'

'Regarding the murders, I take it,' she said, hurriedly getting up from her desk and nearly knocking over the coffee mug in her haste.

'You got it,' Matt said, with obvious enthusiasm.

Lauren followed him into the incident room, her heart racing with anticipation. The air in the room felt charged with the promise of a breakthrough.

'Clem, explain to the DI,' Matt said, gesturing to the officer.

'Ma'am, it turns out that all of our victims were in the same production of the play *The Last Guest* in London's Mayfair Theatre in 1969.'

Lauren's breath caught. 'All three of them,' she reiterated.

'Yes, and not only that,' Clem continued, his words tumbling out faster now. 'Also Cynthia Lewis, Veronica Waite and Bertha Meadows, who are residents in the home, were in the same play. Apart from Cynthia Lewis, who's got dementia, the other two are in the play they're doing now.'

Lauren's mind raced, connecting pieces that had seemed disparate just moments before.

'What about Rita Bird? She told us she'd worked with some of them years ago.'

'She wasn't in the play,' Clem replied.

'Maybe she was really mad about not being in the play and decided to kill off all those who were,' Billy suggested.

'That's a bit far-fetched,' Clem said with a shake of his head. 'I mean, why wait over fifty years before doing something about it?'

'It was just a thought,' Billy replied.

'And we'll bear it in mind,' Lauren added. 'But for now, we've got three other potential victims. Cynthia, Veronica and Bertha.' Lauren moved to the whiteboard and wrote down the new names. The marker squeaked against the board as she underlined each name twice.

'Blunt force trauma, drowning and stabbing, if we don't solve this quickly,' Billy added, pulling a face.

'My thoughts exactly,' Jenna said, nodding vigorously.

'Did anything happen during the run of the play that could be linked to this in any way?' Lauren asked.

'That's what we've been looking at,' Jenna said, swivelling her screen so Lauren could see it. 'There are some articles and magazines online that could provide some sort of link. It turns out that Cynthia Lewis, who went as Thea Drake when she was acting, played Mrs Blackwood in the production – until one night when she had a total breakdown on stage.'

'A breakdown?' Lauren leant forward, squinting at the digital archive of an old magazine article. The headline on the screen read: 'STAR COLLAPSES DURING MURDER MYSTERY'.

'Yes, ma'am.' Jenna scrolled down to show a grainy black and white photograph. 'This is Thea Drake.'

Lauren studied the image. She was a striking woman with intense eyes and high cheekbones. It was like the woman was staring out from the past with an unsettling intensity.

'Okay,' Lauren said, straightening up. 'What else do we know about Thea Drake?'

'She had some amazing reviews when she was playing Mrs Blackwood,' Billy said. 'I'll read one: "Thea Drake delivers a performance of such haunting intensity that one forgets they are watching theatre at all. Her Mrs Blackwood is a masterclass in the portrayal of mounting dread and hidden guilt. When she stands alone on the stage in the final act, her face a mask of beautiful terror, we believe entirely in her doom. Drake is undoubtedly the brightest new star in London's theatrical firmament, and producers would be wise to secure her talents swiftly."'

A heavy silence fell over the room as Billy finished reading. Goosebumps had risen on Lauren's arms. The words seemed to bring the long-ago actress to life among them.

'She was set to become a famous actor, by all accounts. But after the breakdown, which was due to drugs and alcohol, if we're to believe the press, no one would employ her in a leading role. It was a real tragedy,' Clem added, while running a hand through his hair, dishevelling it.

Lauren marched back to the whiteboard, her mind connecting dots with increasing clarity. She could almost feel the pieces clicking into place. She paused, marker in hand, staring at the names before her.

'So that's got to be our link, then.' Matt's eyes reflected the same realisation she was experiencing.

Lauren nodded, feeling the rush that came with a significant breakthrough. She slammed her palm against the whiteboard. 'Whatever's going on is something to do with the play and possibly

Thea Drake.' She grabbed her jacket from the back of a chair. 'We need to get back to the home and speak to Veronica Waite and Bertha Meadows. To let them know what's going on.'

'It's a shame we can't speak to Cynthia Lewis because she's got dementia,' Matt said, heading towards the coat stand to collect his jacket.

Lauren paused, a new thought striking her. 'Are we sure about that?' She turned to face the team, her thoughts going into overdrive.

'What? You mean Cynthia Lewis might be faking it?' Jenna asked, her mouth dropping open slightly. 'You know, that wouldn't be easy. She's been in the home quite a while and surely keeping it up for that time would be difficult, if not impossible. Plus, if her intention was to commit these murders then why wait such a long time. Sorry, ma'am. It just doesn't fit right with me.'

'I'm inclined to agree. Maybe someone connected to her is carrying out revenge on Cynthia's behalf,' Matt suggested.

Lauren's head spun with possibilities. 'Who would have the most to gain from revenge? A family member? Someone whose career was ruined alongside hers?'

'Could it be a child?' Billy called out, typing rapidly. 'I'm checking now if Thea Drake had any children.'

'What about the other actors from the original cast?' Clem asked, adjusting his glasses. 'Maybe someone who was overshadowed by her? Someone who never got the recognition they deserved because she was the star?'

'Ma'am,' Jenna called out, her voice tense with discovery. 'Look at this.'

Lauren moved to the officer's desk. On the screen was an article dated three weeks after Thea's breakdown: 'DRAKE PRODUCTION SHUT DOWN: CAST AND CREW LEFT UNEMPLOYED'.

'The play actually closed after her breakdown,' Jenna explained. 'It says here that "despite attempts to continue with an understudy, financial backers pulled out after Drake's hospitalisation". A lot of people lost work.'

'Revenge is a powerful motive,' Matt said, his brow furrowed. 'Especially if it's been festering for decades.'

Lauren nodded, the full implications hitting her. 'And what better revenge than killing off the cast in the same way they died in the play? It's theatrical. Someone's making a statement.'

'Yes, but why now? That's what I don't get,' Matt said. 'Also, it's not like they're performing the play at the show. They're doing *Arsenic and Old Lace*. There's no connection with that and the Genevieve Hartwell play.'

'True,' Lauren said, with a sharp nod. 'But maybe it's simply that the timing's right.'

'But who's the murderer?' Billy asked, looking around the room. 'Could it be one of the residents at the home?'

'Or a staff member,' Lauren countered. 'Someone with easy access to all the victims. Someone who could slip poison into chocolates, find an opportunity to strangle, gain access to the props cupboard...' She trailed off, mentally running through the staff they'd interviewed.

'Or a staff member's family,' Matt added.

'Check them all,' Lauren commanded, her voice sharp with urgency. 'Remember to look for maiden names of staff and relatives. Anything that might connect them to the original cast or crew. We also need to find everything there is online about Thea Drake. Theatre records, interviews, social media... anything. Can we get a full history on Cynthia Lewis? When she was admitted to the home, her medical records, bank details, everything.' She checked her watch. 'And I want two officers sent to the home right now to keep an eye on our potential victims. If our theory's correct, they're next on the killer's list. Jenna, sort that out, please.'

'Will do, ma'am. But what if the killer wants to finish off Kenneth Blencoe, and stick rigidly to the play?' Jenna replied.

'That's why he's staying in hospital under guard. Matt and I will be questioning Veronica Waite and Bertha Meadows shortly.'

Lauren stepped back, surveying the whiteboard with its web of connections. 'The killer's following a script, but we've just got our hands on the ending. We know what's coming next, and that gives us the advantage.'

Matt nodded grimly. 'Unless they decide to improvise.'

Lauren met his gaze, the weight of responsibility heavy between them. 'Then we'd better solve this quickly. Three people are dead or injured already. I don't intend to let that number rise.'

As the team scrambled to follow her orders, Lauren stared at the digital image of Thea Drake on the screen. Those penetrating eyes seemed to stare right through her, across decades of time. There was something knowing in that gaze that sent a chill down Lauren's spine.

'What happened to you, Thea?' Lauren whispered to herself. 'And what are you trying to tell us now?'

She turned the question over in her mind. Was Thea the victim here, or the mastermind? Was this about avenging something that happened to her, or was she... or someone close to her settling old scores? Genevieve Hartwell was famous for her twists, for making the least likely suspect the guilty party. Was their killer playing by those rules too?

Lauren took a deep breath and hurried back to her office to grab her car keys. One thing was certain, they needed to get to the care home before the killer struck again. The clock was ticking, and somewhere in that home, someone was following a deadly script to its conclusion.

'I asked Jenna to phone on ahead and instruct the care home to get Bertha Meadows and Veronica Waite in a room together and for one of the carers to stay with them,' Matt said as they made their way to Silver Fern to see them.

'Yeah, that's a good idea,' Lauren said, her fingers tapping anxiously against the steering wheel.

'It's unwise for them to be left alone at any time, until we've solved this. Although maybe the killer will wait until Kenneth is dead before moving on if they're going to stick to the play.'

'True, but we can't run any risks,' Lauren said, her voice tense. 'And then there's Cynthia Lewis to consider. She could be the next victim, ahead of Bertha and Veronica.'

'I asked about her when I called and was told that she rarely leaves her room, and to put her in a room with the other two women would upset her too much. Let's hope she'll be okay in her room because I doubt the home could spare another member of staff to sit with her.'

'I've just had a thought,' Matt said, turning to Lauren. 'What if the carer put in with the residents is the killer? Then again... surely they couldn't do anything because we'd know straight away who had done it.'

'It had crossed my mind, too, but then I dismissed it for those reasons,' Lauren said.

'Plus there's been a lot of planning involved so far; it would be out of character to take a chance like that.'

Lauren parked close to the front of the home, and leaves swirled around their feet as they walked briskly towards the entrance, the cool morning air carrying the scent of rain.

They stopped at the reception desk, the fluorescent lights overhead casting harsh shadows across Lauren's determined face.

'We're here to see Bertha Meadows and Veronica Waite,' Lauren said.

'They're waiting for you in the side room off one of the cafés.' The receptionist smiled politely. 'I'll let you through.' She pressed the buzzer and they walked through the security door.

They made their way down a corridor lined with landscape paintings and potted plants. The faint smell of disinfectant hung in the air as they entered the small room. With them were Brian Carson and Gill Trelawny.

'Good morning,' Lauren said, nodding professionally. 'We'd like to speak to Bertha and Veronica alone, so if you could leave us, please. I'll let you know when we've finished so someone can come back and stay with them.'

'Of course,' Gill said.

Once Matt and Lauren were alone with the elderly residents, they sat opposite them.

Veronica appeared frail, her hands trembling slightly on the arm of the chair, while Bertha seemed more alert, her eyes darting between them suspiciously.

'We'd like to ask you about a play that you were in during the 1960s,' Matt began softly, resting his elbows on his knees. '*The Last Guest*. There were several of you living here who were in it. Kenneth, Charlie, Dawn and Cynthia, who was known as Thea Drake then. Do you remember it?'

'Not really,' Veronica said, shaking her head and staring down at the floor.

'Oh, I do,' Bertha said, her eyes bright.

'Do you remember the time when Thea had a breakdown?' Lauren asked.

'Gosh, yes,' Bertha exclaimed, wringing her hands. 'It was... it was awful.'

'It turned out she'd been drinking excessively and taking drugs,' Matt said, studying the women's reactions carefully.

'That's right,' replied Bertha, nodding vigorously.

'Can you remember much about what happened leading up to her breakdown?' Matt asked.

'Yes, I think so. Thea always liked a drink, but she never went on stage drunk. At least I don't think so. Before the night it happened, she'd been taking drugs for about six months or so,' Bertha responded, her gaze drifting as if looking back through the decades.

'Was there anyone in particular who got her hooked on them?' Lauren asked.

'Everyone took something in those days. I wouldn't say that someone deliberately got her hooked on them,' Bertha said with a dismissive wave of a gnarled hand.

'Yes, I've read about the swinging sixties. But do you remember who supplied Thea?' Matt pushed, his voice gentle but insistent.

'Well, she was an item with Kenneth – we all knew that,' Bertha said, a hint of gossip creeping into her tone. 'And Kenneth would freely hand out drugs to whoever wanted them.'

Kenneth? Matt wasn't expecting that.

'So it was Kenneth who got her addicted?' Lauren confirmed, leaning forwards, her eyes intense.

'You can't blame him,' Bertha said firmly, shaking her head. The sunlight streaming through the window highlighted the deep wrinkles on her face. 'He might have encouraged her to use them recreationally, like we all dabbled. He wasn't to know that Thea would get addicted. It was nobody's fault. Things were different then.'

Lauren turned to look at Veronica. 'And you're sure you don't remember any of this?'

'Well, not really,' Veronica replied hesitantly, her shoulders hunched. 'I was more on the fringes. I wasn't one of the "inner circle",' she said, using air quotes.

'But you were part of this in-crowd,' Lauren said, turning back to Bertha, her gaze unwavering.

'Yes, I was a member of the gang.' Bertha sighed heavily, a flash of defensiveness crossing her face. 'And honestly, you can't blame anybody for what happened to Thea other than herself. She obviously had one of those addictive personalities. She drank, took drugs, and couldn't hack it. It's nobody's fault.'

'What about now?' Matt asked. 'Do you ever talk about the past with Cynthia?'

'No, she doesn't really converse about anything. She's got dementia, you know. I doubt she remembers what happened then at all. It's very sad.' Bertha sighed.

Matt glanced at Lauren, who signalled that they should end the interview.

'Okay, well, thank you very much for your insight,' Matt said, closing his notebook with a soft snap, and dropping it back into his pocket.

'We need you to be very careful,' Lauren added earnestly, leaning forwards with intensity. 'Because it seems that the people being targeted were all in the same production of the play. I don't want you to be on your own at all until we get to the bottom of this,' Lauren said, her tone leaving no room for argument.

'But what about at night when we go to bed?' Bertha asked, worry etched across her face.

'Do your doors have locks?' Lauren asked.

'Yes.' Bertha nodded. 'But we don't use them because the carers come in to check us during the night.'

'Well, until further notice, I want you to lock your door. I'll let Gill know.'

Lauren and Matt left the room and made their way to Gill and Brian, who were standing close by.

'Is everything okay?' Gill asked.

'Please make sure someone is with Veronica and Bertha all day. I've instructed them to lock their bedroom doors at night. I realise it's not ideal but until this is solved, we must protect them.'

'Okay,' Gill responded, before turning to Brian. 'You can all take turns being with them. You go back now and someone will relieve you later.'

Brian left, and once he was out of earshot, Lauren turned to the manager. 'We're not ruling out anyone, but by putting these measures in place we doubt the killer will try anything if they're going to be discovered.'

'Do you suspect Brian?' Gill asked, her eyes wide.

'No. I'm just saying so you realise how important it is. We're now going to visit Cynthia Lewis. Where is she?'

'She's on the ground floor in Richardson wing, room four. But I doubt you'll get much out of her, she rarely speaks,' Gill said.

'We'd like to give it a try.'

Matt agreed with Lauren because he'd witnessed people with dementia not being able to string a sentence together one minute and the next, they'd surprise you with moments of clarity. Even if Cynthia couldn't speak there might be something in her room or her reactions that could help. It was a long shot, but in a case like this, they couldn't afford to overlook anyone.

TWENTY-EIGHT

FRIDAY FEBRUARY 14

Once they'd reached room four, where Cynthia was, Lauren paused, took a deep breath and knocked.

'Hello?' a thin and wavering voice called out.

Lauren pushed open the door, revealing Cynthia sitting on a chair by the window, staring out at the garden below. The room smelt faintly of lavender.

'Hello, Cynthia,' Lauren said gently, stepping towards her.

The elderly woman turned slowly, and squinted in their direction, as if trying to focus. 'Who are you?' she asked, her frail hands clutching at the armrests of the chair.

'My name's Lauren; I'm a police officer. And this is Matt.' Lauren gestured to him and he gave a small, reassuring smile. 'We'd like to talk to you about the past when you were an actress.'

Cynthia's face remained blank. 'What about? I don't know anything. Was I... was I any good?' she added after a moment, a flicker of vulnerability crossing her weathered features.

'Yes,' Lauren said softly, crouching down to eye level with the woman. 'Do you remember in the 1960s, you were in a play called *The Last Guest*?'

Cynthia looked at them as if suddenly she remembered something, her eyes widening with recognition.

'Oh yes,' she exclaimed, a light illuminating her face. 'I played Mrs Blackwood, didn't I?'

'Yes, that's right,' Lauren said, encouraged by this spark of lucidity. She exchanged a quick glance with Matt, who nodded almost imperceptibly.

Cynthia's expression suddenly darkened, her eyes growing distant. 'But something happened. It wasn't good, and now I can't play her anymore.' She began to rock slightly in her chair, agitation building. 'Why can't I play her? I promise I'll get better. I promise.' Her voice rose with each word. 'Please let me take part. I promise I won't take anything else. I promise, I promise.'

It was as if Cynthia had gone off back to that time, trapped in a memory that was decades old. Her eyes were unfocused, staring at something, or someone, that wasn't there. A chill ran down Lauren's spine despite the warmth of the room.

'We can't let this go on,' Matt whispered, sounding concerned.

Lauren nodded, feeling a pang of guilt for triggering this distress. She reached out and gave Cynthia a little shake, her hand gentle but firm on the woman's bony shoulder.

'Cynthia, Cynthia, it's me, Lauren,' she said firmly. 'Come on, let's not go back to those days.'

Suddenly Cynthia looked at her, and it was like she was back in her body, the present moment reclaiming her. The transition was jarring, like a light switch being flicked on.

'Who are you?' she said, her voice clear but cold, eyes narrowing with suspicion.

'My name's Lauren – and this is Matt,' Lauren repeated patiently, maintaining eye contact.

'I don't want to speak to you,' Cynthia said flatly, turning her face back towards the window. 'Go away.'

Lauren sighed, a mix of frustration and sympathy washing over her. 'Okay, we'll leave you alone now,' she said, rising to her feet. Her knees ached slightly from crouching.

She gestured to Matt with a tilt of her head, and they left the room, closing the door quietly behind them. The hallway seemed eerily quiet after the emotional turbulence of the interaction.

They hurried to Gill Trelawny's office. Lauren knocked on the door, three sharp raps that echoed her growing sense of urgency.

'Come in,' a voice called from inside.

Gill looked up from her paperwork, over the top of the reading glasses perched on the end of her nose.

'We've just been to see Cynthia,' Lauren said as she and Matt settled into chairs opposite the desk.

'Did you get much out of her?' Gill asked with a hint of resignation.

'Not really, you were right,' Lauren admitted. 'She talked a bit about the past, which seemed to upset her. What can you tell us about her family? Do they visit much?'

Gill's expression softened. 'They used to, her daughter especially. But not so much these days.' She sighed, folding her hands on her desk. 'Now Cynthia's not with it most of the time, they couldn't take it. I don't blame them, it's very hard to not be recognised, or shouted at, any time you're with them. It's distressing for everyone, Cynthia included.'

Lauren nodded, understanding all too well the pain of watching a loved one fade away. 'Please let us know if any of her family do visit because we'd like to ask them a few questions.'

'I can find their contact details, if you'd like. They live a few hours away though.'

'Not for now, thanks. We need to get going.'

The information was scant, but Lauren felt they were getting closer to understanding what connected these deaths. As they prepared to leave, she couldn't shake the image of Cynthia's face, momentarily transported back to a time when everything changed. When her life had changed forever.

TWENTY-NINE

FRIDAY FEBRUARY 14

They left the care home and were walking back to the car when Lauren's phone rang. She glanced at the screen and answered immediately.

'Tamsin? What have you got for us?'

Matt could hear the excitement in Tamsin's voice even from where he stood, though he couldn't quite make out the words. Lauren's expression grew increasingly serious as she listened.

'Are you certain? Right, yes, we'll head over there now. Good work.'

Lauren ended the call and turned to Matt, her eyes bright with the kind of focus that meant a case might be taking a significant turn.

'Quentin Cross has been pawning his mother's jewellery,' she said without preamble. 'A sapphire and diamond ring, a gold bracelet and a pearl necklace.'

Matt's chest tightened. 'That must have been what Tamsin wanted to check before feeding back to us. But why did she think to do so?'

'She'd remembered Natalie's mention of the jewellery in her notes and checked with the home and the pathology department to see if they were there. They weren't. So she decided to contact the local pawn shops. Quentin Cross didn't bother to sell them under a fake name so it was easy to discover what he'd done.'

'That's excellent work. But how does it link him to the murders?' Matt asked, frowning because so far nothing they'd learnt about what was happening was anything to do with jewellery theft. Plus they didn't even know whether it was theft. His mother might have given the pieces to him to sell.

'It might not, but we need to investigate. We're going to his house now.'

They drove in relative silence, both lost in thought. Matt found himself running through the possibilities. Financial pressure was a classic motive for murder, especially when it involved family. But would Quentin Cross really kill his elderly mother for her jewellery? And what about the other deaths? If this was about Dawn's jewellery, how did they fit into the picture? It didn't make sense.

Matt rang the doorbell, and they waited. After a moment, footsteps approached from inside, and the door opened to reveal Quentin Cross.

'Mr Cross – Quentin. We'd like to have a word with you,' Lauren said.

The man paled, and his hands trembled slightly as he gripped the door frame. 'Is this about my mother? Have you found out what happened?'

'May we come in?' Lauren asked gently.

Quentin hesitated for a moment, then stepped aside. 'Of course. Come on through. Would you like a tea? Coffee?'

'We're fine, thank you,' Lauren replied, as they followed him into the drawing room and sat down on one of the sofas. 'Mr Cross, we need to ask you about some jewellery that we believe belonged to your mother and has been pawned recently.'

The colour drained completely from Quentin's face and for a long time he said nothing, simply stared at his hands.

'How did you find out?' he asked, finally looking up at them, his voice barely audible.

'We're conducting a thorough investigation into your mother's death,' Lauren said. 'That includes looking into her financial affairs and personal possessions. Did she give you permission to do this?'

'No.'

'Are you aware that pawning someone else's property without their permission is theft?'

Quentin's head snapped up. 'I wasn't stealing from her, as such. She's my mother – was my mother. I was going to get everything back; I just needed some time.'

'Time for what?' Matt asked.

Quentin ran his hands through his thick silver hair, a gesture that made him look unusually dishevelled. 'I'm in debt. Serious debt. I made some bad investments and took out loans I couldn't afford to repay. The interest kept mounting, and the people I owe money to aren't the sort who are patient about these things.'

'How much debt?' Lauren asked.

'Forty-three thousand pounds,' Quentin said, the words coming out in a rush. 'I know how that sounds, and what you must think of me. But I wasn't trying to hurt Mother. She would have helped me if I'd asked, but she was already worried about money, always going on about the cost of the care home. I didn't want to be another burden.'

'Surely you could have taken out a mortgage against this house,' Matt said, gesturing at their opulent surroundings.

'It already has a second mortgage on it from when I bought my partner out. Unfortunately, when he left most of the clients went with him. I retired not long after that and money's been tight ever since.'

'Yet despite that, you decided to make some investments, which turned out not to be good,' Lauren said.

'Not my greatest moment, I admit,' Quentin said, with a shake of his head. 'I thought they might turn out to be the answer to my money worries. But they weren't.'

Matt leaned forward. 'So you decided to pawn your mum's jewellery to pay back these loans?'

'Yes,' Quentin said, lowering his head.

'Did you get enough money to cover the entire debt?'

'No. But it was enough to keep my debtors at bay until I could get things straight,' Quentin said, drumming his fingers on his knees.

'And how were you going to do that?' Lauren asked, staring directly at the man.

'I had planned on getting some locum work but now...' His words fell away.

'Now your mother is dead, you're going to inherit from her. Is that what you were going to say?' Lauren pushed.

'It's not like that,' Quentin protested. 'If she'd known she would have wanted to help.'

'So why didn't you tell her you'd taken her jewellery?' Lauren asked.

'*Borrowed* it,' Quentin insisted. 'I was going to put everything back once I'd sorted out my finances. Mum hardly wore any of it anymore. Most of it was sitting in that old jewellery box of hers, gathering dust.'

'Where were you on Friday evening?' Lauren asked. 'That's the night your mother died.'

'I was here,' Quentin said immediately. 'You've already asked me this. I told you we got home from the pub at four-thirty and I fell asleep in the chair while my wife did some quilting.'

'Could you have popped out without her knowing?' Matt asked.

'No. She would have seen me leave from the craft room window.'

'What about last Tuesday night?' Lauren asked. 'Do you remember where you were?'

Quentin looked confused. 'Why are you asking?'

'Just answer the question, please,' Matt said.

'We were in London. We went to a show and stayed over in the city.' He pulled out his phone. 'I'll show you the receipt for the invoice. They emailed it to me.' He called up the email and passed the phone over to Lauren, who looked at the screen.

'Thank you,' Lauren said, passing back the phone to him.

'Quentin, are you familiar with Genevieve Hartwell's work?' Matt asked.

Okay, so the man had a receipt but that wasn't absolute proof. It could have been an elaborate plan. Although, he didn't appear to have a motive.

Quentin frowned. 'I believe so. Yes. Why?'

'Have you ever seen the play *The Last Guest*?'

'Oh, that one. Yes, I think I saw it years ago. A local amateur dramatic society put it on. Maybe twenty years ago. I don't remember much about it, to be honest. Something about people being killed off one by one at a house in the country, wasn't it? Why are you asking?'

Before Matt could respond, his phone rang. It was Clem. Matt knew the officer wouldn't be calling unless it was important. He glanced at Lauren, who nodded for him to take it.

'Excuse me a moment,' he said to Quentin, then answered the call. 'Clem, what is it?'

'Sarge, you need to get back to the station. Both of you. We've had a significant breakthrough.'

'Thanks, Clem. We'll be back shortly.'

He turned to Lauren, who was already getting to her feet.

'Thank you for your time, Quentin,' Lauren said. 'We'll need you to come to the station to give a formal statement about the jewellery. I'll be in touch and let you know when.'

Quentin looked between them with obvious anxiety. 'Am I under arrest?' he asked, his voice shaking.

'No,' Lauren replied. 'But I strongly advise you not to leave town without informing us first.'

They left Quentin standing in his doorway, appearing small, despite his height, and defeated. Matt found himself running through what they'd learned. Quentin Cross was clearly in financial trouble, and he'd stolen from his mother to try to solve his problems. But despite the potential motive, something about his demeanour suggested he was telling the truth about not harming Dawn, or the others.

'What do you think?' he asked Lauren as they got into the car.

'He's a desperate man who made some poor choices, but I don't think he's our killer,' Lauren replied, starting the engine. 'If he is our murderer, then why admit to knowing the play, even if his memory of the plot was scant.'

'I agree.'

As they drove back toward the station, Matt's mind was already racing ahead to whatever breakthrough the team had made, hoping that it meant they'd be able to stop anyone else losing their life.

THIRTY

'Hopefully we'll have something I can pass on to DCI Mistry because he's arranging a press conference for later today, and he wants as much information as I can give him,' Lauren said to Matt, while steering into an empty space in the station car park. 'Luckily, he doesn't want me to attend.'

She was anxious to get back to the team. Something important had been found, and her instincts were on high alert. Once they were inside the building, rather than wait for the lift, they took the stairs two at a time to the main office.

'You'll never guess what we've found out,' Billy shouted as soon as they'd got in there, practically jumping from his desk. His excitement was palpable, his face flushed.

'What is it, Billy?' Lauren said, removing her jacket and draping it over the desk next to the whiteboard. The energy in the room from whatever had been discovered was almost tangible.

'Oh well, it's not me,' Billy said, with a grin. 'It was Tamsin.'

Lauren turned towards Tamsin, who sat upright in her chair, 'What is it?'

Pride shone from the young officer's eyes. 'Well, ma'am, we've been researching into backgrounds of the staff working at the care home and visitors, like you asked us to, and something stood out for me. One of the full-time carers, who wasn't on duty during either of the murders, was Melody Wright.' Tamsin paused for a second and lowered her voice dramatically. 'And you'll never guess what...' She paused for a moment as if for further dramatic effect, which irritated Lauren somewhat, but she let it ride. 'It turns out that she's the granddaughter of Cynthia Lewis.'

Lauren's jaw dropped. The connection hit her like a physical blow. Surely it was the missing link they'd been searching for. The room fell silent, all eyes on her, waiting for a reaction.

'How come we've only just found out?' she demanded, not bothering to hide the sharpness in her tone.

She glanced across at Matt, who was frowning in her direction. Did he think she was putting a damper on things? Maybe she was, but surely this was something they should have already discovered?

Tamsin shifted in her seat, spreading her hands. 'It's not like you think, ma'am. Melody has a different surname from the rest of the family. It was just by chance that when researching Cynthia, I came across her daughter Belinda, who has been married three times and has a daughter and son with different fathers. Melody's the daughter and she kept her father's surname of Wright. Her brother and mother go by the surname of Belinda's third husband.' She took a breath. 'It took some unravelling, which is why we didn't discover it immediately.'

Matt whistled softly beside Lauren. 'That's quite the connection,' he murmured. 'Interesting that she didn't try to hide her real name and work at the home under a pseudonym.'

'That wouldn't be so easy because of the police check,' Clem responded.

'True,' Matt said with a nod.

'Sorry, I didn't mean to snap, Tamsin. You're right, it wasn't easy to find her,' Lauren admitted, her mind racing through the new information. 'Have you looked deeper into Melody?'

'We've all been focused on it.' Tamsin nodded. 'She's twenty-seven, single and lives in Penzance. I couldn't discover whether she lives alone or not. She doesn't have a criminal record and she's very quiet on social media.'

'I looked into her education and work background,' Clem said. 'She has a degree in nursing which she got from Bristol University. She's never stuck at a job for more than a couple of years. She's been at Silver Fern for eighteen months.'

'I checked out her finances,' Jenna said. 'She lives within her means and isn't a big spender.'

'It's got to be her. She's clever enough to do all the planning and has taken her time doing so. She could have been working this out for the eighteen months she's been working there. She also keeps a low profile. These are all potential characteristics of serial killers,' Billy finished, with a smug nod.

'That's a rather gross generalisation,' Clem corrected Billy.

'Yeah, well generalisations can be true, you know,' Billy responded.

Lauren sucked in a breath, quickly processing all the information she'd been given. 'Right, okay,' she said decisively. 'We need to get back to the home and have a chat with Gill Trelawny to find out what we can about Melody Wright before approaching her directly.' She pointed at Tamsin and Billy. 'I want you to continue your research into her. But we don't know for sure it's her, despite where it's pointing, so Clem and Jenna, keep up with the other searches and—' '

The office door opened, interrupting her, and in walked an older uniformed officer carrying an enormous brown teddy bear.

'What the…?' Billy called out.

'Yeah, you're right about that, lad,' the officer said, heading over to Billy. 'This arrived for you. Happy Valentine's Day.' He laughed and sat the bear on Billy's lap, before turning and heading out of the office.

'Oh my God,' Tamsin said, doubling up with laughter. 'Where did that come from?'

'I'd hazard a guess at Ellie,' Clem said. 'Am I right?'

Billy peered over the top of the bear, having flushed a bright shade of red. 'I don't know. Maybe.'

'Look, there's an envelope taped to his paw. Open it?'

Lauren glanced at Matt, who had a wide smile on his face. It looked like she'd have to let this play out before calling them back on task.

'Yes, do,' Lauren said, smiling. 'Then we can get on.'

Billy ripped the pink envelope from the paw and opened the card. Another flush crept up his cheeks.

'It's got to be love, if it's affecting you like this,' Tamsin teased. 'Is it from Ellie?'

'Yes, I think so,' Billy muttered. 'It's not signed but there's a cryptic message on the card.'

'Why didn't she send it to your home?' Clem asked. 'It's not like Ellie to want to make a big show, is it?'

'No,' Matt agreed. 'Maybe she wanted to be sure he got it, knowing that we're working all hours at the moment.'

'Right, that's enough,' Lauren said. 'Matt and I are going. Let me know if anything else comes up.'

She grabbed her jacket, already moving towards the door. Matt fell into step beside her.

'Good call to let Billy deal with the bear,' Matt said, once they were out of earshot.

'I didn't have much choice, or I'd never have got them back on task.'

'If you say so,' Matt said, arching an eyebrow.

She knew what he was thinking. That in the past she'd never have been so relaxed about it. But that was then and this was now.

'The look on Billy's face when the bear was on his lap – it was funny, I must admit.'

'Yeah, it did make me laugh. Shame we didn't get a photo,' Matt added with a grin.

'Is the relationship serious? Because if it is, then does that mean we're going to lose Billy to Lenchester?' she asked, not wanting the officer to leave but thinking that it would be inevitable.

'I think it is. Maybe Ellie will come back here,' Matt replied with a shrug.

'I can't see that happening; we don't have a position available.'

'One of the other Cornwall stations might. Anyway, I think we're jumping the gun here. Back to Melody Wright, do you think that she holds all the people in the play responsible for what happened to her grandmother?'

'Quite possibly,' Lauren said, her voice low and intense.

If Melody Wright was their killer, they needed to move fast before she murdered anyone else.

THIRTY-ONE

FRIDAY FEBRUARY 14

Matt and Lauren returned to the care home, and after a brief check-in with the receptionist, who greeted them with a sympathetic smile, they headed straight for the care home manager's office.

Lauren rapped her knuckles against the polished wooden door.

'Come in,' called a voice from inside.

They pushed the door open to find Gill hunched over her desk, massaging her lower back with a grimace. 'You're here again?' she said, wincing as she moved into a sitting position.

'Something urgent has come up,' Lauren said, pulling out a chair and sitting opposite the woman.

'Melody Wright,' Matt added, sitting beside Lauren and watching Gill's face carefully for any reaction.

'What about her? She's great, all the staff and residents love her.' Gill said.

Matt exchanged a glance with Lauren before continuing. 'Well, it turns out that she's the granddaughter of Cynthia Lewis.'

Gill's smile faltered, her forehead creasing into a frown. 'Oh. I didn't know,' she said slowly. 'That's strange. Why didn't she mention it?'

'Is she extra nice to Cynthia?' Lauren asked, leaning forward. 'Does she spend more time with her than the other residents?'

Gill tapped her pen against the desk, considering. 'Not that I've noticed. Melody isn't on Richardson wing often. Unless we don't have the usual staff available. She's mainly on Plowright, than anywhere else.'

'Are you sure that she didn't ever mention being related to Cynthia?' Matt pressed, his voice tight.

'No, absolutely not. I'd have remembered. She might have told other staff members, but it would have got back to me if she did.' Gill's eyes narrowed. 'Why? Is it important in your investigation?'

Matt glanced at Lauren, who nodded at him to continue. 'We've found a link between the victims and we need to speak to Melody about it.'

Gill pushed back from her desk, her chair rolling slightly. 'So what are you saying? That Melody killed these residents?'

Matt held up his hands. 'We're not making any assumptions, but we do need to speak to her.'

'You mentioned that Melody wasn't on duty the day of Dawn's murder. Can we have another quick look at the CCTV together to see if there's anything we missed? You might be able to notice something that we didn't.'

'Well, I did look at it before sending it to you, but it's always good to take another look. Hang on a minute.' Gill turned to her computer, called up the footage, and turned the screen so they could all see.

They sped up the replay and watched the comings and goings for a while, but there was no sign of Melody entering the building.

'Oh, hang on a minute,' Gill said suddenly, pointing at the screen and pausing the tape. Her nail tapped against the edge of the image at a person wearing jeans and sweatshirt getting out of a dark red car, their baseball-capped head lowered. From that distance it was impossible to tell if they were male or female. 'You know, that looks like Melody. It's the way she swings in her right foot slightly when she walks. But I don't recognise the car. She usually drives a blue Nissan with a dented rear bumper. I'm so sorry I missed it before. But what's she doing there?'

Matt's heart hammered against his ribs. 'What's the time on the CCTV footage?'

'Five-thirty, which is the start of evening mealtime,' Gill said, checking the timestamp. 'It's always busy then. Staff will be pushing residents in wheelchairs to the dining room, others helping those who can walk but need assistance. The corridors are filled with movement and noise. Food being brought out, care assistants calling to each other, residents chatting or sometimes becoming agitated with the change in routine. It's noisy, that's for sure.'

'So it would have been easy for Melody to slip in unnoticed,' Lauren said, staring at the screen.

Gill sighed, rubbing her temple. 'Yes, I suppose so. Often the reception desk is left unattended then for a short time as everyone pitches in. Melody knows the code so can come in and out whenever she wants. I expect if she did come in during that time, she might not have been noticed. Or if anyone saw her, they'd have thought she was on duty.'

'So Melody could have gone into Dawn's room without being seen while Dawn was in the dining room?' Lauren asked, her voice tense. 'And the hallway cameras wouldn't necessarily catch her if she knew their blind spots?'

'Well, yes, that is entirely possible,' Gill admitted, looking troubled.

'Is she on duty now, by any chance?' Matt asked, his jaw set.

Gill shook her head. 'No. She's not due in until tomorrow morning.'

'Can you give us her address?' Lauren asked. 'We'll visit her there. But please don't contact her and let her know we're coming.'

'Of course not,' Gill said, her face pale as she reached for her phone. She tapped at the screen briefly. 'She lives in Penzance. I've texted you the details.'

Matt exchanged a meaningful look with Lauren. They were closing in on their suspect at last.

THIRTY-TWO

FRIDAY FEBRUARY 14

Lauren gripped the steering wheel tightly as she drove away from the care home towards Penzance, the car's tyres crunching over gravel.

'This could be it, Matt,' she said, glancing sideways at her detective sergeant. 'Everything's pointing to Melody seeking revenge on all those she believes were responsible for her grandmother's downfall.' She let the words hang in the air.

Matt nodded, his face tense. 'And if Kenneth supplied Thea the drugs, then—'

'She might want to finish him off before moving on to her next victim,' Lauren interrupted, a chill running through her despite the warm car interior. 'But why now? What made her start seeking revenge now?'

She pressed harder on the accelerator, anxious to confront the woman as soon as possible.

They pulled up outside a small, terraced house with a neat front garden. It was a modest home with freshly painted blue trim and potted plants lining the short path to the front door.

'Doesn't exactly scream *serial killer's lair*,' Matt muttered as they approached the door.

Lauren rang the doorbell, listening to it echo inside the house.

There was no response so she tried again, at the same time knocking firmly on the wooden door. The silence stretched uncomfortably.

'Where can she be?' Matt said, peering through the front window. The curtains were drawn, making it impossible to see inside.

Lauren was about to suggest checking the back when the door from the next-door house opened. A tall man with long straggly dark hair stepped out.

'Are you looking for Mel?' he asked, eyeing them with suspicion.

Lauren pulled out her warrant card. 'DI Pengelly and DS Price. We're trying to reach Melody Wright. Is she home?'

The man shook his head. 'Haven't seen her car today. But her partner's in. I saw him about an hour ago.'

As if on cue, they heard movement inside, and the door finally opened. A man in his early thirties stood there, wearing jeans and a faded T-shirt with a game logo on it. His eyes were red-rimmed.

'Yeah? What do you want?' he asked cautiously.

Lauren showed her warrant card again. 'We're looking for Melody Wright.'

The man's shoulders slumped slightly. 'I'm Jason Brand. Melody's partner. She's not here.'

'Do you know where she is?' Matt asked, his voice sharp.

Jason shrugged. 'No idea. I haven't seen her since this morning. She said she was going to run some errands.' He frowned. 'Is something wrong?'

Lauren studied his face, looking for signs of deception, but all she saw was genuine confusion and growing concern.

'When exactly did you last see her?' she pressed.

'Around eight this morning. She had breakfast, said she had a busy day planned, and left.' His worry was visibly increasing. 'Look, what's this about? Mel's never in trouble. She works at a care home, for God's sake.'

Lauren exchanged a quick glance with Matt. 'We need to

speak with her regarding an ongoing investigation. Did she mention where she was going? Any appointments, friends she was meeting, places she needed to be?'

Jason shook his head. 'No, nothing specific but that's normal though. She's not a great sharer and she's been busy at work and...' He hesitated. 'You know, she has been a bit distracted lately. Quieter than usual.'

Lauren felt her pulse quicken. 'For how long has she been acting differently?'

'I don't know, a few weeks maybe? I thought it was stress from work.' Jason's eyes widened. 'Has she done something? Is that why you want to speak to her?'

'We're following up on some information,' Matt said neutrally, but Lauren could hear the tension in his voice.

'Jason, does Melody ever talk about her grandmother? A woman named Cynthia Lewis?' Lauren asked, watching his reaction carefully.

Jason's brow furrowed as if searching his memory. 'She's mentioned a grandmother who was in a care home. Is that who you mean?'

'Did she ever mention that her grandmother was once an actress?' Matt added. 'That she went by the stage name Thea Drake?'

Jason's eyes widened slightly. 'Wait, Thea Drake? Mel has an old photo in a box of keepsakes and in a theatre programme that name's circled. I asked her about it once, and she said it was family history.' He leant against the door frame and drew in a breath. 'Are you saying that's her grandmother?'

Lauren nodded. 'Did she tell you that Thea Drake, or Cynthia Lewis as she's now known, was once considered a rising star in film and theatre? Her career was derailed after a breakdown during a production?'

'No,' Jason said, looking increasingly bewildered. 'Nothing like that. All she said was her grandmother had been in the arts when she was younger but had to quit. I assumed it was for, you know, normal reasons. Marriage and kids... that sort of thing.'

'What about drugs?' Matt asked bluntly. 'Did Melody ever mention that the breakdown was caused by her grandmother being on drugs?'

Jason's face registered genuine shock. 'Drugs? No. Mel's anti-drugs because of...' He trailed off, a dawning realisation crossing his features. 'Because of a family member who had problems with them. She never said who and I didn't ask. She's quite a private person.'

A cold weight settled in Lauren's stomach. Jason clearly had no idea about the full history, which meant Melody had been keeping significant secrets from him. What else was she hiding?

'I think we need to visit the hospital and have a chat with Kenneth,' she said, turning to Matt, not caring that Jason could hear. Time was becoming critical. 'Do you have Melody's mobile number?' she asked Jason.

He nodded, reciting it as Matt noted it down.

'If she contacts you, please don't mention we were here,' Lauren said firmly. 'Just call this number immediately.' She handed him her card. 'It's extremely important.'

'Do you think that's why she specifically got a job at the care home?' Matt asked as they hurried back to the car and jumped inside. 'So she could get close to her grandmother and identify all the people from that production?'

'I've no idea. We don't know the lead-up to it from either side. But we need to speak to Kenneth to find out more. If he really did supply everyone with drugs, then by default he ended her grand-mother's career.'

'And if Melody suspects we're onto her,' Matt added darkly, 'she might accelerate her timeline.'

Lauren pulled away from the kerb with urgency, her mind filled with the image of Cynthia Lewis's broken career and the trail of deaths that had followed decades later. Kenneth Blencoe could be fighting for his life at this very moment.

'Call the hospital, and tell them we're on the way,' she instructed Matt. 'They already shouldn't be letting anyone near Kenneth, but double check they're doing what we asked. No visitors, no staff they don't personally recognise. No one.'

As Matt made the call, Lauren speeded up, silently praying they weren't already too late.

THIRTY-THREE

FRIDAY FEBRUARY 14

When they arrived at the hospital, they hurried down the sterile corridors in the direction of Kenneth's room. The closer they got, Lauren's sense of foreboding intensified, made even worse when they arrived and no one was standing on guard outside.

The door was ajar and she ran in, scanning the room.

'Oh no,' Lauren said, taking in the unmade bed, with the sheets twisted and trailing onto the floor. The IV stand had been knocked over and a cup of water had spilt across the side table. The monitors were disconnected, their cables dangling. Everything about the scene suggested a hasty departure.

'Where on earth is he?' Matt asked, his voice tight with alarm as his eyes darted around the vacant space.

Lauren moved to touch the rumpled bedding. 'Still warm. He can't have been gone long.'

Matt joined her and pointed to a small smear of blood on the sheet. 'Not much, but...'

Lauren's stomach knotted. 'Did his wound reopen? Also, where's the officer meant to be guarding the room?'

She moved back into the hallway, her heart hammering in her chest, and approached the reception desk where a nurse was updating charts on a computer.

'We're here to see Kenneth Blencoe,' Lauren stated, flashing her warrant card. 'But he's not there, and his room looks like there was a struggle.'

The nurse frowned, her fingers pausing over the keyboard. 'He's not due for any procedures. We've been explicitly told that he can't go anywhere without police authorisation.' Her eyes widened as she processed Lauren's words. 'A struggle?'

'And there should have been a police officer stationed outside his door,' Lauren said, her voice sharp with urgency.

Just as she finished speaking, Police Constable Alderton hurried around the corner, looking flustered at the sight of her.

Lauren approached the officer, her posture rigid with contained fury. 'Where the hell have you been?'

Alderton's face flushed deep red. 'I popped to the toilet after someone from the care home came to visit. She said that you'd given permission, and she wanted to give him some personal items that he'd requested.'

'And you didn't think to check with me?' Lauren demanded, her voice dropping to a dangerous whisper. 'You left a vulnerable victim unattended when we specifically told you not to let anyone in without our direct confirmation?'

The officer went pale, beads of sweat forming on his forehead. 'No, ma'am, but... but he seemed very pleased to see her. There was no indication of any problem.'

'Was it Melody Wright?' Matt interjected, stepping forward, his hands clenched into fists at his sides.

'She didn't say her name,' Alderton replied, shrinking under their combined glare. 'All she said was she'd come from the care home and had permission to visit. She was holding a large bag. I was only gone a few minutes, I swear. I'm so sorry, ma'am.'

Lauren exchanged a charged look with Matt. 'Well, those few minutes might have just cost a man his life,' she said, her voice shaking with suppressed rage. 'She's tried to kill him once already, and now she's taken him to finish the job.' She nodded to the door of Kenneth's room. 'Stay there and don't move. Nobody is allowed into the room because it's now a crime scene. I'll deal with your negligence later.'

The officer blanched, nodding silently.

'Come on,' Matt said, placing a steadying hand on Lauren's arm. 'Every second counts. We need to put out an immediate alert for Kenneth and Melody.'

Lauren spun around to the nurse. 'What was his current condition?'

'Stable. But he's still weak.' She shook her head and gave a sigh. 'He shouldn't be outside, especially in this weather.'

'Where's the hospital security? We need to look at the CCTV now,' Lauren said, half turning in the direction of the stairs.

'The security office is on the ground floor and there should be someone to help. I'll let them know you're on the way,' the nurse answered, picking up the handset from the desk and pressing some keys.

Matt and Lauren hurried down the stairs, bypassing the lift entirely. Lauren's mind was racing through possibilities, each more horrifying than the last. Melody had been methodically killing off everyone connected to her grandmother's breakdown. Kenneth was an integral piece of her plan. Would she still follow the play and shoot him? If that was her plan it meant she'd most likely have a gun with her.

When they reached the security office, they found a guard sitting before a bank of screens, already pulling up footage based on the nurse's urgent call.

'DI Pengelly and DS Price,' Lauren gasped out, barely taking time to catch her breath. 'We need to see footage from Hardwick Ward and surrounding areas within the last thirty minutes. A patient has been abducted from one of the private rooms, by someone we believe is intending to kill him.'

The guard's eyes widened, but he worked quickly, his fingers flying over the keyboard. 'I've already started pulling it up based on the alert I received,' he said, going through various camera angles.

The screens flashed with different views and then froze on one showing the corridor outside Kenneth's room. They watched as a woman in a care home uniform approached PC Alderton, engaged him in conversation, then waited until the officer had walked away before entering the room. The timestamp showed 15:37, which was twenty-three minutes ago.

The guard switched to another camera angle, this one partially showing the interior of Kenneth's room from the doorway. They could see Melody enter with a large tote bag and greet Kenneth, who was sitting up in bed. It was clear from his body language that he recognised her and wasn't at all alarmed.

'Speed it up,' Lauren instructed, her nails digging into her palms.

The footage accelerated. Melody appeared to be showing Kenneth something in the bag, then suddenly there was a flurry of motion. Kenneth's arms went up defensively, but Melody had already produced something from the bag. It looked like a syringe. A brief struggle ensued, and then Kenneth went still.

'Oh my God,' Matt breathed. 'She's drugged him.'

The footage continued, and Melody hurriedly disconnected Kenneth from the monitors, knocking over the IV in her haste. She dressed him in a robe over his hospital gown, and transferred him to a wheelchair she'd brought in. She covered him with a blanket, arranged his head to make it appear he was simply sleepy or drowsy, and wheeled him out.

'Where did she take him after this?' Lauren asked, her voice tight.

The guard switched to corridor cameras, following Melody's progress as she wheeled Kenneth towards the service lifts, bypassing the busier main lifts. 'She seems to know the hospital layout,' Matt observed grimly. 'She clearly planned all this.'

They watched as she came out of the service elevator at the ground floor and then navigated through less busy corridors towards a side exit near the staff parking lot. All the time Kenneth remained motionless.

'There,' the guard said, switching to an external camera. 'She's taking him out through the side entrance; that's usually used by delivery people, and staff.'

The footage then showed Melody pushing Kenneth's wheelchair towards a dark blue Nissan, the car that Gill Trelawney had told them about. She positioned the wheelchair beside the back door and then, with surprising strength, slid Kenneth's limp body into the seat. She folded the wheelchair, stowed it in the boot, and drove off.

The timestamp showed 15:42.

'She's got a nineteen-minute head start on us,' Lauren said, her voice hollow. 'And we have no idea where she's taking him.'

Matt leaned closer to the screen. 'Can you zoom in on the licence plate?'

The guard enhanced the image, revealing the registration number.

'Please forward all of this CCTV footage to my email immediately,' Lauren instructed him as she scribbled her contact details. 'Every second matters now.'

'The car's heading west out of the hospital,' Matt said, studying the final frames of footage. 'That's towards the coast – or maybe the care home? But why would she head there?'

Lauren was already on her phone, calling in the vehicle details for an immediate search. 'All units are to look for a dark blue Nissan, last seen heading west from the hospital. The driver is Melody Wright, wanted for abduction and attempted murder. Her passenger is Kenneth Blencoe, unconscious and in medical danger. Consider the suspect dangerous and approach with caution.'

She ended the call and turned to Matt. 'We need to get back to the office to coordinate the search. If she's following her pattern, she'll want somewhere private to finish what she started. But I suspect it will be somewhere with significance. That might give us time to find them.'

They ran towards the car at the same time as Lauren's phone rang. It was the station. 'Pengelly,' she answered sharply.

After listening for a moment, her mouth dropped open. 'Gill

from the care home has been on the phone. Cynthia Lewis, Melody's grandmother, is missing too. CCTV shows Melody escorting her out of the home an hour ago. Cynthia must have been in the front of the car when Kenneth was kidnapped.'

THIRTY-FOUR

FRIDAY FEBRUARY 14

'Sarge,' Billy called out, phone in hand, excitement colouring his voice. 'We've got her.' Melody's car was picked up on the number plate recognition camera. It's parked in the car park opposite a Wave Crest Café in Marazion. I've just called and the owner has confirmed that an elderly woman in a wheelchair and a confused-looking older man in what looked like pyjamas under his coat are sitting on the outside terrace with a younger woman in uniform.'

'Kenneth and Cynthia,' Matt breathed, already reaching for his jacket. 'She's got them both. How long ago?'

'Ten minutes. The owner said Melody ordered afternoon tea for all of them.'

Matt ran to Lauren's office, knocked and went in without waiting for a response.

'We have a sighting of Melody, Kenneth and Cynthia,' he said. 'Shall we send officers there to pick her up?'

Lauren shook her head. 'We'll go ourselves in case she panics and decides to do a runner.'

They took Matt's car, pushing the speed limit on the coastal road to Marazion. The picturesque town with its views of St Michael's Mount seemed an incongruous setting for the climax of a revenge plot.

'We need to be careful,' Lauren said as they approached the town. 'No sirens, no drawing attention. If she has a weapon...'

'Do you think she does?' Matt asked, taking a corner faster than was strictly necessary.

'We can't assume she doesn't. If she wants to shoot Kenneth, to make it true to the play...' Lauren said grimly. 'We need to talk her down. No heroics, do you understand?'

Matt got the message. He already walked with a limp after being shot by a murder suspect while he was undercover.

'Yes, ma'am. I have no desire to be shot again.'

The café sat on a prime spot facing the bay, its blue-painted exterior cheerful against the grey sky. Matt parked a short distance away, not wanting to alert Melody to their presence. From where they stood, they could see three figures at a corner table on the terrace. Melody, sitting upright and appearing tense. Cynthia, frail in her wheelchair, a blanket tucked around her legs. Kenneth, his hospital-issued clothing partially concealed by an oversized coat, his expression confused and frightened. He must have come round sufficiently to walk to the café.

'No visible weapon,' Lauren murmured as they observed from a distance. 'But that doesn't mean she doesn't have one.'

'We'll approach carefully,' Matt replied. 'I'll go first; you circle around from the beach side in case she decides to make a run for it.'

They separated, with Lauren heading down to the beach to approach from the sea-facing side. Matt took a deep breath and walked casually towards the café, acting like another visitor enjoying the coastal view. He was ten metres away when Melody's gaze flickered in his direction, recognition dawning in her eyes.

He watched her body tense, her hand moving instinctively towards her bag. Was that where the gun was?

'Melody,' he called out, keeping his voice calm and even. 'It's over. Let's talk about this.'

Around them, the few other café patrons turned to look, sensing the sudden tension. Melody's eyes darted from side to side, clearly calculating her options. Her hand emerged from her bag gripping a small silver gun.

'Stay back,' she shouted, the gun trembling in her grip but pointing directly at Kenneth. Several patrons screamed and scrambled away from nearby tables. 'You don't understand what they did to her.'

Matt froze, his hands raised. 'I do understand, Melody. I know exactly what happened to your grandmother and the role Kenneth and the others played.'

'No you don't.' Melody's voice cracked with emotion. 'They didn't just destroy her career. They destroyed her mind... her soul. She was the most talented actress of her generation and they couldn't stand it. So they fed her pills and alcohol and told her she needed them to perform. They turned her into an addict because they were jealous. Pathetic and jealous.'

Kenneth whimpered, pressing himself back in his chair. 'Melody, please. I was young. I didn't know—'

'Liar.' The gun swung towards Kenneth and he flinched. 'You knew exactly what you were doing. You all did.'

Cynthia Lewis sat serene in her wheelchair, apparently oblivious to the drama unfolding around her. She hummed softly, a fragment of some forgotten show tune, her gaze fixed on the distant silhouette of St Michael's Mount. But then, something shifted in her expression and her humming stopped.

'Kenneth?' Cynthia's voice was thin but lucid. 'Kenneth Blencoe? Is that really you?'

The effect on Melody was instant. She turned to her grandmother. 'Granny? You remember him?'

Cynthia's eyes moved between Kenneth and Melody. 'Of course I remember him. We were inseparable.' She glanced at the gun in Melody's hand. 'What are you doing, princess?'

'I'm making him pay for what he did to you. I'm making all your so-called friends pay. For the pills and the booze and for ruining your life.'

Cynthia was quiet for several seconds, studying Kenneth's

terrified face. 'I chose to take those pills. To drink. No one made me. I was so stressed out. Taking pills. Drinking. It all helped me perform. But it went wrong. It was nobody's fault but my own.'

Matt stared at the woman. How could she be so with it after all this time?

'No.' Melody shook her head. 'That's not what happened. Mum told me all about it. You're confused. The dementia—'

'It's true,' Kenneth said quietly. 'Thea made her own decisions. I should have done more. Got her proper help instead of enabling her. But we were young and didn't think anything through.'

'But I killed Dawn and Charlie for you,' Melody whispered, staring directly at Cynthia.

'Oh, Melody.' Cynthia's lucidity was fading, and confusion had crept back into her eyes.

While Melody was distracted by the revelation, Matt inched forwards and grabbed her wrist, wrenching the gun from her hand and throwing it over the other side of the café. The woman collapsed, sobbing into her grandmother's lap.

'I did it all for you,' she wept. 'Everything was for you.'

Cynthia's confusion had returned fully now, but her hand still moved instinctively to stroke Melody's hair.

Matt handcuffed Melody, at the same time as Lauren came running over. 'Backup and paramedics are on their way.'

'It's all under control, ma'am,' Matt explained, keeping a firm hold on Melody, who wasn't putting up a fight.

After Melody was taken away in a police car, Matt went over to Lauren and Kenneth, who sat wrapped in a shock blanket provided by the paramedics.

'She told me we were going back to the home,' Kenneth explained, his voice croaky and filled with age and fear. 'Then everything went blurry and when I woke up, I knew she was driving us in the wrong direction. When I asked questions, she just said Cynthia wanted to see the sea one more time.' He shook his head. 'I should have known something was wrong.'

'It's not your fault,' Lauren assured him. 'You're going to be fine. We'll get you back to the hospital.'

While the paramedics were preparing to transport both Kenneth and Cynthia, the elderly woman remained calm throughout. She occasionally patted Kenneth's hand though it was impossible to tell whether she still recognised him.

Matt and Lauren stood in silence, watching as the ambulances carrying the two old people pulled away.

'A fifty-year-old tragedy,' Lauren murmured. 'Built on a misunderstanding.'

'And two people dead because of it,' Matt added, grimly.

THIRTY-FIVE

FRIDAY FEBRUARY 14

Lauren sat across from Melody Wright in the stark interview room. Matt was beside her, his expression carefully neutral. Melody looked smaller somehow, her dark hair pulled back in a messy ponytail, her eyes red-rimmed from crying. The fire that had driven her to commit the murders seemed to have burnt out, replaced by something more fragile... devastation.

'Interview on February 14,' Lauren stated for the recording. 'Those present are Detective Inspector Pengelly, Detective Sergeant Price, and...' She nodded to the accused.

'Melody Deborah Wright.'

'Ms Wright has waived her right to legal representation at this time.' Lauren paused, studying the woman across from her. 'Melody, I'd like to talk about your grandmother, Cynthia Lewis.'

Something flickered in Melody's eyes: pain, confusion, love, all tangled together. 'You mean Thea Drake,' she corrected quietly. 'That was her stage name. Before they... before she...' She trailed off, unable to finish.

Lauren leant forwards slightly. 'Tell me about how you came to work at Silver Fern Care Home.'

Melody's gaze drifted to the wall behind Lauren. 'I hadn't seen my granny for quite a few years. My mother kept us apart because she thought it would be too upsetting for me to see her with dementia. But after Mum died two years ago, I wanted to reconnect.' Her voice was flat, rehearsed, as though she'd played this explanation over in her mind countless times. 'I discovered she was living at Silver Fern and applied for a job there. I was trained as a nurse so it wasn't hard especially as, like most care homes, they were short-staffed. It was a drop in pay, but that didn't matter. I didn't tell them Cynthia was my grandmother in case they thought it was a conflict of interest.'

'So you didn't go with the intention of exacting revenge?' Matt asked.

'No.' Melody's voice cracked. 'I just wanted to be near her, to take care of her. Although it was hard because I was often working on different wings. Granny didn't recognise me most days, but sometimes...' She closed her eyes. 'Sometimes she'd have these moments of clarity. Like the fog had lifted and the real Thea Drake would be there, just for a little while.'

'Like when we were in the café?' Matt said.

'Yes,' Melody agreed.

'When did you first learn about her breakdown?' Lauren asked.

Melody's fingers began to tap a slow, deliberate rhythm on the table, then stopped abruptly as if she'd caught herself. 'It was about six months after I started working at Silver Fern. She was having a good day, and I happened to be working on her wing. I told her who I was and she remembered me. She asked about my mum and got very upset when she learnt that she'd died.' Melody's voice had grown stronger and more animated, as if she was reliving the moment. 'I mentioned to her that mum told me she would've made it big if it wasn't for her friends. And she agreed with me. She told me about her breakdown when she was starring in *The Last Guest* and that she was playing Mrs Blackwood. She said she got fired. So I started researching.'

'What did you find?' Lauren asked, keeping her gaze firmly on Melody, watching for any tells that she was lying.

'Old newspapers, reviews. The infamous performance where

rising star Thea Drake had a "breakdown" on stage. Her career was over after that. No one would insure her for productions. The rumours of drink and drug use followed her everywhere.' Melody's voice hardened with old anger. 'Then I discovered Dawn Cross was also at Silver Fern. She'd been part of the production.'

Lauren nodded. 'And you confronted her?'

'I mentioned it to her and it was like the flood gates opened. She started babbling about "poor Thea" and how sorry she was. That's when I knew Granny had been telling the truth. Dawn knew what they'd done. She was part of it.'

'Then what did you do?' Lauren asked, curious how the revenge plot originated.

Melody gave a hollow laugh. 'I became obsessed with it. I spent every free moment in archives, tracking down people who had been around at the time. Some were dead, of course. But at the home I found many of her friends. And that was when I planned to pay them back for what they'd done.'

'Except you now know the truth,' Matt said.

Melody let out a sound that seemed part laugh, part sob. 'I know. I killed two innocent people and nearly killed a third. I'd spent a year orchestrating their deaths and it was all based on me not fully understanding what had happened.'

Lauren waited a moment before continuing. 'Tell us about the murders, Melody. How did you plan them?'

Melody wiped her eyes with the back of her hand. 'I chose the play because... because Granny was Mrs Blackwood. It seemed poetic. Justice catching up with people who'd escaped punishment.' She laughed bitterly. 'Except there was no justice. Just me, playing God with people's lives based on the confused memories of a woman with dementia.'

'Why was Dawn Cross first?'

'Everyone knew about her chocolates, her love of strawberry creams. It was... easy.' Melody's voice was flat now, emotionless. 'Charlie was harder because of his size, but I knew about his sleeping pills. He was unconscious when I... when I strangled him.'

'And Kenneth was meant to be shot.'

'Yes. Following the pattern of the play. I had my dad's old gun.' Melody looked directly at Matt. 'After he survived the first shot, I decided to make him confess everything to my grandmother first. Make him face what I thought he'd done. But now...' She shook her head. 'Now I know he would have been confessing to something he didn't do.'

'What about the others at Silver Fern? Veronica and Bertha?'

'Blunt force trauma and drowning, according to the play.' Melody's voice was mechanical now, as if she was reading from a script. 'And Granny would have been last. Stabbing. But I was going to sedate her first, so she wouldn't feel it. I thought... I thought I'd be ending her suffering.'

Lauren felt a chill. 'You were going to kill your own grandmother?'

'She has no quality of life. I thought I was being merciful, completing the story, giving her the dignity of being Mrs Blackwood one last time.' She sobbed. 'But she knew me today. She knew me, and she told me the truth, and I realised I was just a monster. A monster who killed innocent people.'

'How do you feel now, Melody?' Matt asked kindly.

The question seemed to physically pain the woman. She was quiet for a long time. 'I regret everything,' she finally whispered. 'I regret that I was so desperate to find someone to blame that I ignored the possibility that there might not be anyone to blame. I regret that I let my love for Granny turn into something twisted and destructive. I regret that two good people are dead.'

She looked up at Lauren with hollow eyes. 'But most of all, I regret that my granny had to see what I'd become. In her moment of clarity, she saw her granddaughter as a killer. That's what I'll never forgive myself for.'

Lauren reached forwards to stop the recording. 'Interview terminated.'

As they prepared to have Melody returned to her cell, Lauren couldn't help but reflect on the tragedy of it all. A talented woman's career destroyed fifty years ago, and now her granddaughter's life ruined by an obsessive quest for revenge.

Outside the interview room, Matt sighed heavily. 'Well, that's it then. Case closed.'

Lauren nodded. 'It's a tragic case of life imitating art imitating life.'

'At least Kenneth survived,' Matt said.

'Thank goodness,' Lauren replied, thinking how easily this could have been another victim on their board. 'Though I doubt he'll ever feel truly safe again.'

THIRTY-SIX

FRIDAY FEBRUARY 14

The pub was buzzing with Friday night energy, but the team had managed to snag a coveted corner booth thanks to Clem having the foresight to call ahead and ask for it to be reserved. The low-beamed ceiling and weathered wood panelling gave the pub a cosy feel despite the crowd, the perfect setting for their impromptu celebration.

'To closing the case.' Matt raised his glass, the amber liquid catching the light. 'And to all of you for your hard work.'

'And to Kenneth Blencoe for not becoming another victim,' Jenna added.

They clinked glasses, the tension of the past week visibly melting from their shoulders. It had been a gruelling investigation. But tonight was about celebrating the win, not rehashing the case.

'Did you see the DCI's face when Melody was brought in?' Billy leant back in his seat, loosening his tie. 'I swear he almost showed an actual human emotion.'

'Careful,' Jenna warned, though her eyes were bright with amusement. 'Walls have ears.' She gestured dramatically to the pub's ancient plaster.

'Also DCI Mistry's okay,' Matt said. 'I've worked with a lot worse, let me tell you.'

'You mean "Dickhead Douglas",' Billy replied, doing quote marks with his fingers and smirking.

'Ah... I see Ellie has told you about him,' Matt said. 'But let's leave that, shall we? Gossip has a way of backfiring when you least expect it.'

'Yes, Sarge,' Billy said, his nod appearing serious if it wasn't for the grin plastered across his face.

'Are you going to Lenchester this weekend now the case is over?' Tamsin asked.

'No because Ellie's working. You know, it's not easy to have a relationship with this bloody job. I'm hoping to go in a couple of weeks.'

'Say hello to her from me,' Tamsin said after taking a sip of her gin and tonic. 'Anyway, back to DCI Mistry, I overheard him mentioning there might be an opening for a Family Liaison Officer soon, because one of them is taking early retirement.'

The table quieted momentarily, all eyes turning to her.

'Are you thinking of applying?' Clem asked.

Tamsin nodded, looking slightly self-conscious under the sudden attention. 'I've been considering it for a while. I love the investigative side of things, but I think working directly with the families will be more fulfilling.'

'You'd be brilliant at it,' Jenna said immediately. 'You've got that way of making people feel at ease.'

'Definitely,' Clem agreed. 'Remember the Wallace family in that hit-and-run case? The grandmother wouldn't talk to anyone but you. It will leave a gap in the team, though,' Clem said, practical as ever.

'It certainly will,' Lauren agreed, nodding.

'We could always get Ellie back from Lenchester,' Billy suggested with exaggerated innocence.

'I'm not sure you can apply on Ellie's behalf,' Lauren said, smiling.

The conversation flowed easily after that, drifting from work gossip to weekend plans. Matt's phone buzzed in his pocket, and he excused himself momentarily to take the call, stepping away from the table towards a quieter corner near the bar.

When he returned a few minutes later, there was a new lightness to his step.

'Good news?' Lauren asked.

'The survey on the cottage came back clean,' Matt confirmed, unable to keep the smile from his face. 'No structural issues, no damp, no surprises. Looks like it's all going ahead.'

A chorus of congratulations rose from the table.

'This calls for another round,' Billy declared.

'I'll help carry,' Lauren volunteered as Matt headed towards the bar.

At the bar, as they waited for one of the bar staff to finish serving other customers, Matt glanced at Lauren. 'How's your aunt Julia doing now she's back home? Still adjusting?'

Lauren leant against the polished wood, her expression thoughtful. 'She's talking about selling the house. She wants to get away from the memories.'

'That's a big decision,' Matt observed. 'She's lived there for what, forty years?'

'Thirty-seven,' Lauren confirmed. 'But I think after everything that's happened with the trial, she wants a fresh start. Somewhere quieter, maybe further up the coast.'

'And Connor and Clint? How are they taking it?'

Lauren's expression darkened considerably. 'That's the complicated part. I'm hoping they'll stay far away. Connor's been sniffing around the house already, talking about helping her sell it. I'm sure he just wants to get his hands on whatever money he can. And Clint...' She trailed off, shaking her head. 'Let's just say the last time he "helped" a relative, their savings account mysteriously emptied.'

'Still skirting on the wrong side of the law, then?' Matt asked quietly.

'That's putting it mildly,' Lauren said with a humourless laugh. 'The only silver lining to this whole situation might be Julia finally getting some distance from the pair of them. They've been bleeding her dry for years.'

'Let me know if they start causing real trouble. We might not be able to arrest them for being terrible sons, but I'm happy to arrange for a patrol car to drive by more often if needed,' Matt offered.

The man behind the bar approached, and they placed their order. .

As they waited, Matt studied the team in their corner booth. Tamsin was animatedly describing something that had Jenna doubled over with laughter. Billy was showing Clem something on his phone that had them both looking impressed. It was a good team. No, a great team. Even with the potential changes ahead, he felt fortunate to work with them.

'You know, even with everything we see in this job, days like today make it worth it,' Lauren admitted.

'Catching the bad guy and saving lives,' Matt replied.

Lauren smiled. 'That too. But I meant this.' She gestured to the team. 'Having people who understand. Who get what it's like.'

The barman returned with a tray of drinks, and Matt paid before Lauren could reach for her purse.

'My treat,' he insisted.

They carried the drinks back to the table, rejoining the lively conversation as the evening stretched comfortably ahead. Next week there would be paperwork to complete, new cases to tackle, and the constant demands of the job. But tonight, in this moment, they were simply a team celebrating a win and enjoying the feeling of a case well and truly closed.

EPILOGUE

'Call for you on line two, Sarge,' Clem called across the office. 'They've been trying your mobile but couldn't get through.'

Matt glanced at his mobile and realised it was on silent. He reached for his desk phone.

'Price,' he answered, then his expression softened as he realised who it was. 'Gill, hello.' He listened for a moment as the manager of Silver Fern Care Home spoke. 'This Saturday? Let me check...'

Lauren, who'd just popped into the office to speak to Matt, watched as he scribbled something on a sticky note.

'That's very thoughtful of you all. Yes, I'll be there and I'll ask the others, too.'

He hung up, a thoughtful expression on his face.

'What was that about?' Lauren asked.

'Silver Fern Care Home's production of *Arsenic and Old Lace* is on this Saturday. Apparently, they continued rehearsing despite everything that had happened. Gill says Kenneth particularly wanted to invite us. They've dedicated it to the residents who died.'

. . .

As they pulled into Silver Fern's gravel car park, managing to secure the last parking spot, Lauren wasn't entirely sure what to expect.

'The whole team's coming,' she told Matt as they walked towards the entrance. 'DCI Mistry thought it would be good for community relations.'

Although she suspected it was more about ensuring the press saw them supporting the survivors. The case had generated significant media attention. Hardly surprising: theatrical murders, a fifty-year-old grudge, the care home setting...

The entrance hall of Silver Fern had been transformed. A makeshift ticket booth staffed by a cheerful elderly resident greeted visitors, while hand-painted signs directed them to the 'Grand Theatre' (usually the Ballroom). Lauren spotted several familiar faces from the team already being shown to their seats.

'DI Pengelly. DS Price.' Gill Trelawny hurried over to greet them. She looked different today. More relaxed in a flowing dress rather than her usual practical trouser suit. 'I'm so glad you could make it. We've saved seats for you in the front row.'

'Thanks for inviting us,' Matt replied, shaking her hand.

'It's been...' Gill appeared to be searching for the right word. 'Healing, I think. For everyone. Kenneth has been tireless with this production, especially considering his injuries. We weren't sure whether to continue, but Kenneth insisted.'

As if summoned by his name, Kenneth appeared from a doorway labelled 'Backstage Access Only' in wobbly handwriting. Despite his age and the recent trauma, he looked animated, a silk scarf draped artfully around his neck.

'Ah. Our distinguished guests from the constabulary,' he exclaimed, making his way over with surprising energy. 'So pleased you could attend our humble production. We're nearly ready to begin. I'm just corralling our actors into their costumes.' He lowered his voice conspiratorially. 'Bertha keeps trying to add a feather boa that most definitely wasn't worn in 1940s Brooklyn.'

Lauren smiled. It was hard to reconcile this enthusiastic theatre director with the frightened man they'd rescued from Melody Wright's revenge plot.

'How are you doing, Kenneth?' Matt asked quietly.

A shadow passed briefly over the old man's face. 'Managing, Sergeant Price, thank you for asking. I'm taking it one day at a time.' He glanced around to ensure they weren't overheard. 'The nightmares are less frequent now. And this' – he gestured to the makeshift theatre space – 'this helps keep the darkness at bay.'

'And the other residents?' Lauren asked. 'Veronica and Bertha?'

'Adjusting,' Kenneth replied. 'Bertha's playing Aunt Martha and she's marvellous, absolutely marvellous. Veronica's more behind-the-scenes. Handling props.' He paused. 'We've all had to face what happened back then. Even if it wasn't our fault. We were there and should have done something.' He glanced towards a corner of the room where a familiar figure sat in a wheelchair, staring vacantly out of the window. 'Not that she understands any of it now.'

Cynthia was dressed in her best clothes, her white hair carefully styled, but her eyes remained unfocused, lost in whatever fragmented world her mind now inhabited.

'She has good days and bad days,' Kenneth said, following their gaze. 'Mostly bad, now. But we've made sure she has the best seat in the house, even if she doesn't quite follow the plot.'

A young care assistant rang a small bell, signalling it was time to take their seats. Kenneth excused himself, hurrying back to his cast with last-minute instructions.

As the lights dimmed, courtesy of strategically placed floor lamps controlled by an enthusiastic teenager who, Lauren learnt later, was Gill's son, a hush fell over the audience. Kenneth stepped out in front of the makeshift curtain, nodding to familiar faces in the crowd.

'Ladies and gentlemen, friends and guests, welcome to Silver

Fern's production of *Arsenic and Old Lace*. Before we begin, I'd like to say a few words.' He cleared his throat. 'The events of recent months have cast a shadow over our little community. We've lost dear friends, Dawn Cross and Charlie Cook, whose memories we cherish. Today's performance is dedicated to them.'

His voice wavered slightly. 'And to Thea Drake' – he gestured towards Cynthia's wheelchair – 'whose talent once lit up stages far grander than this. Thea, who never got the chance to play the roles she deserved.' Lauren glanced over at Cynthia, who seemed completely unaware she was being discussed, her fingers rhythmically smoothing the fabric of her cardigan. 'Finally,' Kenneth continued, 'this performance is also for those of us left behind. A reminder that even in our twilight years, we can still create something meaningful together. Now, without further ado, Silver Fern Care Home proudly presents *Arsenic and Old Lace*.'

The next couple of hours passed in a blur of surprisingly competent acting, occasional forgotten lines covered with impressive improvisation and genuine laughter from the audience. Bertha made a wonderfully sinister Aunt Martha, while the elderly gentleman playing Mortimer Brewster delivered his increasingly frantic reactions to his aunts' murderous hobby with perfect comic timing. Kenneth himself played the menacing Jonathan Brewster with theatrical relish, clearly enjoying the villainous role.

When the final curtain call came, the audience rose in a standing ovation.

'That was actually good,' Lauren whispered to Matt. 'Like, really entertaining. I wasn't expecting to enjoy it so much.'

Matt nodded. 'Who knew there was so much talent here in Silver Fern?'

The reception afterwards was held in the conservatory, with refreshments served by staff and more mobile residents. Lauren found herself drawn into conversation with Gill, who was keeping one eye on proceedings while sipping a well-deserved glass of wine.

'We weren't sure we'd recover, you know,' Gill confided. 'Some families wanted to move their relatives out and some staff were scared to come to work.'

'But you stayed,' Lauren observed.

Gill nodded. 'Someone had to. These people deserve stability, especially after the trauma. And Kenneth helped by insisting that we continue with the play. He said we couldn't let what happened stop them from living their lives.' She shook her head, smiling faintly. 'He claimed it was therapeutic. I thought he was in denial, but he was right.'

'Yes, I'm sure he was,' Lauren agreed.

Across the room, Matt was deep in conversation with Kenneth, Veronica and Bertha.

'They've become close, those three,' Gill noted, following Lauren's gaze. 'Survivors' bond, I suppose. They talk about the old days sometimes. The good parts, mostly. The productions they appeared in. But sometimes I hear them discussing Thea too. How talented she was and what happened.'

'Do they talk about Melody?' Lauren asked cautiously.

'Not by name.' Gill's expression grew troubled. 'She's still awaiting trial, isn't she?'

'Yes,' Lauren confirmed. 'Probably another four months before it goes to court.'

Before Lauren could say more, they were interrupted by Bertha, still in full costume minus the feather boa, who insisted she wanted to talk to 'the nice detective lady who saved Kenneth' to thank her personally.

The rest of the reception passed pleasantly, with residents eager to share their reviews of the performance and their own theatrical anecdotes. Matt found Lauren as they were preparing to leave.

'Kenneth wants to show us something before we go,' he said quietly.

They followed the elderly man down a corridor to a freshly painted wall where a newly installed glass cabinet hung. Inside were theatre programmes, old photographs and newspaper clippings. It was like a miniature museum of productions.

'We decided to create a memorial wall,' Kenneth explained. 'Not just for Dawn and Charlie, but for all the residents who've shared their talents here.' He pointed to a black-and-white photograph in the centre of a striking young woman with intelligent eyes and a commanding presence, caught mid-performance on a proper theatre stage.

'Thea Drake as Lady Macbeth,' Kenneth said softly. 'Her finest role, in my opinion. Before...'

'Before it all came tumbling down,' came a voice behind them. Veronica had appeared, Bertha at her side. 'We should have realised that she couldn't take the stuff like we could and not encouraged her.'

'We were stupid,' Bertha agreed, her earlier exuberance faded. 'Young and stupid.'

Kenneth nodded. 'Yes. We were. But we can't change it.' He touched the edge of the frame gently. 'But we can remember her as she was. Brilliant. Captivating. The talent the rest of us really didn't have. I understand why Melody did what she did. In her position, loving someone that much...' He trailed off, then straightened his shoulders. 'Well. We carry on, don't we? What else is there to do?'

As they finally left Silver Fern, twilight settling over the grounds, Lauren found herself thinking about Melody Wright, now in custody awaiting trial. She wondered if Melody knew about today's performance, about Kenneth's efforts to honour her grandmother, and about the photograph now prominently displayed.

'Strange to think it all began with a play,' Matt said as they reached the car. 'And ended with one, too.'

'Does it ever end, though?' Lauren asked. 'Kenneth will never fully recover from what happened. Cynthia will live out her days without understanding any of it. And Melody...'

'Melody made her choices,' Matt said firmly. 'Just as Kenneth and the others made theirs all those years ago.'

'Choices and consequences,' Lauren murmured. 'Like characters in a play.'

The evening air was cool against Lauren's skin and she glanced
back at Silver Fern one last time, its windows now glowing amber
in the gathering dusk. The truth had emerged after being buried
for so long. Nothing could really be mended, but what Kenneth
and the others had done went a long way.

A LETTER FROM THE AUTHOR

Dear reader,

Huge thanks for reading *The Marazion Murders*. I hope you were hooked! If you want to join other readers in hearing all about my new releases and bonus content, you can sign up here:

www.stormpublishing.co/sally-rigby

If you enjoyed this book and could spare a few moments to leave a review that would be hugely appreciated. Even a short review can make all the difference in encouraging a reader to discover my books for the first time. Thank you so much!

I chose to write about a care home for ex-entertainers because I thought it created a compelling setting where residents possess the theatrical skills to hide their true intentions while also having complex personal histories that can fuel decades-old grudges. It also gave me the opportunity to bring in some humorous situations as the residents all fight to be the 'leading light'.

Thanks again for being part of this amazing journey with me and I hope you'll stay in touch – I have so many more stories and ideas to entertain you with!

Sally

KEEP IN TOUCH WITH THE AUTHOR

www.sallyrigby.com

facebook.com/Sally-Rigby-131414630527848

instagram.com/sally.rigby.author

ACKNOWLEDGEMENTS

The Marazion Murders is truly a collaborative effort, and I couldn't have asked for a better team to work with. Thanks to my editor at Storm, Kathryn Taussig, whose keen eye and thoughtful guidance shaped this story into its final form, and to the rest of the editorial team who ensured every page was polished to perfection. Special appreciation also goes to the marketing department for their creative efforts in connecting this book with readers, and to the talented cover designers who captured the essence of Marazion so beautifully.

Special thanks go to my friend and writing partner Amanda Ashby, who is always there when I need to brainstorm ideas or work through plot challenges. Your support means the world to me. To my sister-in-law, Jacqui, and brother-in-law, Peter, thank you for sharing your invaluable insights into Cornish life that helped bring authenticity to this story.

Finally, thanks to the rest of my family, whose encouragement and belief in my writing continues to inspire me.

Printed in Dunstable, United Kingdom